One of a Kind Christmas

A Christmas Carol
Book 4

One of a Kind Christmas

A Christmas Carol
Book 4

BY

LEXI POST

One of A Kind Christmas:

A Christmas Carol, Book 4

To reach her heart, he must face a spirit, an angel…and himself.

The spirit of Cameron Douglas has totally screwed-up…again. Now, he has to fix his mess in one night with the help of his best friend and somehow encourage his widow to move on.

Holly Douglas is anguished that this is the last Christmas she'll be visited by her late husband, Cameron. For three years he's sent her the spirits of Christmas Past, Present, and Future, and they've helped her cope with her loss. But now all that ends, and she doesn't understand why he must push her away.

Ethan Stewart has been in love with Holly since Cameron's death, but she isolated herself from everyone, including him. Then something changed, and he was welcomed back as her friend. But he wants more— to love her openly, and most of all to make her happy again. Though he loved his best friend like a brother and will do anything for Holly, as he's pulled into the spirit world, he discovers not all is as it seems. If he doesn't figure it out soon, none of them will have a Merry Christmas…ever.

For updates, sneak peeks, and special prizes, sign up to receive the latest news from Lexi Post at http://bit.ly/LexiUpdate

Acknowledgments

For Bob Fabich, Sr., my very own one-of-a-kind man…even if he is a twin. And for my sister Paige Wood, who made this story better by leaps and bounds.

Thank you to my daughter-in-law Rebecca Curran Fabich for answering all my questions on words, food, customs, and everything else in regards to her home country of Scotland. And for those especially hard questions, I had the invaluable help of Alan Curran and Norma Curran. It's truly wonderful to have experts within my extended family. Thank you.

As always, I must thank my fantastic critique partner, Marie Patrick, whose encouragement and kindness has kept me going when I didn't think I had it in me. She is truly worth her weight in gold.

Author's Note

One of A Kind Christmas was inspired by *A Christmas Carol* by Charles Dickens. In Dickens' story, Ebenezer Scrooge, a miserly curmudgeon, is told by the spirit of his former business partner, Marley, that he will be visited by three ghosts and if he doesn't change his ways he will pay for it in the afterlife. Scrooge scoffs at the idea but as he journeys into his past, present, and future with the spirit of each period of his life, he sees the error of his ways and becomes a completely different man when he wakes up on Christmas day.

But what if despite the interference of the Spirits of Christmas Past, Present, and Future, a young widow is still not living a full life? Could the Spirit of her late husband help or hurt? And what about the late husband's friend, who has fallen in love with the widow? Will he help or will he walk away? And most importantly, can love conquer all even in the afterlife?

Chapter One

Deervale, Scotland, December 1

Why was he awake?

Ethan Stewart listened, keeping his eyes closed, his body and mind alert. Something woke him from his dream of walking by Loudon Castle with Holly Douglas.

Despite the fact that all was silent except for the usual screech of the tawny owl outside, he still didn't doubt his senses. Years of studying ancient Scottish hand-to hand combat had tuned him in to his own sixth sense.

Slowly, he opened his eyes. His room remained dark. The heavy damask curtains on his floor-to-ceiling windows were closed except for a slender gap that allowed a sliver of moonlight to slice across the floor.

His bedroom was on the second story of his family's ancestral home, and he doubted anyone could get in without making a noise, but it was still a possibility. Maybe the security system that his parents had been after him to purchase should be moved up on his schedule.

Then again, it could simply be an animal that had scurried in while the front door was open earlier in the day and finally made it up to his room.

Unfortunately, his bed was too high for him to see the floor from where he lay, so there was no help for it but to sit up. Taking a deep breath in case something attacked, he rose in one fluid motion, sending his feet over the side of the bed to land silently on the floor, his knees bent slightly, his hands ready.

He scanned his room, but there were areas in total blackness that his gaze couldn't penetrate. "Who's there?" It was a stupid question, but he asked it anyway. His voice could very well scare a critter into revealing its whereabouts with noise.

"Just an old friend."

Ethan's blood chilled. He hadn't heard that voice in almost four years, but he'd never forget it. "Cameron?"

"Aye."

Ethan turned toward the far corner of his room. He had to be dreaming. Despite the lack of sound, he sensed movement just before the spirit of Cameron Douglas floated out of the darkness and into the sliver of moonlight.

Dressed in his dark green, black and white tartan kilt, black sleeveless t-shirt and black army boots, the spirit's hazel eyes appeared a murky gray and no smile lifted his lips like it had so often in life.

He wasn't dreaming. The man hovering a meter off the floor looked exactly like his best friend, only he wasn't solid, more like a hologram. Immediately, guilt tightened Ethan's stomach. Had his interest in the man's widow somehow called him from his grave?

Refusing to jump to conclusions, he relaxed his stance. "How can you be here?"

His friend floated to the floor, but otherwise remained where he was. "It's time to tell you."

"Tell me what?" As much as he couldn't possibly be speaking to his dead friend, his gut told him he was.

Cameron moved the hair off his forehead. "I need to tell you the truth."

"The truth?" Was the truth from a dead man more or less true?

"Aye. But as braw as you are, maybe you could put on some clothes? You're making me feel woefully out of shape." Cameron's lip quirked up, showing a piece of the personality that had made him who he was…when he lived.

Ethan grabbed up the maroon robe with his monogram on it and slipped his arms into the sleeves. Wrapping it around him quickly, he tied the belt as he stared at the floating shape of his closest friend. "That better? I hadn't expected to have a blether with a ghost in the middle of the night."

"Spirit."

He had to be playing with him. "Excuse me?"

"I'm not a ghost. I'm a spirit."

"Ghost, spirit, no difference." He remained where he was, part of him fearing that if he moved Cameron would disappear, while part of him wished that was exactly what would happen.

His friend shook his head. "There's a *big* difference."

Something told him he didn't want to know what that difference was. So instead of asking the obvious question, he waited. Patience was his forte, not so much Cameron's when he'd been alive. Had things changed?

In no more than mere moments, he had his answer. Nothing had changed his friend, not even death.

Cameron sighed. "I've been visiting Holly every Christmas Eve since I transitioned."

He stiffened. It was typical of Cameron to blurt out the truth, but this truth was a hard pill to swallow. "Why?" Was that why Holly had avoided them all for years? Was that why she'd only recently agreed to do anything with him?

"Because she was hurting. Because of what I did to her. Because I had to." Cameron floated toward the window. He turned to face him, the moonlight shining through his body. "Because I've been selfish."

"Now *that* I believe."

Cameron grinned. "See, I knew you'd understand."

Despite the familiar smile, there was a weariness in Cameron's face that hadn't been there in life. Was that typical of the afterlife? He'd never given it much thought.

"Shit, Ethan. It's just me. You can relax."

Not likely. "I don't make a habit of speaking to my dead friends in the middle of the night, so you'll have to make allowances."

Cameron floated over to him, the mixed colors of his hazel eyes more obvious up close despite his opaque form. "I'm sorry. I know this is weird, but I need your help."

"You need *my* assistance?" As much as he wanted to believe this was all a dream, he was positive it wasn't. "What with?"

"With Holly."

He tensed. He'd always supported his best friends, even when he was trying to curtail their activities. Now, however, his focus had turned to what was best for Holly. "What do you want with Holly?"

Cameron shook his head, his hands coming out in front of him. "Nothing. Nothing for me. I want her to live a full life. I want her to be loved and feel love again." His deep voice softened. "I want her to fall in love with you."

A shiver raced up Ethan's spine. For the first time since he'd woken, he doubted his senses. This encounter could not be taking place. What he wanted more than anything in his life was to have his love for Holly reciprocated. This apparition before him could very well be of his own making, his own soul's deepest wish.

Turning away from the ghost, he strode to the bedside and turned on the lamp, sure that his imagination wouldn't be able to contend with the light. Cameron and Holly had had the strongest love he'd ever witnessed.

After Cameron passed, he'd found himself thinking about her all the time and it wasn't long before he realized the true state of his feelings went far beyond sympathy or compassion. He loved her. He'd probably been falling for her all along and hadn't realized it. For that he was grateful. He couldn't imagine loving his best friend's wife, yet here he was.

When Cameron had died on Christmas day, unexpectedly, and to his mind, needlessly, then guilt had been his constant companion. Seeing Holly's grief had him second guessing his arguments that day and his decision not to go with his friends. Could he have somehow prevented Cameron's death?

It had taken him years to dispel his irrational guilt and even longer to coerce Holly to even let him become a part of her life again in some small way. And now, suddenly, he's woken from a dream about her to find her dead husband in his room telling him that she needs to fall in love with him. That had to be his mind playing tricks on him.

Turning back toward his room, he expected it to be empty, back to normal. Instead, Cameron remained by the window, the golden glow of the bed lamp fading him a bit, but his figure still perfectly clear.

Cameron grinned as he folded his arms. "You don't believe I'm really here, do you?"

"Hell." Not willing to believe what he was seeing, he strode past the apparition and turned on the light in the darkest corner of the room.

His dead friend's laugh filled the space like Charles Dickens' Spirit of Christmas Present. "Ethan. It's really me. What can't you believe? That I'm a spirit come back to ask for your help or that I want Holly to fall in love with you?"

He swallowed hard, still hesitant to believe his senses. Could a ghost exact revenge? "Both."

Cameron's smile faded. "I know it's hard to believe that I could have such unselfish motives, but trust me, they are still selfish. I was the luckiest man in the world to have Holly fall in love with me. I was just as lucky to have two such great friends as you and Brody. Brody has found the love of his life, his very soulmate, just like I did. And you…"

"And I'm still hoping, but why Holly?"

Cameron floated closer. "Because I know you love her."

And there it was, his greatest fear exposed. He didn't want Holly to know. He didn't want anyone to know. If she came to love him, it had to be something she felt, not something people gossiped about. "Why would you think that?" He moved away, but Cameron floated in front of him again.

"Because I sent spirits to visit Holly to help her get over my death and they discovered you love her."

He shook his head.

Cameron scowled. "Don't. I know you love her. I want you to love her. She needs you even if she doesn't realize that yet."

He turned on his heel and strode for his bedroom door. He didn't have to stay in the same room with a dead man. He didn't have to listen to what he most wanted to hear coming from the man who was never to know that he loved Holly. Cameron was dead. He didn't want to feel guilt for loving the man's widow.

He'd always thought of Holly as a friend, but after Cameron passed, something changed. Maybe it was his grief, or hers, but he missed the bright smiles that filled her round face, causing the small dimple in her right cheek to show itself. He missed the sparkle in her chestnut colored eyes and the way she pulled her straight, dark-chocolate hair back into its hairband or barrette.

Opening the door, he headed down the long hallway, wishing for the first time that his parents hadn't moved out of Rawdon Manor and into a cottage near town. His bare feet on the runner made no sound. Even the stairs remained silent as he descended, the study his destination.

Most of all he'd missed Holly's easy smile and quick laugh that seemed to energize her entire curvy body. He wanted to bring that all back, and the longer she'd kept to herself, the more intense his desire to make her happy grew. Finally, he had to admit to himself that he loved her. The only other person who knew was his mum, and he'd planned for it to stay that way until the day, if ever, he could tell Holly.

The screech of the owl outside seemed to echo in the quiet of the empty house. As he opened the door to his study, the hinges creaked, the sound, its simple normality, releasing some of his tension.

Hitting the light switch inside the door, he headed for the bottle of single malt set on the antique bar. Pouring a splash of water from the decanter, he opened the Scotch and filled the glass. Taking a bracing swig, he let the smoky flavor fill his senses before swallowing the amber liquid that heated him from the inside out, dispelling the chill he'd experienced since first waking.

"You can't get rid of me that easily."

At the sound of Cameron's voice, he spun. The ghost appeared to sit on the couch across from his massive desk. Cameron pointed up. "I just floated through the floor. There are advantages to being a spirit." His lip quirked up as if he found the statement amusing for some reason.

Ethan threw back another swallow of Scotch. Obviously, the only way to deal with a dead Cameron was the way he'd dealt with a live one—head on. "Very well. I did fall in with love Holly, but she doesn't love me. She's still in love with you, which is the way it should be."

Cameron seemed to deflate, his apparition shrinking a little. "No, it's not." He moved the hair off his forehead as he'd always done when troubled. "I don't want her to be mourning me for the rest of her life. She has a big heart, and she's still a young, vibrant woman. I want her to live life to the fullest."

Ethan frowned. "I think that's what you did."

Cameron's eyes widened before he smirked. "Aye, and look where that got me." He threw his hand out to the side. "But I was destined for a short life. Holly didn't deserve such heartbreak because of *my* destiny."

"Destiny?" That sounded far more fated than what he liked to believe. "As in there was a plan for you?"

Cameron chuckled. "Hardly. No, it was just my penchant for risk that made it so." He paused, his smile growing crooked. "I probably have you to thank for having made it as long as I did." He shook his head. "It still baffles me how you put up with two crazy lads like me and Brody. You've always been so responsible."

Not exactly, but he'd never told his friends why he'd become so cautious. He didn't think it would mean they'd listen to him any more than they did. They always treated him like the younger one, though he was their age. It was his looks. His dad had always looked younger than his age until he reached his fifties.

Whether it was racing through the highlands or walking through a bad part of the city, hang-gliding or the fateful rock-climbing, Holly and he had always tried to talk sense into Cameron and Brody. Half the time it actually worked.

"Will you help me?" Cameron's words brought his focus back to his strange visitor.

"I don't believe I can help you anymore."

Cameron raised his brows. "You would think that's the case, but I have been granted a special dispensation. If I hadn't, you wouldn't even be able to see me, let alone talk to me."

He could just imagine Cameron's silver tongue talking someone or something into letting him visit the living. He knew Cameron better than most and he'd be foolish to agree to anything until he knew exactly what he was getting into. "What, specifically, were you hoping I could do?" He took another sip of the Scotch, guessing he'd need it.

Cameron clasped his hands on his lap. "I want you to get Holly to fall in love with you."

The Scotch spewed from his mouth as he coughed on it. Swallowing hard, he frowned. "If I knew how to do that, it would have happened by now. She avoided me like the plague the first two years after you passed. It hasn't been until this year that she's actually been more like the friend she always was, but she's very clear about that."

"About what?"

"That I'm just a friend. In fact, she's constantly telling me I'm a good friend."

Cameron grimaced. "That's not a good place to be. We need to change that."

He looked askance at Cameron. "And what do you propose?"

Cameron didn't look him in the eye. "I have some ideas."

He didn't like the sound of that. Suddenly, it was as if Cameron had never died and they were back to their tug-of-war friendship, Cameron leaping ahead while he tried to pull him back with caution. The problem was, this time Cameron was playing in a completely new world, and he'd no clue what the rules were. Nor did he have confidence that Cameron would tell him everything he needed to know. "What kind of ideas?"

Chapter Two

December 10

Holly locked the door of the One of a Kind Christmas Shop and clicked off the outside light before leaning back against the glass and sighing.

"Why don't you go home? I can finish up the inventory of today's deliveries." Brooke Douglas, Cameron's cousin, took off her glasses, her brows furrowed in concern. "You've been going non-stop all week. Didn't you say you had a Christmas tree to put up?"

Holly wiped her hands on her green slacks and pushed off the door to head for the back room. "I know. I'm already a week later than usual in getting it up, but it's so old. Nothing wants to go where it belongs."

Brooke halted her progress by stepping in front of her, her employee's sandy brown hair, so much like Cameron's, fell back over her shoulder. "Don't you think it's time to get rid of that thing? I hear they even make them now where you just push a button and the whole tree rises into position."

Her gut twisted. Brooke was right. The woman's features may be similar to Cam's, but she was far more practical. "I know. It's just that…"

Brooke rolled her eyes. "Is this another one of those fond memories with my deceased cousin?"

She looked away. Poor Brooke heard more about Cameron than anyone. Well, maybe not anyone. Ethan had certainly heard his fair share over the last year, but he didn't seem to mind.

After seeing what her life could turn into when Malcolm and Joy, her spirits of Christmas Future, had visited, she'd begun to notice how some of the people in town reacted when she started to talk about Cameron. It was as if they couldn't get away from her fast enough. Her life really had become stuck in the past, and she hadn't even noticed.

"Listen, I understand memories, but throwing out something that's broken won't wash away the memories. You should buy one of those table top ceramic trees. Then you wouldn't have to decorate it."

She'd seen one of those at Mrs. Bell's house last year. Mrs. Bell said she brought it out for the week of Christmas then put it away to prepare for Hogmanay. Her judgment was that it was perfect for old people like her.

Is that what she'd become over the last four years? Old?

Brooke took her by the shoulders and peered at her. "I want you to turn around, go to your house and get that decrepit old tree out of the closet you have it stuffed in, and I'll call Luca to remove it first thing tomorrow morning."

"But the inventory?" She looked toward the door of the back room.

Brooke spun her around and pushed her toward the door that adjoined the shop to her house. "I told you. I'll take care of it. I came in at noon. You've already put in a full day. Now go."

She looked back at Brooke. The woman's gray eyes were steely with resolve. Raising her hands in the air she capitulated. "Well, fine then. I'm going."

At Brooke's smile, Holly pulled back the tapestry that covered the door and slipped into her house.

"I'm home. Did you have a good day?" Dropping her keys to the shop on the table beside the door, she scanned the living room. "Mac?" In the dark room, she stepped to the lamp next to the side table and turned it on. "Holy crap."

Her living room looked like a tornado had swept through it. The boxes of decorations she'd taken out two weeks ago were toppled over, contents strewn everywhere, broken ornaments and shredded manger hay littered the room. The loveseat that she usually moved away from the bay window in order to set up the Christmas tree had vomit on the cushions. Her anger at her cat immediately turned to concern.

"Mac? Are you okay?"

"Meow."

She switched her gaze to a pile of three boxes. "Mac, are you in there?"

As she walked toward it, the boxes moved. "Meow."

"Oh, you poor thing. Hold on." As she lifted the top box off of the other two, the entire contents spilled out from the bottom. Among the decorations scattered across the two lower boxes, she discovered a gray paw pulling at the still folded closed lid of one of them. "Now how did you get yourself in there?"

She grabbed the two sides and pulled. "Ow!" Pulling her hand back, she put her finger in her mouth and sucked it before inspecting the area where Mac had scratched her. "Hey, I'm trying to help you here. Do you want out or not?"

"Meow."

"Well, it certainly doesn't seem like it." Looking around the braided rug, she spotted pieces of one of the train tracks she used under the tree. Taking two of those, she carefully pulled at the box ends, amid much jousting with Mac's paw. Finally, they separated and the cat jumped free.

When Mac saw that he once more had free reign of the

house again, he scanned his handy work before sitting back on his haunches. He began to wash his attack paw as if it had touched something unacceptable.

"Really? No thank you meow or anything?" She sighed as she looked at the catastrophe that was her living room. She'd obviously left the decorating until one day too late as far as Mac was concerned.

As far as she was concerned, too. She'd like to say it was the unusual influx of Americans this fall, and the increased business at the shop that had delayed her decorating, but that wasn't it. The fact was, she wasn't much in the Christmas spirit knowing that this could be the last year Cam visited her on Christmas Eve. What would she have to look forward to after that?

She looked over at Mac. As a cat mommy, she had to address his behavior, no matter that she understood it. He was upset with her. "Mac, what is this?" She swept her hand out to the side to encompass the whole room. "What were you thinking? If you wanted me to decorate, you've just delayed it even more." Her eye caught a broken glass angel with the words *Second Christmas* across the bottom of the skirt. "Oh, Mac. Really?" Her voice caught as she picked up the ornament she'd given to Cam their second Christmas together. They weren't even married, but it seemed fitting since that was the year it snowed so much in Deervale that it was deep enough at the park to make snow angels.

The cat stopped washing himself and walked over to her, rubbing against her knees as she kneeled on the rug, fighting the tears that threatened. Brooke's words of just a few moments ago came to her rescue—*throwing out something that's broken won't wash away the memories.* Brooke was right.

But as she surveyed the damage done, her gaze found item after item broken or smashed, every one of them connected to a memory with Cam. "You couldn't break something Mom or Sarah gave me?"

Absently she stroked the cat, not really expecting an answer. When a paw came down on her wrist, she turned her attention back to him. "What?"

"Meow."

"You're right. It's time for your dinner. You'll have to excuse me if I was temporarily distracted by your destruction here."

Mac didn't wait another moment. Instead, he trotted out to the kitchen where she had no doubt he was sitting next to his empty bowl waiting to be fed. Letting the broken angel fall to the rug where the other smashed decorations lay, she rose and walked into the kitchen, her heart heavy.

Opening a can of cat food, she scooped some out into Mac's bowl and stood back to watch. "It must be nice to have such a short memory and absolutely no guilt whatsoever."

Mac ignored her, wolfing down his dinner. She really should think about eating herself if she was going to tackle the mess in her living room. Opening the refrigerator, she scanned the contents which included milk, a half bottle of wine that was far too old to drink, three eggs, a half-eaten pastry from the bakery and two bites left of the steak pie she'd bought from the pub six nights ago. She took that out and dumped it in the trash.

Closing the door, she put the kettle on, her appetite having been swept away by Hurricane Mac. Now, not only did she need to trash her Christmas tree, but dozens of ornaments, too, and who knew how many decorations. It was as if the universe was conspiring to make her forget Cam.

She scowled at Mac. "Sorry, Mac. It's not going to work."

He stopped eating and looked at her before walking to his water dish and drinking. The cat seemed to grow angrier every Christmas. Last year he'd toppled the old tree. The year before, he batted decorations off the side table. If he didn't stop soon, he'd be the only thing left from Cam she had.

And what if *he* died? Her heart stopped at the thought, her breath whooshing out of her as if someone had punched her in the stomach. Then Mac and Cam would be together and she'd be completely alone!

Tears she hadn't shed in almost a year gathered, making her kitchen blurry. Wiping her eyes to clear them, she pulled air into her lungs. No, she wouldn't be alone. She'd have Brooke, and Brody and Sarah…and Ethan. At the thought of the man she'd come to lean on in the past year, she balked. Whenever she was around him, she felt happy and guilty, comfortable and uncomfortable. It was too confusing. Instead, she focused on Mac, picking him up despite his weight.

"You're just going to have to stay alive forever. Okay?"

Mac wriggled to be put down, his claws snagging in her green turtleneck.

"Okay, okay. I just wanted you to know I love you." Kissing the protesting cat on the head, she let him go. He immediately sat and proceeded to wash his face as if her kiss had cooties or something.

Throwing her arms up, she moved to the cabinets and pulled out a big mug. Tonight definitely called for a large cup of tea. She had to tackle her emotions and her living room and bring them into some semblance of normality.

The kettle whistled, so she poured the hot water into her mug with the "Christmas Tea" in the strainer. The scent of orange and clove reminded her of Cam's cologne. He always smelled like Christmas to her. Taking a deep breath of the hot tea, she frowned. There was another scent in there that reminded her of something. Was that ginger, maybe? She hadn't noticed it before, but she'd been late in breaking out her Christmas tea as well this year. What was wrong with her?

Again, she looked at the fridge. She really didn't want anything in there. Maybe what she needed was some Christmas music. Oh, and Christmas cookies. Setting her tea on the counter, she opened the cabinet next to the fridge and pulled out the tin of homemade Christmas cookies Mrs. Bell had dropped off just a few days ago. Opening it up, she sighed.

"Now that's what I call Christmas." Stuffing one into her mouth, she bit half and held the rest between her lips as she picked up the tin and her tea and strolled back to her wrecked living room. She'd just reached her comfy chair when the bell rang.

She glanced at the clock. It was only half past six. It felt like nine to her. She set her tea on the small table next to her chair and grabbed the cookie from her mouth. "Coming."

Quickly, she stuffed the rest of the cookie back in and chewed as she approached the front door. Swallowing, she turned the knob, but the door remained closed. *Real smart, Holly.* Unlocking the deadbolt, she pulled again to reveal a bundled-up Ethan on her doorstep. "Ethan. Oh no, did I forget I was supposed to be somewhere?" She racked her brain trying to think of what it could be.

He laughed, his green eyes sparkling in the reflection of her living room light. His hair, wavy now that he'd let it grow a little longer, was sprinkled with a few snowflakes and his teeth gleamed. "No, I thought since you've been working such long hours that a fresh mincemeat pie might be just what you need as you decorate your tree. You did say you were hoping to do that tonight, correct?"

She lifted her brows. "Did I?" She probably had, but she was flustered. To have Ethan in her home seemed more intimate than she was ready for. They always met at public places or at his parents' house in town. He was far too handsome, bearing an uncanny resemblance to Michelangelo's statue of David. He was also kind and good looking and considerate and muscular and tall and…she swallowed, uncomfortable with her thoughts. She shook her head to clear it.

"Aye, you did. But you also said that your tree was broken, so I brought you a new one."

She tensed. Why did everyone want her to have a new tree? "I'm not really interested in one of those new automatic trees. I prefer to put some work into my décor." Though to look at her house right now, no one would believe her.

He frowned, shaking his head. "I hope not. I didn't take you for the automatic-tree type, though that was what was recommended to me."

She relaxed a bit at that. "Good, then what kind of tree did you get?" She was a bit curious now. As nice as Ethan was, he was still a man, and she doubted he had any more taste than Cam. Cam would have bought an automatic tree and a pink or blue one at that.

Ethan handed her the hot pie, and she balanced it on her tin of cookies as he disappeared for a moment.

"Better back up."

Uh-oh. Reluctantly, she stepped back. She really needed to tell him to keep the tree. It wasn't right. Yes, that was the right thing to do. Opening her mouth, her protest died as the scent of spruce wafted in with the cold outside air. He'd brought her a live tree?

She took ten steps back, her memories of New Hampshire and Christmas with her family flooding her as Ethan wrestled what looked like a ten-foot Christmas tree into her house.

Closing the door, he pushed the tree to lean against the entrance and looked up at the cathedral ceiling of her home. "I should have purchased the fifteen-foot size. You still have plenty of ceiling height."

She stared in awe at the beautiful tree filling her living room with its Christmas scent. She plopped her butt on the arm of Cam's chair, her knees too weak to hold her, her heart filled with the warmth the spruce aroma gave her.

Ethan turned to look at her, his ready smile dimming as he

caught her gaze. "You don't like it. I can return and buy the large one. It'd been so long since I'd been in here, I couldn't remember exactly how tall your ceilings were."

Though he'd obviously not meant it as a slap in the face, the sting of his statement brought her to her feet. It was true. She hadn't had anyone into her shrine to Cam in four years. What good were all those Christmas spirits Cam sent her if she still kept him alive in their home and refused to share. No wonder others had moved on with their lives.

Ethan's brow lowered in concern. "Or is it because it's real? They have some very true-to-life looking artificial trees at the hardware store. I think they're still open." He looked at his watch.

She rested her hand on his arm to get his attention. "No, not at all. It's just so perfect, I was stunned."

"You were?"

She swallowed down the sudden lump in her throat at his thoughtfulness. "Yes. I grew up with live spruce trees for Christmas. It reminds me of home." She gave him a small smile, her family suddenly feeling so close. "And that's a good thing."

His brow finally eased, and he relaxed before his eye caught the state of her living room. "Bloody hell, were you burglarized? We need to call the police."

She snorted. "Hardly." She squinted at her traitorous cat, who had hopped down from his chair and was rubbing against Ethan's legs. She removed her hand from Ethan's tan wool coat and pointed. "That's the culprit. He tore this place apart while I was at work then got stuck in a box. Served him right."

"Mac did all this?" Ethan bent over and picked up Mac the Destroyer. "Hey lad, you look like you've put on a little weight since I last saw you."

Just as guilt centered in her gut, Mac pushed his head against Ethan's chin. She'd forgotten how much Ethan adored Mac. "Well, he's spoiled and I don't have a lot of time to play with him. I tried putting him on a leash, but he just fell over and didn't move as if I'd killed him or something."

Ethan's quiet laugh drifted through the room before he set the feline down. "I'm thinking someone needs a few cat toys for Christmas."

She scowled. "Only good cats get presents."

"And fat ones." He pointed to her hands. "Did you already eat? I see a Mrs. Bell cookie tin there."

She'd completely forgotten she'd planned to have cookies for dinner. Ethan didn't say anything, but she was pretty sure she'd gained a few pounds in the past year. Now, with the scent of nutmeg and beef tickling her nose, she found the willpower to wait on the cookies. "Yes, I felt I deserved a treat after walking into this mess."

"I understand." He looked over the living room. "Would you like help cleaning it up? Then I could set up the tree for you. It will probably take two people."

Well, crap. She wasn't being very hospitable. She was sorely out of practice. "That would be great. Have you eaten yet? Are you hungry?"

Ethan unbuttoned his coat and shrugged it off his broad shoulders. He seemed bigger in her house. He turned and hung his garment on the coatrack in the corner next to the door. "I didn't realize I hadn't eaten until I put that in my rented van. Now my stomach is yelling at me."

Thankful to have something to do, she lifted the cookie tin and pie in her hands. "Then let me get this dished out so we can eat before tackling this mess." She beat a hasty retreat into the kitchen. He'd even rented a van to bring her the tree. Holy crap.

She set down the cookie tin and pie. Her kitchen was a small room, cozy. The little two-person table in it had been perfect for her and Cam. At the thought of Ethan sitting there with her, she moved to the cabinet and pulled out a tray. They could eat in the disaster zone.

"Do you have a bucket? I should put this tree in water." Ethan yelled from the living room, though to call it a yell was a bit of an exaggeration.

"Yes, in the closet next to the bathroom."

She dished out the mincemeat pie, very aware that Ethan opened two doors before finding the closet. That she hadn't had anyone in her home besides Brooke and spirits since Cam's passing almost four years ago was a breath-stopping realization. Cam would be so disappointed in her.

At the sound of running water in her shower, she frowned. Picking up the tray, she moved to investigate. She found Ethan filling the bucket with water. Of course. "You better make sure there's enough for a long time. That living room is a real mess."

He stopped the flow of water. "We'll make short work of it with the two of us."

She backed up as he carried the water to the tree.

As he set the bucket down, he looked at her. "Do you think you could move the water underneath as I lift the tree?"

"Oh, of course." Setting down the tray on the side table, she hurried over.

"On the count of three. One, two, three."

As Ethan hefted the big tree, she tried to lift the bucket, but it was too heavy, so she slid it across the floor until it was directly beneath the trunk then stepped back. Obviously, Ethan was still in great shape, and he was a couple years older than her. So, what was her excuse? At thirty-three, she should be perfectly fit.

The memory of Ethan with his shirt off and lying on his couch as the Spirits of Christmas Future had shown her infiltrated her brain. Flushing, she shook her head to dislodge the vision and moved back to their dinner. Ethan was a dear friend and her late husband's best friend. No reason to get hot and bothered over him. *Sure Holly, just ignore the fact that this quiet hunk loves you to pieces, and you're not supposed to know that.*

Ethan rose and brushed his hands against each other as he walked carefully across the braided rug. "I'll just wash my hands."

As he disappeared down the short hall, she moved the food to the small table she often used when eating in the living room. Sitting in her chair, she scanned the room. Usually, by now, she had it fully decorated. She wished Ethan could have seen it at its best.

Looking over at Mac who lay across Cam's chair, she grinned. "Don't get too comfortable. Ethan will be taking your seat."

"Excuse me?" Ethan strode in, one eyebrow raised.

She started, far too used to talking to Mac and having him not answer. She waved toward Mac. "He took over Cam's chair a year ago. Just push him off." She didn't elaborate how she'd avoided Cam's chair until Mac forced her to sit in it, enveloped in his clove scent. Now there was no scent left at all, so she had no problem with the fact Mac had taken it over again.

Before Ethan could touch Mac, the cat sat up and jumped onto the arm.

She stared at Ethan. "Do you communicate with cats now?"

He shrugged after sitting. "Not really. They just intuitively know what I want."

She furrowed her brow, not sure if he was kidding with her or not. Sometimes with Ethan, it was hard to tell. He was so much more serious and even-keeled than Cam had been.

He pulled the plate off the little table and held it. Taking a bite, he chewed as he studied her bay window across from them. He motioned with his fork toward it. "Why did you have an artificial tree in here when you enjoy live trees?"

She finished chewing a savory bite and swallowed, her tummy much happier with her. "Cam always wanted an artificial. He said it was so much easier because we only had to spend time picking it out once, and then we'd have the perfect tree every year."

"Aye, that sounds like Cam." Ethan nodded as he took another bite.

She relaxed as she usually did around him. He was the only one she could talk to about Cam, who didn't lose interest. It simply reminded her that he missed Cam as much as she did. Or maybe almost as much. Even the way he spoke about him was as if Cam was still around. Lucky for him, he didn't know that Cam visited every Christmas Eve and this year would be his last visit.

What would she do then? Knowing she would see him, no matter how briefly, was what kept her going throughout the year. What would keep her going next year?

"Our family always cut down a live tree." Ethan studied the tree by her door. "Dad even planted some so we didn't have to travel so far. He taught me to care for them and to always plant more every year."

She hadn't known that. "Do you still get your trees from your property?"

He sighed. "Nay. The ones we planted before I went to Uni grew too big while I was away, so we cut down live ones at a tree farm. Now that mom and dad are in the house in town, we have to purchase a much smaller one."

"What about that mansion you live in? I bet you could fit one of those big trees from your property."

He chuckled. "I'm not so sure. They are quite tall now. The main hall might be able to accommodate one, but who wants a Christmas tree in the hall?"

She'd only been to Ethan's ancestral home once…or rather three times if she counted her visits with the spirits of Christmas Present and Future. "So where do you set up your Christmas tree?"

He suddenly found his meal incredibly interesting. "I think I'll need to find a reason to stop by Milton's more often. This pie is exceptional."

"Ethan, why are you avoiding my question?"

He watched Mac jump down from his chair before he finally looked at her. "Because it's a little embarrassing to admit to the owner of the One of a Kind Christmas Shop that one doesn't put up a tree and simply goes to one's parents for Christmas Eve night and Christmas Day."

Though his whole demeanor emanated guilt, the mischief in his eyes told her he didn't feel guilty at all.

"Oh, really. Then I'm glad *one* stopped by because *one* is not getting out of it this year. Your mom and dad may have everything set up for you at their house, but you brought me a tree, which means you're going to not only set it up, but string the lights and help me decorate it."

"I'd be happy to. That's little penance for my Christmas oversight."

She grinned before Mac caught her attention by batting a glass snowman against the wall hard enough to break it. "Mac! Stop that." She sighed. "That is if I have any decorations left to put on it." She'd bought that snowman for Cam the year they didn't get a single flake of snow in Deervale. It was to give him the snowman he always liked to build on the town square at night while people slept.

Ethan's laugh surprised her from her dreary thoughts.

"What's so funny?"

He put his empty plate on the table in front of him and twisted his body to face her. "You don't see what was so funny about your statement?"

She shook her head, not even sure of what she'd said, her thoughts straying toward Cam again as usual.

"Holly, you own a whole building filled with Christmas

decorations. I don't think you'll have the slightest challenge creating your Christmas magic in here."

She wanted to tell him that he couldn't understand, but something told her he did, and he was simply helping her to see it from another point of view. She grinned sheepishly. "Well, there is that."

Again he laughed, the sound warming her from the inside out. Maybe having him help her was the best idea she'd had all year. Cam would be so happy to know she'd invited Ethan to help decorate.

Cameron Douglas sat on the edge of his desk as one of his newest spirits of Christmas Past floated through the ceiling and disappeared. When he'd first transitioned and was told he had a lot to make up for, he'd no idea what that meant.

Standing, he walked around to his desk chair and picked up another case file. As it turned out, it meant he would serve as the supervisor to the Spirits of Christmas who worked their magic to help the living. His training had been hard and fast, and he resented every minute of it until he'd been introduced to his "staff."

He had Spirit Guide trainers and Spirit Guides. His main focus was the living. However, one particular living person had called to him from beyond the spirit world, and he'd finally given in and asked if he could help his wife. Little did he know what a landslide of events would take place once he pushed that rock over the cliff.

Remiel, his supervisor, had acquiesced but had made every step as difficult as possible. He'd also demanded long-term problem cases of Spirit Guides themselves be resolved. It hadn't been easy, but he'd done it.

He kept his hand on the closed file. There was no rush. Time meant nothing to spirits like himself. He could go anywhere at any time, except to see his wife and family. For that he had to have permission. Getting permission this time had been more than difficult.

After visits from three sets of spirits, it was deemed that Holly should have moved on. That she hadn't made better strides rested on his shoulders. This was his last chance to help her let go, so they could be together for eternity. He shook his head at the irony of it.

Remiel had set hard rules, such as no more than fifteen minutes with Holly at a time. His and Holly's bond was so strong, that the Arch Angel's protection was the only way he could even converse with her. Otherwise, he might turn into a ghost and be trapped on the living plane for eternity while she passed on.

He was also limited to Christmas Eve to see her, and he was forced to stay within that time frame once again. Remiel had indicated there would be other limitations, but refused to expand on them.

His boss may think he'd fail, but he had a secret weapon, thanks to his Spirit Guides. Ethan Stewart—his best friend and the man who loved Holly as much as he did. He'd learned in the afterlife that love was the most powerful force of all, and he planned to make good use of it.

Visiting Ethan had been a stroke of genius. He was confident in the plan they'd agreed to, or rather the plan he set up and Ethan would follow. A twinge of doubt knocked on his brain, but he shook it off. Ethan had as much to gain and lose as well. If all their ideas bore fruit, Holly would be ready to love Ethan come Christmas Day, and then come eternity, they'd be together again.

He looked at the name on the file beneath his hand but couldn't seem to read the letters. He was too excited to get started. He'd just come back from his visit with Ethan and was ready to get started. Luckily, moving forward or backward in time was easy for him. He wanted to find out if Ethan bringing Holly a brand-new artificial tree with the fancy lighting had made a difference in her future.

Without another thought, he floated out of his office and into the ether toward the future. He slowed as he came to the divergent timelines for Holly. Only he could see the multiple futures of every living assignment. He simply kept the ones open that his Spirit Guides could show to insure the best outcome and closed the ones he felt detrimental. It meant the Spirit Guides still had a choice based on their plans.

Before him were Holly's five openings in the gray mist. Two showed colored lights in the distance. They were the two possibilities Joy and Malcolm had shown Holly.

The other three openings showed only darkness. Was that because there were still only two possibilities or was it because he wasn't being allowed to see all five? When he'd sent the spirits of Christmas Future to Holly, there had been three possibilities. That there were five now made him nervous.

Did that mean the other two were better or worse than those already in place? A chill passed through him, and he glanced around. What the fuck was that?

Not seeing anything nor sensing another being, he turned away. He would come back here and check again after Ethan and he had spent some time with Holly. Hopefully, instead of more future possibilities, there'd be only one…the right one.

Chapter Three

December 20

Ethan held the ladder as Holly reached over to the top of the tree and placed a pink and purple fairy on top. Her sweet scent that reminded him of cinnamon apple pie tickled his nose…and his desire. He forced himself to look past her shapely ass and the temptation to touch it.

"Where? Oh, I found it." She sounded excited, which was a far cry from three days ago when they started the project of changing her living room into a Christmas haven. "It's really beautiful lit up." She started to back down the steps.

Ethan kept one hand on the ladder to hold it steady and let go with his other hand, well aware that she seemed averse to touching him.

"Crap!" Holly tilted on one foot, the ladder trying to go out from under her.

His choice was the ladder or her, and that was no choice at all. Grabbing her around her waist, he pulled her off before she could fall. The ladder clanged as it hit the floor causing Mac to run out of the room.

Lowering her to the ground, he quickly stepped away.

She spun around, her eyes wide.

Blast, now she'd be angry with him.

After a moment, she stepped toward him. "Thank you." She touched his shoulder as she stood on her toes to kiss him on the cheek. "I'm so glad you're that strong or I would have crushed all our handiwork."

He stood stunned, unable to move as she strode past him to set the ladder right again.

What happened to all the flinches he'd seen from her over the last year whenever he inadvertently touched her? He'd received the message loud and clear. They were *just* friends. He wanted so much more that his body ached with it as he lay awake at night imagining what it would be like to make love to her.

He gritted his teeth. It was Cameron's fault for making him think he could have something more. He'd tell him so next time his friend showed up. Cameron dangled his heart's desire in front of him, only he was wrong…again.

"Ethan, don't you like the tree?"

At Holly's tug on the sleeve of his turtleneck, he blinked. "What?"

"You're scowling. I don't think I've ever seen you scowl."

He looked into her chocolate brown eyes and easily relaxed his expression. She had a baby spruce cone stuck in her hair. Reflexively, he pulled it out, and luckily, she didn't move away. "I was scowling at this." He held it out to her. "You don't need any kind of decoration to look Christmassy."

She grinned. "You're just saying that because I own a Christmas Shop, but that's okay. I'll take it."

He wanted to tell her he never said anything he didn't mean, but he clamped his mouth shut as she held onto his arm with both her hands and faced the tree, the warmth of her fingers permeating his sleeve.

"I don't think I've ever had a prettier tree."

At her words, he forced his gaze from her happy face, her cheeks rounded with her smile, and looked at the tree. "The new decorations compliment the old ones well. You did a brilliant job decorating it."

"No, *we* did a great job decorating it. I forgot how much more fun it is to decorate with someone. Cameron used to help a little, but mostly he distracted me." She flushed. "Sometimes it took me over a week to get it done."

His heart stammered over her phrase. He was torturing himself being around her. He should be entered into the masochist club to be going along with Cameron's plan…or mostly going along with it.

Holly sighed. "Cam will love this."

He wasn't so sure since Cameron thought a new mechanized tree was what she needed. Suddenly, her use of the word "will" registered. He turned to face her. "You said Cam *will* love this. Not *would* love this. You know he's gone, right?"

She wouldn't look at him. In fact, she let go of his arm. "I know, but he always seems so close at this time of year. I think I miss him most now."

That made sense since Cameron died on Christmas day, and Ethan would have accepted Holly's explanation if he didn't know better. At least he *thought* he knew better. Had Cameron really visited him two weeks ago? Their conversation while planning how to aid Holly in moving forward with her life had felt so normal, the way it had always been, that he doubted his own senses now.

"Do *you* still miss him?" Holly's voice held a note of hope.

His heart squeezed at how alone she must feel. "I do. He was one of my two closest friends. When he died, he left a void." Yet as much as he hurt at losing Cameron, he hurt for Holly more, knowing instinctually the pain she endured, recognizing the constant sorrow in her eyes. But she'd pushed him away. She'd pushed all of them away.

He tried for three years to remain her friend, but she'd avoided him and Brody for the most part. The pain of losing Cameron and her rejection had been hard to live with. Then last year, just as he'd given up hope, she'd accepted his invitation to his parents for Christmas dinner.

At first, she'd been very stiff and clearly uncomfortable, but his mum had a way of making people feel welcome, and Holly soon relaxed, even playing some of their silly games.

She finally looked at him again. "I'm so glad I'm not the only one that misses him. It seems like no one else does. I never truly understood how you could be so close with Cameron and Brody. They were the complete opposite of you."

Less opposite than she realized, but he wasn't about to explain. "I think we rubbed off on each other. I tempered them a bit and they forced me out of my shell." Like him being in Holly's home decorating a Christmas tree he'd brought her. He wouldn't have been so forward if Cameron hadn't pushed him into it.

"Oh, I never saw you as being in a shell. It was more like you were their older brother, ever cautious, even if you always did look ten years younger."

He grimaced. "I think that put me at a disadvantage with them."

"I don't know." She walked around to the back of the two chairs facing the tree to view it from there. "I know Cam has a lot of respect for you."

There it was again. She spoke of Cameron as if he were still alive. Either Cameron *was* visiting Holly from beyond the grave or she was mentally ill. He wasn't sure which he hoped was true.

He strolled over to where she stood to view the tree as well. It reminded him of the trees he had as a child, but with an American flair. Holly insisted on stringing popcorn for garland, and he'd bought her the chocolate ornaments she'd never had before. While she set up her two trains under the large spruce, he'd selected the lighted fairy with wings that fluttered at uneven intervals for her tree top. The entire tree looked like something from a fairy tale.

The night he brought the tree, they'd spent cleaning up Mac's mess. That she'd relaxed enough to invite him to help her decorate it had been a clear sign she was lonely. He hated that she felt so alone. If only she'd let him in.

"I'm so glad you let me ramble on about Cam. The minute I bring him up, everyone else in town puts on this polite look and finds an excuse to leave the conversation. I think I'd go nuts if I didn't have you to talk to about him."

What she didn't realize was that she didn't talk about Cameron as much as she used to. It was only as Christmas approached that she'd become more fixated on him. There was an air of desperateness about it that concerned him. Cameron said this was his last year to visit her. Then what would she do?

Holly crossed her arms. "Cam never told me about putting a fairy on top. Then again, he was less focused on the details than I was. I think he just likes the feel of Christmas."

Likes? He couldn't let it pass this time. "Has Cameron visited you since his death?"

Her gaze snapped to his. "Why would you ask that?"

Cameron told him not to reveal to Holly that he'd visited, but Ethan wouldn't lie to her, especially if there was a chance, even a sliver of one, that she might come to love him someday. This was his chance.

Not one to rush into things, he quickly went over the pros and cons of getting her to admit she saw Cameron's spirit. Since they had no relationship beyond friends, there was little risk.

He'd prefer she tell him, but they weren't close enough for her to confide in him, which meant he had to admit it first. Taking a deep breath, he looked her in the eye. "Because he visited me."

Her mouth opened then closed then opened again. Then she

moved around what she called Cam's chair and plopped down on the arm. "You saw him?" Her words were barely a whisper.

He didn't move, afraid she would tell him he'd lost his mind. Maybe he had. Maybe that ghost really had been his imagination and the whole Christmas Eve plan just wishful thinking on his part.

Except he wasn't excited by the whole plan and would insist on changes because, once again, Cameron hadn't thought it through.

"I did." He didn't move a muscle as she studied him. If he hadn't really seen the ghost then Holly would think he was crazy.

Her eyes suddenly lit with excitement. "You *have* seen him!" She jumped up and grabbed his hand, tugging him over to the chair she'd just vacated. "Sit. You have to tell me everything."

He did as she requested, but tensed at the thought of telling her everything. She wouldn't be happy if she discovered the purpose of this year's visit was for her to fall in love with him. He'd attempted to convince Cameron that love took time, but the man brushed him off, telling him that something called "soulmates" could fall in love in an instant.

Holly knelt on the rug at his feet, a position his body immediately noticed, but since it caused him discomfort, he focused on her eyes. Would she ever be as excited to talk about him as she was to talk about Cameron? The answer his gut gave him cooled his desire.

"When did he come? Did he say anything about me? Did he take you across time? Do you like flying? Did he say if he can come back next year? Did he miss you?"

He gently placed his finger on her lips. "That's far too many questions for me to answer at once." He realized his mistake too late as her warm breath brushed over his finger, reawakening his need to kiss her.

Instead of recoiling, she grasped his hand and pulled it away from her mouth, but she didn't let go. "I'm sorry. I'm just so excited that someone else has seen him. Do you think he's visited Brody and Sarah, too? What about his aunt and uncle?"

"He didn't say anything about visiting others. I had the impression he was very limited by his superiors in what he was allowed to do."

She frowned. "He does seem under a lot of pressure from them. Did he look stressed to you? Last year he seemed very stressed. Then again, I'm sure it was hard for him to learn that you…" She pressed her lips together and quickly dropped his hand.

"Learn that I what?" He had a sinking feeling he knew what Cameron learned, but he hadn't mentioned Holly might know as well.

She looked away. "I can't tell you."

It had to be that he was in love with her. If that was the case, then it explained why she'd kept her distance and didn't want him to touch her. She knew he loved her, and didn't want him!

Suddenly, the room felt too small—the train whistle as it chugged around the tree trunk, the flickering lights around the room, Holly's closeness. They all combined to make him feel stifled.

He rose. "I should probably leave. Your living room is well decorated now." He clamped his mouth shut at the next words he wanted to utter. *Now your ghostly husband will be happy with you.* No matter that he resented Cameron right now, he wouldn't hurt her by uttering a word. Instead, he started for the coatrack.

He hadn't taken two steps before Holly grabbed his arm. "Don't go. Please."

If he looked at her, he'd stay and then what? "Why?" The word was out of his mouth before he could stop it.

She let go of his arm. "Because I was really looking forward to this evening." Her voice turned soft. "Coming home to an empty house every night is hard, but since you've been visiting, I feel… happier. Like Christmas is real again."

If she'd said anything else, he would have found the willpower to leave, but her admission burrowed under his agony and forced him to turn around. He studied her, trying to stay detached, but her honesty was clear in her gaze. He forced down the spike of hope that rose in his heart. "Christmas *is* real."

"Then stay." She gave him a half-hearted smile. "I even bought a steak pie from the Black Raven for dinner. A little birdie told me it's your favorite."

"A little birdie by the name of Mrs. Branson?" He tried to keep his tone light, but could tell he wasn't very convincing.

Still, she didn't give up trying to be cheerful. "Maybe. Or it could have been your mom. You do know that she comes into the shop every now and then. I guess you'll never know." She shrugged her shoulders, then lost her smile. "Please stay."

He was the biggest fool there was, but he couldn't resist her plea. "Very well."

A smile lit her face. "Great! You're probably hungry after all that talk of steak pie. I'll go heat it up."

"Meow." At Mac's rather demanding call, she faced the cat.

"Yes, I'll get you your dinner, too." She shook her head as she walked toward the kitchen. "Men and their stomachs."

Surprisingly, the cat didn't follow her out of the room. Instead, it sat on the floor looking at him.

"What?"

At the cat's continued stare, he rubbed the back of his neck. "Yes, you're right. I'm an idiot."

As if that was all Mac needed to hear, he turned around and trotted out of the room to find his dinner.

Ethan looked at the ceiling. "Cameron, you better be right."

Christmas Eve

Holly stepped out of the shower and dried off. Wrapping an old beach towel around her, she walked into her bedroom and opened the closet. She'd planned to wear her sexiest nightgown to see Cameron again, but that was out of the question now that Ethan would be coming over.

Ever since the night she'd made him uncomfortable, and he'd almost walked out, she'd made an extra effort to have him over. They'd even gone to dinner but only as friends. Part of her didn't want him to love her as it made it awkward, but part of her couldn't resist his company. After all, he was the only one truly interested in what she had to say about Cam. Often, he even joined in adding to a memory. They had all been so close.

So, what to wear tonight? Ethan said her rose red sweater complimented her brown eyes. That had to be why so many people commented on it. But she'd been wearing that sweater a lot with the Christmas rush. Thankfully, Brooke had offered to stay and wait for Mr. Branson, who would stop in at the last minute to buy an ornament for his wife like he did every year. Otherwise, she wouldn't have had time enough to shower, eat, and be ready when Ethan arrived.

She couldn't wait to see what Ethan thought of seeing Cam. She had no idea what spirits Cam would send this time, but she hoped they could include Ethan. She loved that she could talk about this secret side of her life with him.

Scanning her wardrobe, her gaze lit upon the red dress she'd bought at an after Christmas sale last year. She hadn't been able to resist. It was so much like Joy's, her Spirit of Christmas Future. Only Joy's had been a Kelly green and this one was a warm red. It was cut narrow at her waist and flared out from there, but it was longer than her Spirit friend's, coming to fall at mid-calf. She wasn't nearly as slender as Joy, whose dress had white fur trim. Hers had bling around the hemline, as well as at the end of the fitted sleeves.

She'd looked for ankle boots but didn't find any, so she'd bought a pair of knee-high ones that were black. She only wore them with her black leggings, but maybe tonight she'd wear them with the dress. She had to have a black belt somewhere. Still wearing just the towel, she rummaged through her drawers and checked the hangers in her closet.

Where had she put that wide black belt she had? She couldn't have given it away. Rechecking her drawers and even her hope chest, which was filled with her summer clothes, she still couldn't find it.

She sat down hard on the chest. "Doesn't that suck?" Tears of frustration gathered in her eyes. How stupid to be on the verge of tears over a stupid belt. She could wear another one or another dress, but the more she contemplated a different outfit, the more she wanted to wear the red dress.

Pull yourself together, Holly. Just because it's the last time you'll see Cameron doesn't mean you have to look stunning. He loves you no matter what you're wearing. Despite her conscience, she still pouted. Why couldn't she wear what she wanted for the last time she would see him? Why did it have to be the last time? Why—

Mac jumped up on the chest and walked onto her lap.

"Really? Can't you see I'm upset?"

The cat butted its head against her chin.

"How could I forget how selfish cats are?" She stroked Mac, and he started to purr. "You always know when I need you, don't you?" She gave the big cat a hug. When she let go, he jumped down.

"So much for your giving nature."

Mac wandered into her closet.

"Hey, you know you're not allowed in there. You'll get locked in like you did last time." Jumping off her hope chest, she strode for her closet, but Mac had already disappeared into it. "You're not helping, Mac."

She pushed the door wide open and the light from her room reflected on Mac's amber eyes. "Ah-hah. I see you." Getting on her hands and knees, she crawled under her clothes to the far corner.

As she reached for Mac, he jumped away causing her towel to come loose. She grabbed it. About to swear, she stopped, eyeing something on the floor where Mac had been. "What's this?" Grasping the dark object with one hand, she backed out and sat on the throw rug outside her closet. It was her black belt!

"Mac, you're awesome!" She looked under her clothes for him but didn't see him. Great. Now she'd have to leave her closet open until she found him again. Standing, she held the belt up. She couldn't be mad at Mac. He deserved to sleep wherever he wanted tonight. It wasn't as if she'd be home.

Grabbing the hanger with her red dress, she brought it to the bed and put it on. In the four years of seeing Cam on Christmas Eve night, this was the first time she was home early and had the chance to freshen up. She wanted to be ready and enjoy every second she could get with him.

After checking herself in the mirror on the back of her closet door, she left it open and walked into her kitchen to pour herself a ginger ale. She didn't dare have any of the left over wine that Ethan had brought two nights ago. That would make her fall asleep. She was such a light weight.

Taking a sip of the soda, she glanced at the clock with the Douglas tartan in the background. It was almost half past seven. Ethan would arrive any minute. He was always on time, so unlike Cam.

She wandered into the living room to make sure all was ready. She'd turned on all the Christmas lights as soon as she walked in the door after work, but it had still been light out. Now the cozy room was aglow, the gas firelight barely competing for attention.

The huge spruce tree smelled heavenly, and she closed her eyes as she inhaled. Memories of her as a teenager helping John and her mom get ready for family, flew through her mind, warming her heart. They were quickly followed by memories of the days she and Ethan decorated her new tree.

He'd helped her carefully gather all the broken ornaments that meant something to her and Cam and put them in a box to try and repair later. She'd hoped to fix them before Cam arrived, but it had been even busier in the shop than usual and Ethan had enticed her to go to the town square tree lighting, a Christmas cèilidh, and a Christmas concert put on by the choir at the Parish church.

She hadn't been in years and people said they were happy to see her and how great it was she'd hired Brooke. She'd only done that because of the Spirits of Christmas Present. They had made it clear that she couldn't hide away in her shop if she ever wanted to be with her husband again.

She perched on the arm of Cam's chair. It no longer smelled of him. She breathed deeply. No, now it smelled like the Christmas tea she'd been drinking. How odd. She took another sip of her soda and watched the trains beneath the tree chug along, one crossing over the other on an arch that Cam had made.

She lifted her gaze, not wanting to dwell on the fact that tonight would be her last time seeing the man she loved. Her eyes fell on a new ornament. It was one of three that Ethan had bought for her, saying she needed to continue to receive ornament gifts even if she owned her own shop. She'd no idea where he'd purchased them, but each was lovely in its own right. That he'd done so because he loved her wasn't lost upon her, though he never let on how he felt, and for that she was grateful. Her feelings for him were mixed up enough as it was.

The ornament at the front of the tree had the year's date from four years ago, her first Christmas without Cameron. It was a large sprig of holly with two berries on it that gave off a soft glow, catching the fake snow sprinkles on the holly leaves. Ethan said it was to celebrate her Christmas spirit with or without Cameron by her side.

She rose from the arm of the chair, put her glass on a side table, and strolled to the other side of the tree. Ethan had hung the second ornament on a higher branch. It was a little gingerbread house with a large front window and over it were the words "One of a Kind Christmas Shop." That he'd gone so far as to have the artisan customize it so much touched her heart. She couldn't wait to show Cam.

She crossed her arms, her emotions starting to swirl. Her anticipation and fear were building equally. She couldn't wait for Ethan to meet the spirits. Her guess was Cam wanted Ethan to learn something. She'd certainly learned a lot from her three visits.

But she also feared saying goodbye to Cam forever. He'd obviously been slowly building up over the years to tonight, knowing they would finally have to part. Her heart ached just thinking about it.

Movement outside her bay window caught her eye, and she breathed a sigh of relief as Ethan's Mercedes pulled up in front of her house. He was exactly what she needed—a distraction. Walking around the tree, she opened the door before he could knock.

His eyes widened as his mouth broke into a smile. "Happy Christmas Eve."

She stepped back to let him in. "Happy Christmas Eve to you." Too excited to contain herself she threw up her arms and gave him a hug.

It took a couple seconds before he hugged her back, but he did and the scent of cold air and ginger enveloped her. It was familiar for some reason and made her feel safe and warm inside. Finally, she stepped away, and he closed the door.

"Now that's a true Christmas welcome." He unbuttoned his coat and hung it on the coatrack. He wore an ivory wool sweater over a green collared shirt that matched his eyes, not to mention the dark kilt he rocked. Her gaze wandered down past his muscular calves covered in the Scottish socks with flashes and stopped at the dark dress shoes.

Ethan was a handsome man anyway. She'd never take that from him, but dressed in his blue and green Old Stewart tartan, reminded her of exactly how Scottish he was, and her heart beat a bit faster. She stepped farther into the living room, suddenly unsure. All the other times Ethan came over, he helped her with something, but now everything was done, and they just had to wait for Cam.

He turned to face her, rubbing his hands together to get them warm. "Don't you look bonnie tonight." His gaze ran from her boots to her face and finally to the holly barrette in her hair.

She felt heat rise in her cheeks. "Well, you said red complimented my eyes, so I thought for this very special night, it was appropriate."

His gaze softened, reminding her once again of what he felt for her. She looked away. Why did it have to be so awkward? They were just friends.

"Did Mrs. Bell make you another clootie dumpling this year?"

She nodded. "She did. Would you like some?"

"Aye, I would."

Happy to have something to do, she strode into the kitchen to pull out the dessert. Ethan's footsteps on the hardwood floors let her know he was coming before she'd even taken out the dishes. "Here, let me help."

She stepped away from the counter, the kitchen seeming to grow two sizes smaller with him in it. Opening the fridge, she took out the sweet, pudding-like dessert. The first time she'd ever tried the Scottish specialty, she'd fallen in love with it but could never seem to make it herself. Luckily, Mrs. Bell had supplied her and Cameron with them since their first Christmas in their new home.

She set the dish on the counter next to Ethan and unwrapped it.

"Ach, Mrs. Bell is an angel." At Ethan's exclamation, she grinned.

"I think the same thing every Christmas." She pulled out the drawer with her silverware and handed him a knife. "Would you like a big spoon or a small one?"

He took the knife from her, his fingers brushing hers for a moment. She quickly moved her hand next to the drawer and waited. When he didn't answer, she looked up at him. "Well?"

Ethan glanced at her, his left eyebrow raised. "I thought that was a rhetorical question."

"Right. Big spoon it is."

He chuckled as he turned his attention to the dumpling before cutting into it. After setting a large slice on each plate, he rinsed off the knife and set it in her sink.

The man was certainly neat. Cam would have left the knife on the plate and walked away with his portion.

"Do you have any custard to go with it?" Ethan sounded hopeful.

She grinned. "Not exactly custard, but I do have some French vanilla ice cream. Will that do?"

"Aye, it will. Do you like yours warm or cold?" He moved toward her microwave, completely at home in the kitchen.

"Warm please." As he heated their dessert, she put the remainder in the fridge then pulled out the ice cream. When she turned around, he was taking one dish out and putting the other in. She couldn't help satisfying her curiosity. "I thought you had a cook at Rawdon Manor."

He shrugged. "I do. But she's not around at half past ten when

I get hungry again." He took out the second plate and set it on the counter. "I've become an expert with the microwave."

She gave them each a scoop of ice cream then put it away. When she turned back, he held her plate like a butler, one of her paper napkins over his arm. "Shall we adjourn to the living room?"

"Most certainly." She attempted to keep a straight face, trying to match his formal tone, but she couldn't, and she laughed as she took the plate from him. "Sorry, I guess the American in me just can't seem to stay stuffy."

He followed her out of the kitchen with his own plate. "We'll have to work on that. We Scots are experts at both. Our wild ancestry has us eating with our hands, and our neighbors to the south have us drinking tea with our pinkies out straight."

"Hah, I've seen you drink tea, and you do not stick your pinky out."

He winked. "But I do know how."

Feeling more relaxed, she settled into her chair facing the Christmas tree. As Ethan sat beside her, the Christmas scent she'd smelled earlier wafted over her. Holy crap, it was Ethan. He smelled like Christmas! That's why the chair reminded her of her tea. "Did you want something to drink with that?"

He shook his head, his mouth full of dumpling.

Taking a cue from him, she dug in. It wasn't as if they sat in silence so much as they ate without talking.

The room was filled with activity, even the new manger she'd purchased had the animals bowing their heads, and the fairy on the tree glowed from a pale pink to a deep purple and back again, its wings fluttering inconsistently. The trains chugged on their tracks, and three cardinals perched in the tree chirped sporadically. There was only one thing missing.

"Meow." Mac sauntered in and sat at Ethan's feet.

Nope, nothing was missing now…except Cam.

Ethan put his plate on the side table next to his chair. "Are you looking for a lap?"

"Meow."

She chuckled. "I think he's telling you that's his chair. He's not big into laps, but once in—"

Mac jumped onto Ethan's lap, walked in a circle and lay down.

She scowled at the cat. "He's just trying to make me out to be a liar."

Ethan chuckled. "I don't think you're a liar. I think Mac just does what he wants when he wants to. I had a cat like that when I was a child. I had to respect that."

She stared hard at Mac as he turned to look at her as if to say she should respect him, too. "I'd respect him more if he hadn't destroyed half my decorations."

Ethan absently stroked the cat as he scanned the room. "I'm not sure where you put all those decorations before, but I think the room appears fully decorated now."

He was right. It felt decorated and homey, but not cluttered. Maybe she *had* been going overboard. Then again, Cam had liked it that way. *But Cam won't be here to see it next year.*

She ignored the voice in her head. "You must have all your staff working overtime to decorate Rawdon Manor. That must take months."

Ethan waved his hand and Mac gave her a perturbed look. "I don't decorate Rawdon. Who would see it? Mum used to, but now that they're in town, and I stay with them for Christmas, there's no need to decorate at home."

"Not decorate?" She stared, flabbergasted. She never pegged Ethan for a Scrooge.

He focused on Mac. "Nay. Like I said, I go to my parents."

She rose and faced him. "Ebenezer Stewart, you're a hypocrite."

His eyes widened. "Now you sound like Mum. It's not that I

don't like Christmas. It's just that no one would see the decorations but me, and that's only if I went into the parlor, but I never use that room."

She crossed her arms and frowned at him. "So, what's wrong with putting a tree in your study and decorating that room? You spend most of your time there, don't you?"

His gaze finally met hers. "Because I didn't think of that? Mum always decorated her parlor."

She threw her hands up. "Men. Next year Ethan, we're going to get you a live tree, we're going to decorate it *and* your study."

He grinned like a little boy who had just been told he could have clootie dumpling for breakfast. "I'd like that."

She picked up his empty dish, shaking her head. "Sometimes, I just don't know where your head is at." Adding her empty plate to his, she walked out of the room.

Chapter Four

Ethan grinned. He hadn't thought about making Rawdon festive, but now with Holly planning it as a project for next year, he was grateful for his oversight. She may wonder where his head was at, but sometimes it was best she not know, like when she bent over to pick up his dirty dish. Her scoop-necked dress was demure when she stood, but bending over, she revealed a lot more of her substantial bosom than she probably realized.

He generally stifled the urge to compliment her since she tended to grow uncomfortable when he did, but tonight she was a stunner. In his gut, he knew she'd dressed up for Cameron, but that she'd taken into account what he'd said about the color complimenting her eyes took the sting out of that fact. That he'd played some role in her decision meant she valued his opinion.

"That's enough attention, Mac." He lifted his hand from the cat and the feline calmly rose and hopped onto the arm of the easy chair.

Rising, Ethan walked to the gas fireplace and set his hand on the mantle as he watched the flames. He was skeptical about tonight. It felt as if he was at a tipping point with Holly and this adventure could cause her to go either way.

He wasn't sure what he'd do if she shut him out again. As much as he wanted to love her openly and have her feel the same way, the risk was too great. He'd rather be Holly's friend than not have her in his life at all.

He grimaced. What had he let Cameron talk him into? Visits to the past, present, and future that Cameron chose. Few of them felt right to him, but his friend insisted they would work and asked him to trust him.

It wasn't that he didn't trust Cameron. The man always had the best of intentions, but his plans didn't necessarily have the results he expected them to.

Of course, that was assuming this spirit that had visited him really *was* Cameron Douglas. What if it was some other entity? What if Holly was in harm's way? No matter what he thought about the evening's activities, there was one thing for certain—he would protect Holly with his life if he had to.

Holly's high heeled boots clicked on the wood floor as she entered the room before the sound was swallowed up by the braided rug. "The waiting part is the hardest. Every year I fall asleep only to be woken by two spirits." She glanced at the clock and frowned. "That's around nine or ten, but Cam always arrives first to let me know what he wants help with. Usually, he's come by now."

Ethan rubbed the back of his neck. He needed more information. When Cameron had visited and explained his plan, he'd said he'd return, if he could, to fine tune it, but he hadn't. Would he show up now? If he didn't, how would that affect Holly?

He dropped his hand and looked at her as she adjusted an ornament on the tree. He'd bought her a fourth one to represent this year, but he wouldn't give it to her until Christmas day at his parents, assuming she would still come. The uncertainty of her future didn't sit well with him. He needed to do something to influence the outcome, but he was woefully unprepared. "Tell me about your visits with the Christmas ghosts."

Holly spun at his voice as if she'd forgotten he was present. "Oh, they aren't ghosts. They're spirits. Those are nothing alike."

I'm not a ghost. I'm a spirit. Cameron's words echoed in his brain. He hadn't given it much thought at the time. "How are they different?"

Holly perched on the arm of her chair, a place she seemed to gravitate to regularly. "A ghost is a soul with unfinished business here on Earth, and because of that, is stuck among the living for eternity."

A chill filled him at her words.

She continued. "A spirit is just someone who has passed. I'm not sure of all the distinctions, but I think spirits help the living." Her faced glowed with pride. "Cameron is in charge of lots of spirits."

That the afterlife had distinctions like she explained had never occurred to him. Though in truth, he hadn't given the afterlife a lot of thought until the night Cameron had visited him. "And you say you've gone with two spirits every Christmas?"

She smiled. "Oh, yes. The first year it was Duncan and Jessica. Duncan was from way earlier in Scotland's history and Jessica had actually been my mom's and my social worker after our apartment building caught on fire one Christmas Eve. I was just a teenager then."

"And what did they show you?"

Holly's eyes lit with excitement. "They didn't just show me. They brought me to that awful night, my first Christmas with Cam, and a whole bunch of other events from my past. They proved to me that instead of being sad about losing Cam, I should be happy that I had the time with him I did. They showed me what I had with him was something some people never experience."

Spirits from her past helping her cope with Cameron's loss? "And what about the next year?"

Holly crossed her arms. "Now that was Ian and Coco. At first,

I didn't really care for Ian. I think he was some kind of Scottish aristocracy, but Coco was from Kentucky and so warm. Those two constantly argued."

Ethan let go of the mantle and leaned his back against the wall next to the small fireplace, his mind organizing the facts. "And what did they show you."

"They *brought* me around town that Christmas to see how other people were celebrating." Holly's gaze flitted away from him. "Thank you for not letting the crowd at Brody's come to my house to force me to attend."

She'd seen that? He'd been thinking she'd dreamed it all, but this made it real. Every nerve-ending in his body came to attention. "You're welcome." That was actually the year she'd come to the party, though later in the night.

"I had been thinking that people were all happy and wouldn't want this sad face around them, but Ian and Coco revealed to me that other people had their troubles, too." She frowned for a moment and gave him a quizzical look. "Have you seen Sophia lately?"

"Sophia?" He thought for a moment, the change in subject throwing him off balance. "The last time I saw her was at the bakery. She was ordering trifle for Christmas day. She invited me to her home, but I told her I celebrated with my parents." He reflected on the conversation. "I think she was hoping for an invitation. I was tempted to offer it since it appears she'll be alone for the holiday, but Mum only invited you, and I didn't feel it was my place to extend another invitation."

Holly nodded. "Thank you. I do feel for Sophia, but I think she'll have somewhere else to go tomorrow."

"I didn't know you'd become friends with her."

"I didn't though I tried. I just learned something about her when I was with Ian and Coco as well as with Malcom and Joy."

"And was Malcom from Scotland and Joy from America?" There was definitely a pattern here.

She snorted. "Why, yes they were. But Malcolm was from the future."

Now that didn't surprise him. Spirits from the past, present, and future. He'd like to put the whole unbelievable story down to a Dickens novel and an active imagination except for two things—his visit from the ghost, no, spirit of Cameron Douglas and what Holly saw at Brody's party before she'd even arrived.

Then again, someone could have told Holly he'd stopped them all from dragging her to the party, and the spirit of his best friend could still be his own imagination.

"Malcom and Joy showed me the future of my parents, my friends, and myself." Holly's excitement dimmed. She dropped her arms and rose to walk over to the side table where she picked up a sheep from a manger scene. "They showed me two, forty percent possibilities for my future."

His heartbeat hitched. Forty percent? That was too specific for comfort. He wanted to ask what she saw, but he swallowed his question. If she felt something for him, she'd tell him. He counted the seconds as he waited for her to continue.

Just as it seemed she wouldn't, she put down the sheep. "Some of what I saw I didn't like. I'm hoping that the changes I made in my life this past year will have changed the odds. Maybe that's it. Maybe I'll simply have another set of spirits."

It took a lot of willpower not to cross the room and take her in his arms and assure her she could have any future she wanted. For fuck's sake! What the hell was Cameron doing to her? On one hand, Cameron said he wanted Holly to move on, but something about what she related didn't feel right.

Holly suddenly smiled. "The best part about the spirits is the flying."

"Flying? You mentioned that once before. Cameron didn't say anything about flying."

She strode toward him. "Well, first you have to get phased. That way you are just like a spirit. Then they take your hand." She took his hand in hers. "And we fly out of this house, right through the wall. It's really fun. Except for the gray mist." She wrinkled her nose. "I don't like that part, but it doesn't last long. Then we get to fly around the new place and phase into wherever we're going."

He lost track of what she was saying the second her hand had clasped his. All he could think of was how right it felt.

"Ethan? Don't you want to fly?"

He blinked and snapped his gaze from their clasped hands to her lips. Quickly, he looked into her eyes. "I don't know. I've never done it before. Did you like it the first time you flew?"

She gave him a reassuring smile. "Oh, yes. It's better than a rollercoaster."

He returned her smile. "I like rollercoasters."

She literally beamed, taking his breath away. "Then you'll love it."

He was sure that anywhere he went with her he would love. He tensed as reality reminded him of what the experience was supposed to bring about and what could be on the line for them.

Holly let go of his hand and walked back to the second chair where Mac lay. She absently stroked the cat, whose purring became loud enough to hear from where he stood.

Based on what Holly told him and his *conversation* with the spirit of Cameron, there would be no more spirits. She said herself this was Cameron's last visit. It was clear to him, as an outsider, that his friend had been trying to help Holly move on from his death with his spirits, but unlike in the Dickens novel, that hadn't been enough. Something about the process had not been successful. This felt like a last-ditch effort to help her.

Holly couldn't see it. She was too close, too emotionally involved to see the patterns and the failure of her experiences. She was simply focused on making it through a year to see Cameron again, which begged the question, what would support her through the next year? His gut twisted in fear. He had to find a way to reach her heart.

She looked up at the clock again, her brow furrowed in worry. "I hope this doesn't mean he's not coming. He said he would, but it's getting so late." Her voice cracked on her final word.

"He'll come."

At his voice, she snapped her gaze to him. "But he should have been here already."

He pushed away from the wall and strode toward her, wanting to take her in his arms and reassure her, but he stopped on the other side of the cat's chair. "He's coming later because there will be no spirits. He will be your guide for tonight."

"Really?" She latched onto his arm across the chair, Mac looking up at her in what seemed to be annoyance. "Are you sure?"

Was he? He didn't want to give her false hope. Reviewing the facts, such as they were, he spoke with renewed certainty. "I'm sure."

She breathed easier, letting him go. "I don't know what I would do without you."

You never have to find out. "I'm sure you would manage." He tried to sound nonchalant but wasn't sure he pulled it off.

She stepped around the chair and stood in front of him. "No. Really. You've been a better friend than I."

I don't want to be a friend. I want you to let me love you. "You've been a great friend."

Holly smiled. "I've really been trying. We all had so much fun together when Cam was alive. Adjusting is…hard."

"I know. But you're strong. We all are. If Cam were here, and I was gone, he'd persevere."

She cocked her head to the side, an unusual occurrence for her. "I'm not so sure. He depended on you so much."

"Me?" At her serious face, he squelched the chuckle that rose.

She pointed her finger into his chest. "Yes, you. You don't give yourself nearly enough credit."

He grasped her hand and placed it on her chest. "And you don't give yourself enough credit."

She smirked. "Some pair we are. No wonder we needed Cam."

"Did someone call my name?"

"Cameron!" Holly's eyes lit up, and Ethan spun around.

Standing in front of the fireplace was Cameron Douglas in spirit form dressed as he'd been just a few weeks ago. His gazed softened. "Merry Christmas Eve, hen."

Holly walked toward her late husband, but stopped short of embracing him. "I was afraid you weren't coming."

He looked past her. "But Ethan told you I would, right?"

She glanced back at him and smiled. "Yes, he did." She faced her husband again. "You visited him."

Cameron nodded. "Aye, I did."

"How come you can visit him and not me?"

Ethan couldn't see her face, but he could picture her pout. On other women that look irritated him, but with Holly, it was part of her charm, her honesty.

Cameron floated around his wife and greeted him. "Thank you for coming with us."

He nodded. "Of course."

Holly marched over. "Cameron Douglas, don't you ignore me. Why were you able to visit Ethan and not me?"

Cameron grimaced at him before facing his wife. "I couldn't. You know our connection is far too strong. You don't want me to turn into a ghost, do you?"

She crossed her arms. "Of course not, but you're here now, so why couldn't you have visited me earlier this month like you did Ethan?"

Ethan held back his smile. Holly's backbone was one of the characteristics he admired about her. Here she stood, facing off with the spirit of her late husband, not letting him off the hook as if he were still alive.

Cameron moved his hair off his forehead. "I have to follow the rules, love. And this time there are a lot."

At Holly's clear skepticism, Cameron continued. "But that's because I get to go with you myself. No other spirits this time."

Her eyes widened as she looked past her husband to him. "You were right!"

He smirked at that. "It happens on occasion."

She chuckled. "Sorry, I didn't mean it the way it sounded."

He shrugged it off as he walked around the spirit and stood next to Holly. He was still uncomfortable talking to his dead friend, but for Holly, he'd do whatever he had to. "You said there were many rules. I think you should share them so we are all well aware of yours and our limitations."

Cameron raised his hand to slap him on the shoulder, but it went right through him, causing a strange sensation. "Sorry. It's habit. You're right as usual. The rules I can tell you about are that I will only be able to stay with Holly for fifteen minutes of living time. Then I can't come back for an hour. This will mean that our transit will need to be fast, and that you will need to keep Holly safe." Cameron stared hard at his wife. "And in one place where I can find you both."

Holly looked away clearly guilty. That meant she may not be as obedient as Cameron liked. Ethan found that concerning in this situation, but in general, he was glad she didn't bend so easily.

He pulled Cameron's attention back to the issue at hand. "Are there other rules we should be aware of?"

"Aye, anything you see in the present and future, you must not reveal to anyone."

Holly dropped her arms. "Well, of course. Malcom and Joy made that very clear."

"Why?" His question obviously surprised Cameron.

His friend's brow furrowed. "For one thing, you'll make things very difficult for me. I've had to jump over hurdles to be able to come here tonight. I've also made some agreements, and one of them is that you both will not reveal what you see. If you can't agree to that, then you can stay here."

Ethan bristled at Cameron's tone. "Aye, I can keep what I'm shown to myself, but what I want to know is why did you have to do so much to come here? Is this unusual?" He refused to back down. He needed to know, and for Holly to hear the truth before he entrusted both of them into the hands of a spirit.

Cameron threw up his hands and walked toward the fireplace, through it and the wall, disappearing from sight.

"No, Cameron, come back!" Holly stepped in front of him to chase after Cameron.

He grabbed her by the arm. "No. Stay here. He'll be back."

The fear in her eyes as she looked at him tugged at his heart, but he stood fast. Cameron would be back because it was the last chance for him to fix what he'd screwed up.

Holly pulled her arm from his hand and plopped into her chair. Mac, who'd sat up at Cameron's entrance looked at him before settling down and curling back into a ball where he was.

Ethan knelt at her feet. "I know you don't want to think about this, but what will you do after tonight?"

She wouldn't look at him. "I don't know. He has my heart. To love someone so much and not be able to have that returned is torturous."

"I know." The words were out of his mouth before he could recall them.

Holly's gaze rose to him.

He laid his hand on the arm of the chair. "I know how much you suffer from missing him. I hate to see you sad. I want you to be happy. We will have to work on a way to make you happy every day in the coming year."

She shook her head. "I'm not sure that's possible." Then her lip quirked up. "Even with Cam, I wasn't happy *every* day. He could be so frustrating."

He chuckled. "I can't disagree with you there."

Her lips moved into a sad smile. "I'm sure you were more frustrated than I was. I think he liked to push your buttons just to see how you'd react."

He widened his eyes in fake surprise. "Did he now?"

She giggled. "I should have known you could see right through him."

Unfortunately now, that was literally true. "Aye, but I still let him rile me. I guess it was a sort of game we played."

A twinkle came into Holly's eyes. "If you want, I could be unreasonable toward you."

He grinned. "Only if I can frustrate you."

She pretended to seriously think about it before laughing. "No, I don't think either of us could be as good as Cam." She grew pensive. "Besides, frustration can be wearing."

He didn't respond, recognizing their conversation as a step forward for her. If she could see life without Cameron as having some positives, she might be able to open her heart again, which was his own fervent wish.

She finally returned her gaze to him. "You don't have to kneel on the floor. You can sit right here." She placed her hand on the chair next to hers. "Just move Mac."

"I'm not sure that's a good idea." He noticed that at the mention of his name, Mac's ears perked up. The cat was obviously not asleep as he pretended.

"Mac, move so Ethan can sit down. He's our guest."

The cat's ear twitched toward the sound of Holly's voice, but he remained curled in a ball.

Ethan grinned. He liked Mac. The animal was smart and made Holly smile, which is why he was still baffled as to why Mac had destroyed half of the ornaments. Could it be curiosity, that he wanted to play with them, or was it that he'd had enough of the Christmas clutter? Could he be that intelligent?

Holly's hand on his own immediately switched his attention. "Tell me he'll come back tonight."

That was an easy request. Grasping her hand in his, he stood. "He'll come back and probably soon. He needs you to go on this journey."

She didn't pull her hand away, but she did stand. "How can you be so—oh, wait. You know what he has planned, where we're going." She studied his face, looking for reassurance. Having her gaze focused on him was such a pleasure that he delayed answering for a few more seconds.

He loved looking at her round face, her pert nose, and especially her warm brown eyes. He was so thankful he hadn't truly appreciated all her attributes while she was still married. That would have made it hard to be with Cameron, even now, with him as a ghost—no spirit. He had to remember that. Now it felt odd, not just that Cameron was with him and Holly, but that Cameron wanted his wife to love him, his best friend.

"Ethan?"

He finally nodded. "Aye, I do."

She didn't stop staring into his eyes. "And you think that no matter how mad he is that he'll come back?"

"Aye, he has to."

She tugged on his hand. "Why? Tell me."

He sighed. "I can't, *mo chridhe*. You need to hear it from him."

She pulled away and strode to the other side of the tree. "Well, that's going to be a little hard with him not here. Now *you're* being frustrating."

He loved her spirit, and he wanted to give in, but playing with her emotions was Cameron's expertise, not his. All those spirits he'd sent to help her move on may have been successful, but Ethan was sure Cameron was the problem. If the man hadn't visited Holly, she might have continued to live by now.

He remained silent, glancing at the clock. How long would it take Cameron to blow off steam? Not that it mattered because according to him, time meant nothing, so was the man purposefully hurting Holly or was he trying to make his pique known.

The train whistled, a sound he'd noticed Mac didn't care for, but other than that, there was only the ticking of the grandfather clock in the corner nearest to Holly. He let her have her space. She wasn't one to hold a grudge for long, and she wasn't one to stay still for long either.

Within seconds, she walked back to where he stood. "I'm sorry. I'm kind of up and down when Cameron is around. It seems like the rest of the year is such an even keel and then tonight comes, and I'm the happiest I've been all year and I'm the saddest. Does that make sense?"

He wanted to take her in his arms and tell her he'd spend his life keeping her happy if she let him. Pushing his own feelings aside, he connected with what she said because that was how it was for him any day he was with her. "I understand."

"You do? It's such an odd situation. I'm not sure anyone can truly understand."

He put his hands on her shoulders and was pleased when she

didn't flinch. Why was that all of a sudden? "I do, and if there was anything I could do to make it easier for you, I would, but I think this is something only you can take control of."

She stood straighter. "You're right. I'm tired of being pathetic."

He laughed and reluctantly removed his hands. "You're far from pathetic." He was the pathetic one. Not having the guts to tell the woman he loved how he felt. His mum thought he was a lost cause.

She gave him half a smile. "Oh, you should have seen one of my futures. It was beyond pathetic."

"What about the other one? You said you saw two that were equally likely to come to pass."

Just as Holly stiffened, Cameron floated down beside her. "Is Ethan making you feel uncomfortable, love?"

She snapped her head to the side. "You're back." Her smile was wide. "I'm so glad."

Cameron gazed at his wife for a moment before looking at Ethan. The look was hard, but not unfriendly. "Ethan has a way of making us see things we don't want to see."

He shrugged. "The truth about ourselves is sometimes difficult to face." And he, of all people, was well aware of that.

Cameron floated over to him and faced his wife. "Holly, I screwed up…again."

Her brow furrowed. "What are you talking about? You can't mess up anymore."

Cameron gave a self-deprecating chuckle. "Oh aye, I can." His face grew serious. "And I'm afraid I may have wasted some of your time."

"No, not at all. I only have Brody's party to go to tonight." She pointed. "I'm going with Ethan."

Cameron looked at him as if to ask if he really needed to tell her.

Ethan had seen that look enough in their Uni days to know it. He gave one definite nod.

Cameron sighed then turned back to his wife. "No, what I meant was, I should have let the spirits of past, present, and future do their work without coming to see you. Because you've been able to see me, you haven't moved on with your life like you were supposed to."

"No, that's not true." Holly shook her head. "I've learned a lot from them, and I helped you accomplish what you needed them to accomplish. You said so yourself. We make a good team. Always have. Always will."

Movement in the corner of his eye had Ethan glancing to his other side only to find Mac perched on the arm of his chair watching Cameron. A chill raced up Ethan's spine.

"Yes, I mean no." Cameron brushed Ethan's arm as he walked to his wife. "We can't be a team anymore. You need to stand on your own now."

Chapter Five

Holly's heart squeezed, making it hard to breathe. She didn't want to be strong. She'd done everything the spirits expected her to, but she still wanted Cameron in her life. Even if it was just one night a year.

She looked into Cam's hazel eyes, now a mellow gray, and they blurred. "But I don't want to stand on my own. I did that before I met you. I wasn't supposed to have to do that again. It was supposed to be until death do us part."

Cameron's hand rose to touch her cheek, but he stopped before making contact. "Hen, death did part us."

Seeing his spirit made that hard to accept because she knew he existed on some other plane. "But that was supposed to be after decades together."

He shook his head. "No. That was never my destiny. You heard Malcom. That I was graciously given a few years with you was a bonus. I was just not wired to live a long life. Sometimes I wish we'd never met to spare you this heartache."

"No! I love that we had our time together. Duncan and Jessica did make me see how special that was." She wanted him to hold her, and that he couldn't was killing her. She craved his comfort, feeling the need deep in her soul.

A strong arm wrapped around her shoulders, and she turned her head to look at Ethan, who now faced Cam as well.

"I think what Holly needs is a distraction right now. Something to set her sights beyond the past."

Cam looked at his friend and floated back a few feet. "You're right. And what better place to start than in the past?"

She wiped her eyes with her sleeve. Leave it to Ethan to calm the situation. He was so good at that. It was one of the reasons they all loved him. If she'd never met Cam, she could see herself falling for Ethan, but she had met Cam.

Knowing Ethan loved her, even if he wasn't sure she knew that or not, should have made it uncomfortable. But there was a certain comfort in that because he loved Cam as well. "That means were going to fly." She looked at Ethan, whose green eyes had become a lighter shade.

He took his arm from her shoulders and straightened. "I'm not sure how this works, but I'll trust in you."

She flushed. Ethan didn't trust easily because he had to judge everything for himself. This was a leap of faith for him, and she was honored. She gave him a smile before looking at Cam. "We're ready to be phased."

Cam floated to her first and touched her. At first, she didn't feel his hand, just the usual tingle as his unearthly form met hers, but then the coolness emanated from where his hand was and spread through her whole body until she could see through her own hands.

Excited, she turned toward Ethan whose gaze was wide and panicked. That he was new to the whole experience, cooled her energy, and she gave him a reassuring smile. "I know it seems strange at first, but you get used to it. This is the only way we can fly. I can't wait for you to experience it."

Ethan gave a curt nod, but she could tell he was tense. She'd grown used to his body language over the past year. While Cam tended to fist his hands, Ethan was so much more subtle. His shoulders tightened up, making him look like he was ready to take on an incoming army, which considering his study of ancient Scottish combat, probably wasn't that odd for him.

"Ready, my friend?" Cam held his hand above Ethan's stiff shoulder.

"I am." Ethan looked Cam in the eye as he began to phase.

She'd never seen anyone phase before. Watching it happen to Ethan, she shivered. No wonder he'd been apprehensive. If she'd seen that before she was ever phased, she'd probably have refused.

Who was she kidding? If it gave her a chance to see Cam, she would have done it in a heartbeat. Still, she was glad she hadn't had to witness it.

As soon as Ethan was fully phased, he floated over to her, his face unreadable, which was unusual for him.

Cam grinned. "Are you ready to relive the past?"

Holly smiled. "Of course." She grabbed Ethan's hand. "This is where we get to fly." She squinched up her face. "But we have to go through the gray stuff first. That's a little eerie, so don't let go."

Ethan still didn't say anything as he looked down at their clasped hands.

She'd little time to think about that oddity because Cam took her other hand and headed for the ceiling. Her heart melted at his touch. Last year he'd held her briefly in her phased state and that memory had comforted her after many a hard day. To hold his hand now was a dream come true that she planned to enjoy to the fullest.

She looked below to see Mac watching them. "Don't worry, Mac. We'll be back."

As they cleared the roof, she thought she heard a meow.

Cam floated them down Main Street and into the gray matter she didn't like.

Ethan's hand in hers tightened just before he spoke to Cam.

"What happens if we let go of you?"

Cam looked back. "In the ether? You'd simply float here until

I came back to get you. In here, you have no control of when or where you go."

"Has any living person been lost in here?"

Ethan's thought sent a chill racing down her spine. She didn't like the ether anyway.

Cam raised his brows. "Not that I know of, but I never bring the living through this. That is the purpose of the Spirit Guides I direct."

She smiled at Ethan. "He's a supervisor with lots of Spirit Guides reporting to him."

"Like a job?" Ethan's own brow rose.

Cam looked forward again. "No. It's more like they depend on me."

She'd always thought of it like a job. Could that be why Cam seemed tired in the afterlife, because so many depended on him?

She was about to ask when the grayness cleared like coming out of a fog, and they flew along the same street they were on moments ago. Then Cam took a left turn along Donniebristle Lane. "We're still in Deervale."

"Why are we still here?" Ethan's tone was accusatory.

She looked back at him in consternation. "Aren't we supposed to be here?"

"No."

She turned her head to see what Cam would say to that, but he just kept flying. Now, why would he bring them somewhere besides where he told Ethan he would? Then again, why wouldn't he? This was Cam.

She looked below them. They passed along stretch of connected houses before slowing as they went by a double house with a large yard and came to stop above a white-washed cottage with a black sign out front and a large picture window to rival the one at the One of a Kind Christmas Shop. "I know this place. It's the Black Raven."

Ethan let go of her hand and floated over to Cam like a pro. How'd he learn to fly so quickly?

"This isn't the university."

Cam grinned. "No, it isn't." He turned his head toward her. "Ethan didn't like my idea of showing you what an immature ass I was at Uni, so I took his advice." He gave Ethan a fake punch in the shoulder. "See, I still listen to you once in a while."

Ethan didn't budge. "So why here? I can think of a number of times you were here that Holly doesn't need to see."

"Relax, this isn't me being a buffoon."

Her heart warmed. It was so like Ethan to not want her to see what an idiot Cam could be sometimes, but she knew what he was like. It wasn't as if he were like that all the time, and his kindness, caring and protectiveness all made up for it. "Don't worry. I'm well aware of my husband's faults."

Ethan rubbed the back of his neck, a sure sign he was seriously troubled.

She took his hand again. "Come on. Believe me, I've seen some very harsh scenes. I doubt that Cam at the Black Raven can even come close. Besides, it's not like I'm a wilting flower. I do have a backbone, you know."

He finally gave her a smile, the first since he'd been phased. The relief she felt at that was confusing but welcome. No sooner had he agreed than Cam floated them through the roof of the local pub and over to the highest corner against a rock wall with a fireplace.

She spoke to Ethan to explain. "He doesn't want our spirit forms to come in contact with living people because we'll both feel it, and it's very strange."

He gave her a nod, but didn't say anything, his focus on the people across the narrow room.

Curious, she scanned the men sitting at the dark wood table.

A wall of the same wood rose behind them with the boards set vertically and a Glengoyne Highland Single Malt Scotch painting, highlighting the local burn took up most of the space. It was an old advertisement. She'd been in the Black Raven more than a few times, but never noticed it.

Then again, the walls in that pub were covered with pictures and paintings, mostly of Loudon Hill or the castle ruins, but also of old lace factories and other buildings that used to be in town.

It was no surprise to her that it was Cam, Ethan, and Brody sitting in that dark corner. The surprise was how quiet the conversation appeared to be. "Can we move closer?" She pointed to a lower spot where an old lace loom sat covered in Rangers memorabilia, one of the Scottish football teams and obviously a favorite of the proprietor.

Cam scanned the entire pub before answering. "Aye, it looks safe enough."

The three of them drifted over, Cam leading the way.

The Cam sitting at the table looked about the age he'd been when he proposed. They'd been renting a flat on the edge of town. Ethan's hair was short and curly, exacerbated by the humidity outside, which flowed in the open windows at the back of the pub. Brody was smiling as usual, his light brown hair, which was barely darker than Ethan's, was shorter than it was in her time. "This was about six years ago, right?" She looked at Cam. "Before we bought the shop and the house?"

Cam grimaced. "Aye."

Now why would he be unhappy about that time? It was a great time in their lives. She studied the three men at the table.

"I'm telling you, I haven't seen anything like it." Brody was barely staying seated, his body shifting in his chair.

"I'm all in. This is just what we needed." The younger Cam's eyes sparked with his excitement.

The younger Ethan shook his head. "This isn't a good idea. You've worked hard for that money. It's too great a risk."

Cam frowned. "You think everything's a risk. We need to jump on this stock before it slows."

"If it slowed that would be good. This is unmitigated growth. It can't last. Don't do it." Young Ethan stared hard at Cam and then at Brody. "Either of you. You have others to think of now."

Brody scowled. "Hey, I'm not married or anything. I can risk what I like. I haven't known Sarah that long. Don't attach a ball and chain to my ankle yet there, Ethan."

"What about Holly?" Ethan returned his attention to Cam. "Are you going to ask her what she thinks? After all, part of that down payment is hers, right?"

She sucked in her breath and stared at her late husband. "You risked our down payment in the stock market? Is that why we were able to buy the shop as well?"

"You need to watch."

At Cam's unusually serious tone, she turned her attention back to the men at the table.

The young Cam moved his hair off his forehead. "I'll only leave it in for a few days."

Young Ethan scowled. "And what if it drops in two days."

Brody jumped in. "It won't. I've had mine in there for a couple days already. It just keeps rising. I'll let it ride one more day and take it out."

"Listen to you." Young Ethan scowled. "You make it sound like a bet. The London Exchange isn't a game. It's influenced by the world economy." He refocused his attention on Cam. "Don't do this. Aren't you supposed to meet with the bank next week about the house you found in town?"

"Exactly. I'll take the money out by that meeting and go in with a much larger down payment. Holly will be so excited to hear we can buy the shop next door, too."

"You're not listening." Ethan shook his head, his frustration evident.

Brody lifted his glass. "Let's toast to a good week on the Exchange."

Cam lifted his ale, but Ethan frowned. "Oh, come on, Ethan. At least you can wish us well."

Ethan finally lifted his glass. "I *do* wish you well."

Brody grinned. "Here's to the London Exchange soaring to new heights next week."

The three men tapped glasses and drank.

Holly glanced at Ethan floating next to her and recognized the set of his jaw. He was even less happy than his younger self. Why, when obviously everything had turned out well? Maybe he just didn't like not being listened to.

Cam clasped her hand. "We need to go right now. I only have a few more living minutes."

Quickly, she grabbed Ethan's hand again and Cam flew them through the pub. After a few seconds in the gray mist they came out flying toward the outskirts of town. With both men so focused, she didn't say a word as Rawdon Manor, Ethan's ancestral home, came into view.

She'd been there with her Spirits of Christmas Future to witness an unhappy scene, so she hoped she wouldn't have to see another. Her heart went out to Ethan. He squeezed her hand, obviously not liking what they were about to see.

Cameron flew them down through the roof and into Ethan's bedroom.

Now she'd seen the family rooms when she and Cam visited, but she'd never been in the private quarters. It was eye-opening. It was obviously Ethan's room since there was a robe on an easy chair with his initials embroidered on it, plus there were two books on the side table next to the chair and one was titled The Battle of Loudon Hill and the other was one of Sir Walter Scott's novels, both interests of his.

Ethan let go of her hand and drifted to the side of his bed.

It was an impressive bed. It was a four-poster with dark maroon curtains gathered at each post, and above the mattress was the same velvet material. The mattress itself was so high that she couldn't imagine climbing into it without the aid of steps.

Suddenly uncomfortable, she turned away from that thought and scanned the room. It was very masculine and simply decorated, but what was in it seemed of very high quality. The vase on a side table looked like it could be a Ming Dynasty piece and the painting over the fireplace reminded her of a piece by the English Romantic poet and illustrator, William Blake, but if that were true, it had to be worth a fortune.

Her gaze finally rested on Ethan, who hovered near the far side of his bed looking down at a book on his end table. He was such a regular guy that she often forgot he came from money. And since he handled all his family's financial investments, he'd probably remain that way.

"Ach, in my rush I misjudged."

At Cam's exclamation, she drifted closer to him. He hung near one of the twelve-foot windows. "Why? Did we arrive too soon? What's going to happen?"

"I want you to see. It's important."

"No, it's not. I think we should leave."

At Ethan's reply, Cam stiffened. "Trust me. She needs to see this. It's important if—"

At that moment, the door to the bedroom opened and the younger Ethan strode in. He wore a pair of light gray sweat pants tied at the waist, a similar color sleeveless t-shirt and he held a towel in one hand and a water bottle in the other.

Kicking the door closed, he set the bottle on the side table and wiped the sweat from his face. Then he dropped the towel next to the water bottle as well and headed for a large dresser at the opposite end of the room from the fireplace.

His bedroom door swung open again. Since she was looking at him at that moment, she witnessed his reflexes in action. He spun around and bent his knees in some kind of fighting crouch then just as quickly straightened.

"Ethan, I need your help." The young Cam had panic in his eyes as he stopped, his face flushed, and his shoulders drooping.

She'd never seen him like that and her heart tightened with worry before she remembered everything must have worked out since the scene was from the past.

Cam grabbed her hand and squeezed. "I have to go. I'll be back in an hour of living time. Don't leave these grounds, okay?"

She nodded, not wanting him to leave, but very much aware of the danger of him staying. "I'll be here."

He nodded toward Ethan, who had drifted closer. "Ethan will explain everything." With that, he was gone. No flying through the wall or upward through the roof. Just gone, as if someone had snatched him up.

Instinctively, she floated over to Ethan, glad she wasn't left in her phased state by herself. It had never bothered her before, but then she had Spirit Guides to rely on and they *had* to keep her safe.

"Take a breath, Cam." The young Ethan strolled toward Cam. "Nothing's going to get worse in the next two minutes. Sit down." He motioned to one of the two easy chairs that flanked the fireplace.

Young Cam didn't do either. Instead, he started to pace. "That stock dropped. I didn't think it would."

"But it just dropped today. I've been watching it. You were right, it did have three days of growth in it. It actually had five."

Cam shook his head as he paced. "But I thought it would continue to go up."

Young Ethan froze. "You sold it at the close on Wednesday, right?"

Cam kept pacing, shaking his head.

"For fuck's sake, Cam. When did you sell it?"

Cam stopped. "This morning."

"What?" Young Ethan grabbed his laptop out of a satchel leaning against one of the chairs. Turning it on, he quickly typed. "Bloody hell."

"I know." Cam finally dropped into the other chair, completely defeated. "There's hardly anything left, and we're supposed to give the down payment tomorrow."

Holly's chest tightened. How could that be? They put a down payment on both the house and shop the very next day.

Young Ethan took his own advice, his chest rising with a deep breath as if he'd practiced it a hundred times. Then he sat in the adjoining chair. He didn't say anything, but he was clearly reviewing a number of possibilities.

She relaxed. Ethan must have come up with a way for Cam to get his money back. Maybe a stock he knew would jump? She glanced at her companion, but his brows were lowered as if it pained him to watch. That was not reassuring.

He caught her staring, so she asked the obvious. "You came up with a plan?"

"Aye."

When he didn't say anything else, she returned her gaze to the two men sitting in the easy chairs. Cam had to be devastated. She'd only seen him sit still that long a few times, and it always meant he'd given up.

Young Ethan finally spoke. "Did Brody lose his shirt, too?"

"No, he sold on Wednesday."

"That's more than three days."

Cam threw up his arms. "I know. He held onto it for five days. He'd bought two days before me, so I figured I'd hold onto it for five, too. Then sell today and I'd be able to put half down tomorrow."

"That didn't work out so well."

Cam glared at Ethan. "No shit."

Again, silence ensued. Cam sunk lower into the chair, his whole body like a wet autumn leaf while Ethan remained alert.

"She'll leave. Go back to America. I know it." At Cam's dejected tone, she wanted to reassure him, but that was silly. This event had already passed. She found herself focusing on Ethan, both the younger one and the older one. As she did, she noticed a few differences.

The older Ethan had lines around his mouth that weren't on the younger version, and as she looked closer, she noticed his lower lip had developed a deep crease in the center. She found that oddly attractive. Licking her own lips, she returned her gaze to young Ethan.

She couldn't help smirking as she found that despite all his thinking, young Ethan was not happy. Between his right eyebrow and hairline, he had a small tic that was obvious now. Of course he wouldn't be happy. Once again, he'd warned Cam and the warning had been ignored. That had to grow tiring, and yet he'd remained a steadfast friend.

And here he was, helping Cam again. She warmed with a new appreciation for the man beside her.

"Did you hear me? She's going to leave me." Cam's tone bordered on whining, which he'd never done in her presence. He had to be feeling desperate. She would be heartbroken right now if she didn't know the future, but she did. The next day Cam made the down payment on both properties, so it all ended well.

"Aye, I heard you, but I'm trying to think."

Cam closed his open mouth. He understood the value of Ethan. She thought she had, but she was learning there was even more. She'd seen the bond between the three men, so to see these two together without her was riveting.

Young Ethan rose and went back to his computer. "How much do you have left?"

Cam immediately perked up and told him.

She gasped. Despite knowing the outcome, she was still shocked. How could he have risked so much of their future?

Ethan typed away at the keys.

"You know how this resolved. We can leave now if you like." Ethan's voice, so close, startled her. She'd been so intent on *the boys*.

As she gave him her attention, she could sense his tension. "I'd like to see how it came about. I'm guessing you worked some of your magic." She smiled, wanting him to know how much she appreciated him. He was her rock now, but it appeared he'd been so all along. She just hadn't known.

He looked into her eyes as if trying to read her thoughts then finally gave a single nod. He returned his focus to the past, so she did the same.

Why was he reluctant to stay? Did he not like being the hero?

Young Ethan stopped typing and faced Cam. "I have a solution, if you want it."

Cam jumped up. "Of course, I want it."

"I've never done this before because I don't want it to become awkward between us, but I think I can keep that from happening if you'll hear me out."

"Tell me. I'll do anything to keep her." Cam's desperation tugged at her heart.

Didn't he know she wouldn't have left him over a stupid decision and a couple buildings? Their love was so much stronger than that. It actually hurt that he would think she could possibly leave.

"You give me the rest of your down payment."

"What? How the hell is that supposed to help! You did hear me correctly, right? I don't have the money I need."

That young Ethan didn't respond in kind told her a lot about him. Had he'd always had so much control? If Cam had spoken to her like that, she would have yelled right back at him that she wasn't stupid.

In fact, Ethan just stared at Cam, not saying a word.

Cam finally got the message. "I'm sorry. I'm just fucked." He walked behind the chair and grabbed it with both hands. "I'll shut up until you finish. Promise."

"Good." Ethan pointed to his computer. "I ran some numbers, averaging market trends, potential for growth, and a few opportunities coming down the line. If I invest your money tomorrow, it should be back to where it was in roughly thirty months, assuming no serious world events."

Cam opened his mouth, but then shut it.

She was proud of him for that.

Ethan continued. "Obviously, that doesn't help you with tomorrow. So here is my solution. I will give you the down payment money."

"What?" She couldn't help herself. She looked back at the older Ethan who was watching her. "You gave us the money?"

Instead of answering her, he switched his gaze to his younger self.

When Cam didn't say anything to that, she turned her head, too.

"I'll take the money you have, invest it in what I think appropriate, and when it has reached the amount I gave you, I'll keep it. This way your debt will be paid without you having to feel like you owe me anything. I don't want money to come between us."

Cam stared at Ethan, his eyes wide.

Unexpected anger filled her. "Holy crap, you did it, didn't you?" She floated toward the young Cam, who opened his mouth, but nothing came out.

She snapped her head up and scowled at the phased Ethan. "He took your loan, didn't he?"

"Aye, he did. And in thirty-one months it was paid off."

Cam's yell had her spinning back around, just in time to get out of his way as he strode around the chair and gave Ethan a bear hug. He laughed. "You're a genius! I knew you always got the best grades of all of us, but you're a fucking genius."

Ethan pulled back. "I do have one condition."

"Anything. You name it. You just saved my future."

"You promise that you will never buy another stock until we're even."

"Done." Cam held out his hand and the two men shook.

Holly turned away from the young men and the Ethan that was with her and floated through the ceiling. Her shop, her home, her short marriage to Cam had been made possible by Ethan. Cam had always said he wouldn't marry her until he could put a roof over her head that he owned. And then they almost didn't have one.

Why had Ethan done it? Had he loved her then? Even if he didn't and did it just for Cam's happiness, she felt indebted to him. Crap, just when she'd finally become comfortable having him for a friend, knowing how he felt about her, now she wanted to get away from him. He confused her.

Quickly, she rose through the ceiling and floated above the roof, the overcast skies mirroring her mood. She wished she were back home with Mac instead of on this journey, or better yet, in Cam's arms. They were both phased now, but he hadn't touched her except for holding her hand.

The scent of Christmas floated toward her, not as strong as in her house, but it was definitely there. "I'm sorry you know about that now. It wasn't what we'd talked about."

She didn't turn to face him. Instead, she kept her gaze on the green lawn below that stretched out as far as any grand estate she'd seen in Scotland. Beyond it were spruce trees, no doubt planted by Ethan and his dad. It was the home of a wealthy family. One that could give a loan to a friend, so why was she so upset?

Refusing to look at him, she spoke to the landscape. "Why did he want me to see that?"

In the silence that followed, she knew he was weighing the pros and the cons of telling her. Frustrated with that, she spun around. "Tell me."

Ethan lifted his hands up and to the side. "He didn't tell me, but I think he wanted you to see how imperfect he was."

"What? Like I don't know that? We were married for two years and were together two years before that. Cam was anything but perfect. Does he think that for some reason by me seeing him at his worst that—"

Ethan opened his mouth to interrupt.

She wagged her finger at him. "Oh no, don't defend him. That was definitely one of his worst moments. But reminding me of his imperfections isn't going to make me love him any less."

Her anger was wearing off and already she felt her eyes tearing up. "Why does he want me to stop loving him? Why does he want me to forget him? He keeps telling me I need to move on. Why is he pushing me away?"

The sympathy in Ethan's eyes was too much. Her tears started to fall, and she couldn't help it. "It's like he doesn't want me to be his wife anymore."

"Ach, *mo chridhe* don't cry, please. We don't know that's why he brought you here. He may have had another reason and now it has backfired. He doesn't expect you to stop loving him any more than he could stop loving you. That's why he's here. He just wants you to hold onto him as a happy memory and keep living."

At Ethan's words, she tried to focus on him, but her sight was blurry. "Why does it have to hurt so much?"

He drifted closer. "I don't know. I wish I could take the pain away."

Wiping her eyes with the back of her hand, she glimpsed Ethan's pain before he opened his arms and she floated into them.

Chapter Six

Holly's heart ached and to be held again after so long was too much to resist. She wrapped her arms around his waist and hung on like he was her only lifeline. Despite their phased state, he felt solid, an anchor amidst her turbulent emotions.

Her tears fell, the ache in her chest a hard throb, like the beat of a bass drum, every hit taking her breath.

Ethan's hand rubbed back and forth across her shoulder blade, his other arm around her waist. Her ear against his chest picked up the beat of his heart. She focused on that, shying away from the pain, keeping his slow steady rhythm her centerpoint. She was tired of hurting.

They hung above the grand roof of Ethan's home for who knew how long. Finally, she lifted her head to find him staring at the scenery behind her, his eyes suspiciously moist.

How could she forget how much he'd loved Cam, too? She wasn't the only one who hurt. That realization took the edge off. Misery must truly love company. "I'm sorry. I forget that you knew Cam even longer than me."

His gaze moved to hers, the green of his eyes, even in their phased state appeared even brighter. "It's not about the length of time, but about feeling. Your hurt is as deep as anyone's."

She almost nodded, but stopped in time. Again, she was only thinking of herself. "I know Cam depended on you a lot."

Ethan moved his gaze back to the landscape. "I depended on him, too."

"Really?" It had always seemed like a one-way street to her.

"Aye. He always pushed me beyond my comfort zone. Sometimes encouraging me, other times daring me, and sometimes guilting me into going beyond my safe life. My life has been richer because of him."

Her heart warmed again, Ethan's words soothing it in ways she'd never thought they could. "I never learned how you two met. I know he and Brody were in the Polo club together at the university, or Uni as you all call it. That was no surprise to learn. But I don't take you for that kind of sportsman." She cocked her head and smirked a bit. "I see you more as a golfer."

His chest against hers vibrated with a silent chuckle, reminding her she was still in his arms, but it felt so good to be held again that she didn't move away.

"Ach, that was not one of my more stellar moments. In fact, if it hadn't been for Cameron, I would have quit school altogether."

"What?" She leaned back a bit, begging him silently to look at her. "But you're the smartest. Why would you quit school? You always said you enjoyed your courses."

"Oh, I did love my classes, but in my first few days, it was obvious to a few of my classmates that I was a bit of a geek."

She rolled her eyes. "Now you're just playing with me. You're way too muscular and handsome to ever be considered a geek."

That got his attention. She flushed as he gave her a quizzical look, but he continued. "To put it politely, there were a few bullies in my history course who preferred to show they were better than I was via intimidation. There were six of them, all on what you Americans would call the 'soccer' team, our football. It was beyond immature, so I chose to ignore it, but one day they went too far."

She held her breath, gazing into his eyes as he remembered the incident. His brows had slowly lowered, and she could see the anger there. She'd never seen Ethan angry. At his look, she understood exactly how accepting he'd been of all his friends.

"They crowded me toward the stairs between the second and third floors of the classics building. They were doing the usual verbal taunts, which I ignored, but I think that was the wrong way to handle it because they were clearly looking for a reaction. When I turned around to head down the stairs, one of them shoved me."

"Oh!"

He shook his head, his lips quirking up in a smirk. "I didn't fall that far. Cameron and Brody were coming up the stairs, and I literally fell into them." He sobered. "But if they hadn't been there, I would have broken a few bones and possibly my neck."

Her chest suddenly tightened at the idea of Ethan being hurt. If he'd died that day, she would have never known him. And she and Cam would have never married before he died because Cam had lost their down payment. Crap, her husband probably would have died even sooner!

Ethan shrugged. "I decided right then that I'd quit school, but Cameron wouldn't let me. He said I couldn't let those football team members influence my life like that. Then he told Brody to take notes for him and skipped his next class to walk with me to the Dean's office and tell him what happened. Cameron explained what he saw, that he'd never met me before the incident, then ended with the fact he'd been thrown against the wall by my fall. He made it all sound rather dramatic."

She opened her mouth to respond, but her indignation over the whole event made her throat close over the jumble of words that wanted to come out.

"The football coach was livid and benched them all. Two quit school soon after that and the rest stayed away from me." Ethan's gaze returned to her. "From that day onward, Cameron and Brody stuck with me. I always wished that I had had enough historic combat training to have taken them all on, but as I matured, I understood that wasn't why I had been studying it in the first place."

He grinned at her. "Studying ancient Scottish warfare qualified one as a geek back then. I'm not sure that's changed." He removed his arms from around her and held his hands out to the side. "I blame my interest on living here."

Uncomfortable that she hadn't moved out of his embrace sooner, she floated back. "What do you mean? What does living here in the countryside have to do with being what *you* call a geek?"

"Look behind me. What do you see?"

She floated to the right, to look past the front drive. "I see the ruins of Loudon Castle."

He nodded. "Exactly. I grew up with that in view. As a boy I made up stories about living there. Then when I learned to read, I read every book I could find on castles in general and that one in particular."

It was certainly a sight most American children didn't have growing up.

"And if that wasn't enough to keep my active imagination occupied, all I had to do is look out beyond our back lawn." He pointed past her.

She turned around at the sprawling countryside that was his family's estate. If she looked past the spruce forest, Loudon Hill stood out, a high promontory in the middle of pastures. "The battle of Loudon Hill." She shivered as she remembered the ghosts she'd seen at the bottom of that particular hill.

"That was a bloody battle." Ethan's voice was closer now.

She shivered again, this time on purpose. "I know. Robert the Bruce fought it in 1307. The dead still haunt it."

Ethan floated by her and faced her. "You know of it?" His excitement was clear in his face.

"Not much. But I saw the dead when I was there with the spirits of Christmas Past. It was awful. Their wounds and faces and…" She couldn't continue as her memory of the images filled her mind.

"You saw them?"

She nodded. "You can only see them in a phased state."

Ethan looked over his shoulder. "I'd like to see that."

She grabbed his arm. "No, you don't. Really. It's gruesome."

He studied her, his indecision clear. Finally, he sighed. "I won't go without you, so I guess I'll have to forego it."

Oh, no. She couldn't do that to him. This was his one chance to see a battle he'd studied his whole life. An event that made him part of the man he was today. She took a deep breath. She could do this for him. It was the least she could do. "No, let's go. I can stay on top of the hill."

He searched her eyes. "Are you sure?"

"Yes. I just won't look down until we reach the hill."

Ethan's smile was wide. "I will be forever in your debt."

Before she could reply, he grabbed her hand and flew toward the hill. She kept her gaze on the top plateau where Jessica had brought her to relive the day Cam had proposed and they'd found Mac. There had been no ghosts up there.

They floated down next to the small monument that marked the top.

"Are you sure you'll be okay if I leave you here?" Ethan's concern was heartwarming.

"I promise. Just don't stay down there too long. I'm not used to being phased without Spirit Guides around."

He squeezed her hand before letting go. "I'll be quick."

She watched as he flew over the ledge, obviously knowing exactly where the battle had taken place. When he'd disappeared, she looked around the plateau that was the top of the hill. The tree where she and Cam had sat when he proposed was to one side and the bush where he found Mac wasn't far away, but she didn't move.

Those spots had happy memories for her, but since seeing the ghosts below, the whole area felt cold. Shouldn't Cam be arriving soon? She'd ask Ethan what time it was when he returned.

Cam's last words to them before he left drifted through her mind. *I'll be back in an hour of living time. Don't leave these grounds, okay?*

Well, crap. They'd forgotten they were supposed to stay at Ethan's. She should call him. But even as she opened her mouth to yell, she shut it again. This was an amazing opportunity for him. She didn't want to cut it short. He'd be the only living person, besides herself, to ever know what that battle had looked like, or rather what the men looked like.

Besides, he had a watch. He could tell time. Cam said one hour.

She looked up at the sky, which had turned darker and felt gloomy, not that that was that uncommon in Scotland. It was as if her nervousness had conjured up a depressing sky.

"You're right. That's not something you want to be viewing." Ethan floated over the top of the hill.

Relief washed through her. She may not have any Spirit Guides, but she had Ethan. He'd never let anything happen to her.

She had Ethan. The thought caught her up short. She forced a small smile. "Was it what you hoped?"

He came to a stop in front of her, his brows lowered. "Aye and nay. It was different from what I imagined, harsher." His face brightened. "But it was fascinating to see the clothing and weaponry. They weren't fighting, but the wounds told their own story."

Another shiver raced through her.

"I'm sorry. I'll keep my observations to myself. Come. Let's head back to Rawdon." He held out his hand.

She looked at it and couldn't help thinking how strong it was, like the body it was attached to. But Ethan was more than hard-bodied, he had strength of character and mind. She placed her hand in his, expecting him to direct them. When he didn't move, she looked up at him.

"Are you all right? Did something occur while I was below?"

"No, I just don't like this place anymore."

"Of course." He turned his head toward Rawdon Manor and pulled them upward.

She glanced back at the tree that had been so pivotal to her life. Now it just seemed like a tree. It wasn't the place or events but the memory of the person that was important.

Gritting her teeth with determination, she made a silent pledge. No matter what Cam showed her, she'd always remember him as the person she knew he was—loving, kind, enthusiastic and flawed.

Ethan locked away the images in his mind for further perusal at a later time. That Holly had been willing to give him this unique opportunity despite her own fears, made him love her all the more.

Was this what Cameron had wanted to happen? He hoped it wasn't what they thought, that he was trying to show Holly how much he'd messed up in the past. On the next visit, he'd ask him outright because the guessing game he had them playing was unacceptable.

To see Holly in so much emotional pain had cut like a *sgian-dubh*. She was supposed be healing, moving forward, not being subjected to her worst fears. He had to figure out how to protect her from that.

As they approached his home, a ray of sun broke through the clouds and highlighted Loudon Castle just a short distance away. He looked back at Holly. "Have you been to the castle in phased form?"

"No. Did anything bad happen there?" Her trepidation was obvious as her eyes widened.

He quickly reviewed what he knew of the castle's history. "Nay. It used to house William Wallace's sword, which I'm sure has a bloody history, but that sword is long gone now, so there shouldn't be anything untoward there."

"Then let's take a look. I haven't been there since the day all of us went for a picnic on the lawn in front of it."

He halted in mid-flight. "You haven't visited it since?"

Holly gave him a crooked smile. "You know Cam had no interest in it because he couldn't climb it, and since he passed, I've had my hands full."

She held up her other hand to keep him from speaking. "And before you say anything, it wasn't because I was moping, well not after the first year. Losing Cam meant twice the work for me. We had just started our life together, but it was long enough for us to have divided the work. Suddenly, he was gone and all the chores he used to do fell on me. It's time consuming."

That detail had never occurred to him. He was single and had a staff at Rawdon Manor. Brody, on the other hand, was married, and now that Holly pointed it out, instances when Brody stopped at the store, or tied up the trash, or set the table, came to mind.

Immediately, he wanted to offer to help, but his gut told him that wouldn't work with their current relationship. "I understand. We'll just have to plan to take you over there after Hogmanay."

Her brow lifted. "I'd like that, but we can also see it right now." She pointed to their destination.

"Yes, we can." He squeezed her hand and started for the castle again. "In our current state, we can explore inside. It's privately owned and closed now, so normally we could only see it from the grounds."

As they approached, she flew next to him. "Wow, I didn't realize how big it is or was." Her excitement at seeing his *favorite place on Earth*, as his mum called it, pleased him.

To have her love it as much as he did would somehow mean something. It wasn't logical, just as his connection to the castle wasn't logical. He'd learned long ago in his ancient studies that logic had its place, but sometimes it needed to step aside.

"Can you imagine growing up here?" Her voice was full of wonder.

They floated over the center of the ruins, which dwarfed his own home. "I can and I did when I was a wee boy. Do you want to see where I decided my bedroom was?" He smirked, the memory a happy one for him. In his imagination, he also was part of a big family with lots of siblings and not the only child that he was.

"Oh, yes. You have to show me."

He pulled her toward the east corner of the roofless structure and descended inside the square tower, one of many with a tree growing inside it. "This was my room." He grinned. "Actually, it was me and my twin sister's room in my youthful imagination. We had eight other siblings."

She laughed. "Oh, my. You did have quite an imagination." She floated around the space he always considered *his* room. He'd never told anyone about it, not even his mum. "What was your twin's name?"

"Frances. She actually existed in her time and we are related, but she was born almost two hundred years before me. I called her Franny. I guess you could say she was my imaginary playmate."

Holly turned and looked at him. "I wish I had that kind of imagination. Luckily, my mom married me into a bunch of cousins. Wait, you said she once existed. Did you research that as a boy?"

He swallowed. He hadn't meant to give away that particular oddity of his childhood. "Nay, I learned that much later." He shrugged. He didn't believe in coincidence, but that wasn't something he wanted to discuss right now, especially in a phased form. He'd always felt that Franny had let him know she'd lived there through their shared DNA.

"So, you were related to the people who built this? It must be reassuring to be able to trace your roots back that far."

He wasn't unaware of the wistfulness of her tone and tried to lighten the mood. "My mum says that's why I'm so taken with it. She says I feel this place in my blood." He tensed ready for her to laugh at the fancy, but she didn't.

"I know what she means. It was how I felt when I first arrived in Deervale, like I was coming home." She shrugged. "Who knows, maybe my biological father had Scottish roots."

At the idea that her ancestors may have been living near his own, a feeling of rightness brushed through him. It had to be true. Maybe they were meant to find each other in this odd way. He may be grasping at straws, but stranger things had occurred just in the past year, so he wasn't going to ignore it.

Holly floated through the tree trunk to the other side of the room, reinforcing the very strangeness he was thinking of. He joined her by going around, not as comfortable in his state as she was.

"Are these your initials?" She pointed to the letters EAJS scratched into the inner wall.

He cringed. "Aye. I can only blame my youth for this vandalism."

"Ethan Alexander James Stewart. If I'm not mistaken you've got a bunch of royal names in there. Where did the Ethan come from?"

He stared, shocked that she knew his full name. Even Cameron would be hard pressed to rattle it off so easily. "You know my name?"

She didn't look at him, her gaze focused on the wall. "Sure. Of course, the initials make it easy to remember— almost like an acronym. That makes it—Oh, look!" She pointed to lighter scratches in the wall below his. "It looks like FSAR. No, there's another letter. I think it's another A. Oh wow, this is Franny's initials, right?" She rose and spun. "She really was real. You put your initials above hers. Do you know what they stood for? Did I get them right?"

Holly's excitement erased any embarrassment he felt at having defaced the property. "You're close. The last letter is an H. She was Frances Sophia Adelaide Rawdon-Hastings when she lived here."

Holly chuckled. "That little girl had an awfully long name."

He agreed. "What was your biological father's family name?"

She rolled her eyes. "Campbell. Like there has to be millions of Campbells in Scotland."

His gut tightened. "Aye, but Deervale was founded by a Campbell."

Her eyes widened. "Really? Wouldn't that be amazing if I was able to trace my roots back to the founder of this town? That would definitely explain my weird coming-home feeling." Her smiled faltered. "Or maybe it would be too weird."

"Not weird at all." He needed to play it off as unimportant because it obviously bothered her. "That we're floating in some kind of phased state in our past, now that's unique."

She crossed her arms. "Good point. Oh, crap, what time is it?"

He glanced down at his watch. "I don't know. My watch appears to have stopped. Why?"

She dropped her arms and started to float upward. "Cam is supposed to come back in an hour and he told us not to leave your property."

He quickly caught up. "Should we be concerned?" He wished he knew more about the rules of this strange experience.

"I'm not sure, but I think it's very important that he not lose us and vice versa. He's the only one who can make us solid again." She crinkled her nose. "I do like flying, but I'm kind of attached to my solid form."

The precariousness of their position hit home hard. If Cameron were to miss them, they could be stuck in the past for at least another hour and maybe even longer. From his conversation with him, it was clear that this trip was pushing the patience of whoever made the rules for Cameron.

But feeding into Holly's fear wouldn't help anything. "Not to worry. Technically, we haven't left my family's property since the Rawdon-Hastings are my family."

Holly looked askance at him. "Wow, you can rationalize better than most men I know. I'm going to have to watch you. You're way too smart."

He chuckled, appreciating both the compliment and the gleam in her eyes.

"Cam likes to fly in from the rooftop, so we should see him as soon as he arrives if we stay up here." She slowed to a stop next to one of the nine chimneys that dotted his family home.

He hovered near her. "I now understand what you meant about enjoying the ability to fly."

She grinned. "See, I told you. You should trust me. I'll never lead you astray."

Though she was obviously having fun, he took her seriously. "I do trust you, or I wouldn't be here."

She sobered and reached out her hand. "Thank you for coming. I would have been terrified hanging out here by myself."

He took her hand in his, wishing he could always do so. "And thank you for letting me know about ghosts. I didn't see any at the castle. I wonder why."

She was back to smiling in an instant and disengaged her hand to wave it about. "Oh, that's easy. That's because none of the people who lived there or died there had any unfinished business. You can rest easy that your ancestors had happy lives." She paused. "Or at least they didn't die feeling so strongly about something that they never left the living plane."

His understanding of the difference between ghost and spirit was becoming more solid. "And that's why Cameron has to leave us because he'll turn into a ghost?"

She nodded.

"But if you were unfinished business, wouldn't he have become a ghost immediately instead of a spirit?"

She frowned. "That's a good question."

The appearance of the man they spoke of as he floated down behind Holly appeared to be fortuitous.

Ethan pointed. "Then let's ask him."

Holly spun around. "Cam!" Without giving the man a chance to react, she flung herself at him.

The look of terror in Cam's eyes before he gently pushed her away had Ethan tensing. What could scare a deceased man that much?

"Ah, hen, I can't. It will lessen our time together tonight."

Holly looked ready to ignore Cameron's warning, so Ethan drifted over. "We were going to ask you an important question, right, Holly?"

She pouted, but nodded.

"That's fine, but ask as we fly. We have a couple stops to make, and I don't have much time."

The relieved look Cameron threw him made him more determined to find out what his friend was so afraid of.

"Will you not take my hand, love?" Cameron held out his hand, and at first, it looked like Holly wasn't going to grasp it, but finally she sighed.

"Fine." She held her other hand out. "Come on, Ethan. It appears we're needed elsewhere."

He took her hand in his, and she held tight as Cameron flew them up and directly into the gray mist.

"Actually, hen, we're headed for the present."

She frowned, still obviously unhappy with her husband.

Ethan gave her hand a squeeze. "Didn't you want to ask Cameron something?"

She shrugged, obviously no longer interested in the ghost-spirit issue.

But he was. "We wanted to know why you didn't turn into a ghost the minute you passed."

That caught Cameron's attention.

"Holly says that people who pass away with unfinished business stay with the living."

Chapter Seven

Cameron scowled at Ethan. Why did his friend have to make him look like a jerk? Ah, but then again, that was perfect. He needed to remind Holly of that side of him. He smirked. "I didn't have any unfinished business. I had a happy life, so I became a spirit, and not just a Spirit Guide, but the director of them."

"Then why are you afraid of turning into a ghost now?"

Holly's question stumped him. The truth would make him look too good in her eyes. Throwing away one possibility after another, he finally gave up. "Because you and I had such a strong connection in life that seeing you now could cause me to change. Remember what happened with your Spirit of Christmas Present."

"Had?" She frowned. "I thought we still have that connection. Isn't that why you only have fifteen minutes?"

He looked past her at Ethan, who appeared as confused as Holly. Shit, he was messing this up. He was here to break that connection, not make it stronger. He had to, or he'd be stuck in limbo forever. "It's hard to explain. There are a lot of nuances in the spirit realm."

The gray mist parted and he smiled. "First stop, Milton's Restaurant."

"Cameron Douglas, I know when you're stalling. Don't think I'm going to forget about this."

He was well aware she wouldn't, but it could give him time. "Of course, but first I wanted you to see what's been happening on Christmas Eve day. You know how much I love the anticipation."

She finally smiled. "I do." She turned to Ethan. "He's so wound up by Christmas day that he would rip through his presents before I even finished choosing one to unwrap."

Ethan looked at him with raised brows.

He shrugged. "Hey, you know how low key this holiday is in Scotland. It was fun to be an American for a change."

Ethan didn't let it go. "That's why you were ready to leave before Christmas dinner to try your new equipment."

"Ouch. That hurt old friend."

Holly snorted. "Ethan's right. If you had taken your time like a civilized person, there's a chance the ice would have melted by then."

He shook his head. "Don't you see, it doesn't matter? I'm gone. And if not then, then in a couple weeks, or months. You said yourself, Malcolm knew I was destined for a short life."

"Sure, you had to remind me of that."

He squeezed her hand, holding her in any way was a balm for his soul. "I was very lucky to have you in my life, but you deserve a long, happy life after putting up with me."

"You can say that again."

At Holly's disgruntled reply, Ethan laughed. "If that's the reward for putting up with you, I'd like a long, happy life, too."

He smirked at his friend. "With the way you review every possible angle about everything, I'd be surprised if you didn't live to be two hundred."

Ethan grimaced.

Holly was shaking her head as they floated through the roof of the restaurant. "You two are like two pieces of a whole. One too adventurous and one too cautious. If we could have melded you both together, I could have had the perfect man."

Cameron glanced at Ethan to see the man swallowing hard. Ethan was so in love with Holly. Maybe even more than he was. He couldn't have chosen a better man to love her if he'd been asked. That they were soulmates like he and Holly had been made an odd kind of sense. But that wasn't something he was allowed to reveal, so he'd just have to show them.

The local restaurant was packed. Situated a couple blocks down Main Street from One of a Kind Christmas Shop, it was in an attached building nestled between the hardware store and a pet supply place. It was double the width of their own shop and boasted at least twenty tables and a counter.

On one wall was a mural of Loudon Hill. On the opposite wall, high above the customers heads, were a variety of light-colored wooden shelves full of various knick-knacks. Everything from trowels and pipe fittings to lace handkerchiefs and baby bottles were propped up on them.

Holly let go of Ethan's hand. "So why are we in Milton's?" She floated in front him, curiosity clear in her brown gaze. "I didn't go near this place today because I knew it would be packed with last minute shoppers." She looked below them. "Boy, was I right."

Cameron smiled. That was so Holly. She liked the people in town, but very crowded places weren't her thing. She always said she didn't mind it in their shop because she could escape to the space behind the counter. He nodded toward the customers. "We're going to eavesdrop."

Her brilliant smile was his reward. "This is even better than being here in person." She let go of his hand and turned toward Ethan. "We'll get to hear what's going on, but don't forget, we can't let on that we know any of it."

Ethan nodded solemnly, but there was a glint in the man's eyes. He obviously found Holly's excitement as enchanting as he did.

Once again, he was reassured that she'd be in good hands. "Who do you want to check on first?"

She scanned the busy room filled with wooden tables, the noise of people talking and dishes rattling drowned out any particular conversation. She pointed to a corner table. "Let's see what Mr. Wrenford and Mrs. Bell are talking about." She wiggled her brow. "Maybe love is in the air."

He shook his head. "You already know that's not what's in store for these two."

"Hey, a girl can dream, can't she?"

Ethan chuckled and opened his arm for her to float by. "After you."

When Holly had drifted a bit, Ethan leaned in. "Are you sure this is a good idea?"

Was he? He was second guessing everything now. "No, but I think it's a good place to start."

At Ethan's nod, he felt a bit better about his decision. They floated up behind Holly.

She looked back at them. "They're going to Brody's tonight, so that's something."

He winked. "Hope springs eternal."

She chuckled and turned back to watch.

Mrs. Bell put down her coffee cup. "Do you think Ethan will bring Holly this year?"

Mr. Wrenford finished buttering his scone before answering. "That would be my guess, why?"

The older woman sighed. "I just so wish those two would fall in love. They both lost someone very special, and I think it would be a beautiful testament to Cameron Douglas if they married and named a son after him."

Mr. Wrenford's hand paused on the way to taking a bite. "Only a woman would think that way."

"I beg your pardon. What's wrong with hoping two young people fall in love? Especially two such lonely people?"

"Nothing, as long as hoping is all you're doing. Most women I know meddle. If it's meant to be, it's meant to be."

Cameron was about to reiterate that sentiment when Holly suddenly headed for another table.

He looked at Ethan. "At least the thought is in her head now." He made to follow, but Ethan grabbed him back.

"I received the impression the thought was already in her head."

The angry whisper came out almost like a hiss, and Cameron cringed. "What do you mean?"

"I mean I've been given the impression that Holly already knows how I feel."

He pushed the hair off his forehead as he contemplated the best way to answer.

"So it's true." Ethan turned away.

This time, he grabbed at him. "Wait, you need to know, I didn't tell her. The Spirits of Christmas Future revealed that when…when they showed her what your life would be like in the future if she continued to push you away."

"Blast, so that's why she suddenly accepted my annual invitation to dinner on Christmas day with my parents."

Ethan's upset wasn't lost on him. "Aye, but that's good. She changed her behavior because she cares so much about you."

"As a friend." Ethan shook his head. "That's why she jumps away every time we accidently touch. She wants to keep it that way."

He frowned. "But she's holding your hand now. I saw it."

"I know. It's odd." He rubbed the back of his neck. "Since I brought the tree, there's been a change."

He smiled. "See, I told you to bring a tree. Of course, now you're going to have to bring a tree every year since you didn't get the one I said to get, the one that folds down and packs away in a jiff."

"Exactly. Now I have an excuse to visit her every Christmas season." Ethan's gaze found Holly hovering above Luca and Milly, two young people who were in the beginnings of their relationship. "Thank you for pushing me to show up on her doorstep."

Cameron punched his friend in the arm. "Told you. She needs to know you want her. She loved that about me. I was a bloody nuisance, calling her every day, asking her to go out with me for every meal."

"I prefer not be considered a nuisance."

His heart warmed as he remembered pieces of his stay in America. "I had to be. I fell hard and fast and was returning home to Scotland. I had to get her to love me." Even as he said the words, the images faded from his memory, leaving a chilly void.

Ethan shook his head. "Luckily, I don't have a time limit."

Cameron sobered. "Aye, you do. Not as hard and fast as I did, but if Holly isn't starting to fall for you by the end of my visit, it won't go well for any of us."

Despite his phased appearance, Ethan's face paled considerably. He may not know much about the spirit world, but he knew enough to understand the significance of their task. "You didn't tell me that when you planned this."

"I know. I was afraid you wouldn't come. I need your help. I must get her to see her future without me, or I'll be stuck where I am and never see her again."

"For fuck's sake, Cameron! You know I'd help you no matter what. You're the brother I never had. You should have told me."

He held his hands out to the side and shrugged. "Sorry. I just can't think straight when it comes to Holly."

"*That* I understand. Very well, now that I know what needs to be done, maybe I can be more helpful." Ethan gave him a hard stare. "And maybe you'll listen to me."

He gave a quick nod. "Speaking of listening, let's have a listen to what she's hearing."

Ethan didn't answer. Instead, he floated up to Holly, who looked at him briefly before moving to another table.

Cameron cringed. That wasn't good. He made for his wife, who now hovered over the Bransons, an elderly couple who'd been married for years. "So what juicy gossip have you learned so far, love."

She scowled at him. "That *I'm* the center of the gossip. Here you sent Coco and Ian to me to get me more involved beyond simple gossip, and I find myself the center of it now. It's all your fault."

He held up both his hands and floated back a bit. "What did I do? I've only been trying to help."

She sighed. "I know."

"I understand, hen. Ethan's been in love with you since I transitioned. Though he's told no one that I know of, just seeing you two as friends is going to cause people to talk."

She glanced over her shoulder and lowered her voice. "Are you sure it was *after* you transitioned?"

As opposed to…oh. "Ach, yes, I'm sure. While we were married, Ethan only thought of you as a friend."

"That's a relief. Still, I just…I don't like being pushed into something I'm not ready for yet."

Though he should have frozen at her words, that she said the word "yet," made him want to jump up and down, but with Ethan approaching, he held his excitement in. "You don't have to do anything you don't want to do. It's your life."

She relaxed at his words. "Thank you. Does that mean I don't have to—"

"This should be interesting." Ethan joined them and pointed to Sophia Dunlap who had entered the restaurant followed by Brody and Sarah.

Cameron grinned. "Shit, he looks good in Present Day." Brody was built much like him and had always been his partner in crime when it came to rock-climbing, hang-gliding, and any other rush they could find. That Brody had married the beautiful svelte blonde on his arm, hopefully meant he'd be a bit more careful than he'd been.

Holly touched his arm, sending a spike of yearning so strong, that he turned to look at her just to break the contact. She pointed. "Brody and Sarah are soulmates."

"Soulmates?" Ethan's question took her attention and Cameron drifted away a bit more.

"Yes. When I was with Coco, one of my Spirits of Christmas Present, she told me she had the ability to see soulmates. Isn't that awesome?"

She didn't wait for an answer, but pointed back to Milly and Luca, drifting toward them. "These two are soulmates as well. Did you know a person can have more than one soulmate? Luca actually had two in the same room. I didn't know the other woman, but I knew Milly, so I made sure to introduce them." She grinned triumphantly. "Barring any unforeseen intrusion, they should be married in another year."

Ethan stared at her in awe, and Cameron swallowed a chuckle. He kept forgetting his friend was new to this world. He hovered a bit closer. "She's correct. Coco was able to see soulmates and then my Spirit of Christmas Future, Malcom, was able to see possible futures. These two marrying has a ninety-three-percent chance of occurring."

"Ninety-three?" Holly's eyes had gone wide before she clapped her hands once. "That's excellent! I'm so happy for them."

Milly's laugh caught their attention. "Oh my, do you think he'd be interested in Iona Napier. I mean, Ethan is Holly's friend, but if Iona is interested in him that would be brilliant. That man has mourned as long as Holly. He needs someone to make him happy again. Do you think I should introduce them?"

Luca wiped his mouth with his napkin before answering. "I don't think you should get involved. Let things happen naturally."

Milly gave Luca a shrewd look. "If Holly hadn't introduced us, we would have never met. Remember, you'd planned to attend university in the Netherlands. We wouldn't be sitting here today."

Luca speared a sausage link with his fork then halted. He looked at Milly, love shinning in his eyes. "Do it."

Milly reached her hand across the table and squeezed Luca's free hand. "I will."

Holly turned on Ethan. "Are you going to go out with this woman?"

Ethan shook his head and Cameron frowned at him. Luckily, Ethan caught the silent communication. "I can't say. I haven't met her yet."

Holly's eyes narrowed before turning away.

Cameron grinned behind her back. A little jealousy couldn't hurt.

Ethan stared at him with the calculating look that always made him uncomfortable, so he quickly turned their attention to his other old friend. "Holly, let's see what's new with Brody and Sarah."

Holly changed direction and the three of them hovered over the couple.

The two were talking about their party that evening as Sophia stepped up to the counter to pick up a to-go order.

Holly pointed to the thin red head. "I tried to be her friend last year, but she's just not interested."

"You did? I've spent the last few years trying to avoid her." Ethan shook his head. "She's very persistent."

Cameron could tell Holly wanted to say something. "Go ahead."

She spun back to Ethan. "It wasn't that I wanted to be Sophia's friend so much as that I want to try and save her little sister."

Ethan frowned. "Sophia Dunlap has a little sister?"

"Yes, but it's a secret and you're sworn to keep it. Her little sister Thea is supposed to have a bone marrow transplant. But while she's home after kemo, her boyfriend will go over to see her, even though the doctors said she had to stay away from everyone. It turns out he will have the flu virus and Thea won't make it. I still haven't figured out how to keep this boy from visiting her when Sophia won't let me be her friend or even acknowledge she has a sister."

"I didn't know."

Ethan's concern was genuine, but Cameron didn't miss the small look of irritation that crossed Holly's face at Ethan's interest in Sophia's life. Could that be more jealousy rearing its beautiful head?

Brody's voice caught their attention. "I've got Ethan bringing Holly tonight. I figured he could use a nudge since Cameron isn't here anymore to do it."

Sarah's gentle smile lit her face. "Don't be getting your hopes up. They're just friends, you know."

"But it could be so much more. I just want to spell it out for the man. She's lonely. He's lonely. And they both miss Cam a lot."

"Yes, but so do you." Sarah placed her hand on Brody's arm.

"But I have you, dove. They don't have anyone except they could have each other. I just know Cam would go for it."

Cameron wasn't unaware of how Holly stiffened and moved close when Sophia decided it was her place to join the conversation.

"Holly and Ethan, really?" She looked up, right at them then looked back at Brody. "Nope, I don't see it. Ethan needs someone with a little more drive. He needs someone to get him out of that mausoleum he lives in and into the real world. If those two ever got together, they'd probably sit in that Christmas Shop of hers and play chess."

Brody's brows lowered as he opened his mouth, but Sarah spoke first. "I'm sure whatever Ethan needs, he'll find. After all, he's a grown man and can make his own decisions."

Sophia smiled slyly. "That he can. We've been dancing around each other for years now because he's so reticent to take action, but I think when I see him next, he will definitely be ready to jump."

Cameron clamped his teeth together hard to keep from laughing at his wife. She looked ready to "jump" on Sophia and tackle her to the floor. Then again, Holly knew how Sophia's mind worked from her visits to the future, so it may not be jealousy.

Holly spun toward Ethan. "Don't listen to her. She's a selfish bitch…" She paused, obviously thinking of what she'd seen in Sophia's future. "Mostly she's selfish, but when it comes to you, she'd down right devious."

Ethan's surprise was evident as he raised his brows. "She is?"

Holly nodded vigorously. "Trust me. You need to stay far away from that woman."

She scanned the room and before she even spoke, Cameron knew exactly what she was thinking. Shit, he loved that woman. His wife—no widow—had the biggest heart.

Holly leaned toward Ethan as if the living could hear them. "I think we need to let people think we're a couple, so Sophia stays away from you. Either that or it will make her reveal her hand."

"Reveal her hand?" Ethan looked toward Sophia, completely confused. The man just hadn't been privy to the future like Holly was.

"Yes. Sophia Dunlap has something up her sleeve when it comes to you."

Ethan moved his gaze to Cameron for confirmation.

He nodded. This could be a big step in the right direction. *Thank you, Sophia Dunlap.*

Ethan shook his head, but before he could say anything, Brody's voice got their attention. "Ethan is my friend, and I'll be damned before I let him fall for the likes of you."

Sophia lifted one shoulder. "We'll see." She turned to pay for her food then took the bag and waved at Brody and Sarah.

"Did you hear her?" Brody spoke to Sarah, but at least half the shop was listening now.

"Yes, I heard her, but she's all talk. Ethan has no interest in her. You shouldn't have let her get you so riled up."

Brody took a deep breath. "I know." His voice lowered and people in the restaurant went back to their own conversations. "It's just he's the only one I have left besides you. Cameron and Ethan are the brothers I never had. Then Holly joined us and then you. Cameron is gone and Holly only sees us but three times a year. I don't want to lose her or Ethan."

As Sarah patted Brody's arm, Holly drifted forward. "I promise you won't lose me, Brody. I'm so sorry. I didn't know you felt that way."

Cameron started to move forward, but Ethan had the same thought and they bumped into each other. Irritation had Cameron clenching his jaw before Ethan backed away. A chilling cold whipped through him and he backed off. Fuck, he'd messed up again.

Holly turned back, tears glistening in her eyes as she gazed at them both. "I always thought you men weren't entirely happy when I came along." She threw her arm back. "Especially, Brody. I thought I was the one who broke up the boys' club."

This time as Ethan stepped forward, Cameron held himself in check, but it wasn't easy. He had so little time left with Holly, every minute was precious.

"Lass, we never resented you. We gave you a ribbing because you were so good at taking it. You would sass us right back, and we enjoyed that. If you hadn't mellowed us, then sweet Sarah would have never had a chance. You weren't a fourth wheel. You became the center of our group."

Holly's hopeful expression as she turned to look at him, made it twice as hard to stay where he was. "It's true. You were the glue that held us together."

Her beautiful brown eyes almost glowed. "And I've left you all rudderless."

Ethan put his hand on her shoulder, and Cameron grit his teeth. "We are a bit scattered and broken, but that was because Cameron left us. No one expected you to shoulder our grief. But now, if you're willing, Brody, Sarah and I would love to have you back. You're one of us."

She turned and gazed at him. "And what about Cam?"

Yes, what about him? No, he would be fine if she could move on. Then he could have her again for eternity. He waved aside her comment, forcing himself to appear unaffected. "I'm fine. I'm in a place where I don't need my brothers until they make the transition. You need to focus on who's left."

Her full bottom lip came out as she pouted in response.

He used to kiss her pouts away. *Ach, Remiel, you are really making me pay, aren't you?* "Now that we've settled that, we better move to the next visit because I only have a few minutes left."

Holly immediately grabbed his hand, soothing his angst with her touch. She held out her other. "Come on, Ethan. I'm going to need you when Cam's gone."

His heart skipped a beat at her sentiment. If he could just get her to see that need beyond tonight, they might have a chance.

Chapter Eight

Ethan felt his hope rise at Holly's words, no matter how casual they were. If only she'd let him in, not just let people think she had. He'd discuss that with her after tonight. He didn't want to propagate false hopes for anyone, including himself.

Grasping her warm hand in his, he held on as they flew through the roof of Milton's and sped across Scotland, heading north. He was pleased to see that Cameron hadn't changed his plans for the present-day visits. Then again, he had no reason to, since they benefited him as well.

Whether Cameron realized it or not, he was gaining a lot of insight and knowledge from this *adventure*, as he'd called it. Maybe that would help them in their goal.

Ethan still didn't understand clearly why Holly falling in love with him was so pivotal to her and Cameron's afterlife. It also begged the question about what he could look forward to then as well? Would he be relegated to having Holly only in life? Would that be enough for him?

At the moment, it was a moot point. First, she had to love him. She definitely did on a friendship level, but could they really move their relationship forward to another level in one night with her late husband as a guide? If anyone had asked him that question before Cameron's spirit had visited him in the dark of night, he would have said it was impossible. And now?

"Oh, I know where we are." Holly's excited voice pulled him from his thoughts. "Cam, this is the area of Inverness where Lorna's father lives." She looked back at him. "Remember, I told you about her."

"Aye. I found her address and gave it to Cameron when he visited me." He'd planned on telling her that he'd found Cameron's older half-sister's whereabouts, happy to help her, but those plans changed when Cameron decided on this visit.

She laughed. "I should have known you'd be one step ahead of me."

If he had his way, they'd always be in step together.

Cameron slowed, and they hovered over a brick townhouse on a long winding street with dozens of them. "This is where Lorna lives."

"Did you find out anything else about her?" Holly let go of his hand to face her husband.

"I was hoping you could do that for me."

She let go of Cameron's hand and tugged on Ethan's arm. "Yes, Ethan and I can find out everything after you leave."

He relaxed at her attention. "Aye, that we will."

"Thank you. You can tell me all about it when I return. She's inside getting ready to go to her father's Christmas Eve gathering. Since she's alone at the moment, you won't learn anything because she has no one to talk to. I was hoping you wouldn't mind spending this visit in the living time."

That hadn't been the plan, but Ethan was more than happy to be solid again. Flying was enjoyable as Holly had said, but he'd rather give that up to be solid once again. "I'm happy to return to the living state."

Holly's brow puckered. "Are you sure? She won't be expecting us and Malcolm said her dad didn't want her to know her mother."

Ethan didn't miss the pain that crossed Cameron's face at the mention of his mother. Why would he—Ach. It made sense now. Cameron skirted the issue, but he'd said enough that it finally made sense.

Cameron couldn't be with his mother either because he hadn't achieved something. What had Holly said? *A ghost is a soul with unfinished business here on Earth and because of that is stuck among the living for eternity. A spirit is just someone who has passed. I'm not sure of all the distinctions, but I think spirits help the living.*

There must be another level of the spirit world. He'd bet his life on it, and Cameron hadn't reached it yet. He was in some kind of limbo, but his mother wasn't.

Cameron sighed. "I know. But you're not exactly my mother, right, hen?"

"I guess." Her hand squeezed his arm harder, a sure sign she wasn't entirely comfortable with openly visiting Lorna.

He placed his hand over hers. "Don't worry. We won't stay too long if you prefer not to. Inverness is a big city. We can walk about a bit."

Cameron frowned. "Just be sure you're back here within an hour. I only have fifteen minutes from the time I appear and if I have to spend ten minutes hunting you down that means less time to get to our next stop."

"Then let's get started before you have to leave." Holly looked hopefully at Cameron. "Maybe you could eavesdrop a bit. You know, be nearby as we meet her?"

Holly's lack of faith in him had Ethan tensing. He forced himself to relax. It *was* Cameron's relation they were visiting, so it made sense she'd turn to him, even if he was a member of the spirit world now.

Ethan took her hand. "Aye, let's go meet Ms. Lorna." He pulled Holly with him as he flew down to street level.

Cameron followed, facing them as they hovered on the sidewalk. "Are you ready?"

He nodded at the same time Holly did. In the next instant, he was holding Holly's solid hand.

She stepped forward and pushed his hair to the side. "There you go. You're presentable. How do I look?"

Beautiful.

Cameron spoke before he could. "You look perfect, as always."

She smiled at her husband before looking back at him. "Really, Ethan. Is everything in place?"

He took a moment to gaze at her, enjoying the view. He had to find something she could fix or she wouldn't be satisfied. "Your holly looks to be falling to the side."

Her hands flew to her hair. "Oh, I can take care of that." With expertise from long practice, she let her hair down a moment before pulling the sides back up.

It was only a glimpse, but Ethan caught his breath at how quickly she turned from cheery Christmas shop owner to seductress.

"How's that look?" She gazed at him expectantly.

"Very smart."

She blushed. "Thank you." She faced her husband again. "We're as ready as we'll ever be."

Cameron didn't smile. Instead, he opened his arm toward the walkway. "Remember, one hour." He nodded at Ethan. "Your watch should be workin—"

"Oh, wow." Holly looked at the empty space where Cameron had been then looked up at the sky and shivered. "They really do have him on tight leash. Do you think he's alright?"

He squeezed her hand. "Aye, he's fine. But he's depending on us to continue on for him. Shall we?" He lifted their clasped hands, pleased that she hadn't released his since he'd taken it.

She swallowed. "Let's do this." Her chin came up, and she threw her shoulders back.

He bit down on the grin that wanted to emerge. This was the Holly he'd fallen in love with.

As she stepped forward, he matched his stride to hers until they were at the front door. Without hesitation, she knocked.

It took a couple minutes before they heard footsteps, and Holly's bravery lessened, but as soon as the inner door started to open, she lifted her head again and put on a smile.

The woman who stood behind the glass outer door looked so much like a female version of Cameron that Ethan was positive they had the right house. Her face was oval like his. Her sandy brown hair the exact color of Cameron's was pulled back in a ponytail accentuating her high cheek bones, also like his. Even her nose was a bit large like Cameron's, but her eyes, which crinkled at the corners were a muted gray. "Jing scrivens help ma boab, you're Holly!"

Lorna threw open the door and stepped out onto the walkway in a robe and slippers. "I can't believe you found me!" As the scent of lilac mixed with the savory smells flowing out of the house, Lorna embraced Holly before the glass door slammed shut.

Ethan chuckled quietly as Holly squeezed his hand, her eyes as wide as a tawny owl's.

Lorna pulled away but kept her hands on Holly's shoulders. "I'd know you anywhere. I have your wedding picture from the paper. I can't tell you how excited I am to finally have you here."

The woman turned toward him. "Hello, my name is Lorna Munro."

He had to release Holly's hand to shake or be very impolite. "I'm Ethan Stewart, a friend of Holly's."

The woman's eyes rounded. "Of course, Cameron's great friend." She looked behind them. "Is Brody here?"

"You know Brody?" Holly's question echoed his own.

Lorna shook her head. "Oh, no. I've never officially met any of you, but I've wanted to." Suddenly, her hand flew to her chest. "Oi, look at us, meeting out in the middle of the street, having a good blether when I'm half dressed. Come, come."

She opened the door and waved them inside.

They stepped into a warmly decorated parlor that rivaled Holly's for Christmas décor.

Lorna closed the solid wood door and brushed by them. "Please, sit. Can I get you some tea? That's a long drive all the way from Deervale."

Holly still appeared dumbfounded, so he led her to a couch. "Tea would be perfect, if you have some made. If not, water is fine."

"Do I have some made? Of course, I do. It's tea time." With that, Lorna bustled off into the other room to fetch the tea.

Holly sat. "I don't understand. Malcolm said her dad didn't want her to know about Cameron. Cam certainly didn't know about her before he…transitioned."

That she used the word Cameron did concerned him. Would she ever accept that her husband was gone? "I'm sure she'll tell us everything as soon as she comes back in. I don't see her as the shy type."

Holly gave him the glimmer of a grin, but still she took his hand as he sat next to her.

He grasped it firmly, happy to have her depend on him. Before he could reassure her further, Lorna was back with a complete tea tray that included shortbread and Christmas cookies.

"Most of me goodies are packed to take over to Dad's later, but I keep a few baked goodies for Christmas day. Everything I bring is wolfed down by the kids."

"Thank you. This looks very festive." Ethan glanced at Holly as Lorna handed them cups of tea. She seemed to be recovering from her surprise. There was that look in her eye that she had when she grew determined.

Lorna pulled an upholstered rocking chair closer to the coffee table in front of them and scooped up a couple cookies. "Please, help yourselves and save me. They have to all be eaten. If you don't do the honors, I'll be forced to." The woman gave a short laugh, clearly enjoying herself.

Holly took a sip of tea before setting it on the table. "How do you know about us? We didn't know about you until a couple years ago. Is that when you discovered you had a younger half-brother?"

"Oh, no." Lorna licked the crumbs from her fingers. "I've known about Cameron since I was small, maybe eight or nine I think."

"Your father told you?" Holly released his hand and leaned forward.

Lorna grimaced. "Not exactly. I had a tummy ache one night and came downstairs for comfort when I heard them talking quietly, so I stayed around the corner. When I realized they were talking about a boy who was me brother, I ran into the kitchen. I'm sorry to say me dad was not happy."

"What did he do?" Ethan asked the question before Holly could, as anxious to hear the story as she was.

"He scowled." Lorna laughed, which didn't make much sense. She waved away their surprised looks. "Oi, you don't know me dad. He's always scowling. He was born that way." She nodded conspiratorially. "I've seen his baby photographs."

Holly's quiet chuckle next to him meant she was finally relaxing. "Did he explain Cameron to you then?"

Lorna finished chewing the bite of Christmas cookie she'd taken. "Nay, but me Mum did. Me Dad's second wife is the only mother I've known, so she took me up on her lap and explained that me daddy had been married before and that his former wife had remarried and had a boy. Of course, I was too young to realize we had the same Mum, especially because I had me own Mum."

"So how did you figure out that Cameron was your half-brother?" Holly finally picked-up her tea and took another sip.

"It wasn't until I was a teenager and questioning everything, especially when me and me Dad argued. It was one of those yelling matches when I told him I was going to go live with his other wife to get away from him."

Ethan swallowed his piece of shortbread almost whole. "What did he do?"

Lorna gazed at the Christmas tree set up against the wall opposite them, her lips turned down for the first time since they'd walked in the door. "I had pushed him too far, but in me defense, I didn't have all the facts. He started to turn red. Then his face twisted in pain, and I thought I'd given him a heart attack. Luckily, Mum heard the sudden quiet and ran in."

Lorna looked at them, her own gaze filled with pain at the memory. "She glared at me before stepping between us and getting me Dad's attention. He finally focused on her, his breathing slowing. Then he threw out his hand toward me and told Mum to do something about me or he would. He stomped out of the room and out of the house."

Holly remained quiet. That she felt for Lorna so much as not to intrude and immediately ask what he knew she wanted to know was a testament to the empathy she had for all those around her.

Finally, Lorna shook her head and took a sip of tea before continuing. "Me Mum sat me down and told me everything. She felt that if they had told me about my biological mother and brother earlier, the fight would have never gone so far." Lorna looked at them. "She was right. After that, I knew I could never search out either me brother or our Mum while me dad lived. I needed to honor his feelings."

She lifted her cup. "And quite frankly, the thought that I almost gave me Dad a heart attack, pretty much cured me of disobeying for a very long time." She winked before finishing up the last of her tea.

Holly let go of his hand. "I don't understand why your dad

wouldn't want you to know about us? Was it because of his new wife?"

"Nay, she's the best. She actually tried to talk him into letting me meet me mother, but he was having none of it. I guess my biological mother was a bit of a daredevil. Mum said that Dad was afraid she'd rub off on me, and I was energetic enough as it was."

Understanding dawned as Ethan put the pieces together. "Is that why he divorced Cameron's mum?"

Lorna nodded. "Oh, aye. Once I was born, he thought she'd calm down, but that didn't happen. I was barely a year old when he left her. I was nary two when he married Mum."

He could feel the tension radiating off Holly. He'd no doubt she was ready to yell at Lorna's father, too. He needed to distract her. "But how did you know who we were?"

Lorna's smile was back. "I respect me Dad, but that didn't mean I couldn't learn all there was to know. I did me own investigating. It didn't take long to find me mother and her new husband. The internet is a wonderful thing." She frowned. "Unfortunately, I only found one photo of our mother. She wasn't that bonnie, but she had guts. The picture showed her hanging from a rock face with one hand, dangling over a chasm. I couldn't even look at it that long."

His gaze met Holly's in understanding. That had to be why Cameron had never shown any of them his mother's photo. Holly said she hadn't even learned there was a photo until the Spirits of Christmas Present visited her. Cameron would not have wanted her to see what his mother was like. It would have only made her more nervous.

Holly turned back to Lorna. "And you followed all of us?"

The woman blushed. "Oh, aye. I was heartbroken when I found out me mother had died in a car accident, and I had never met her. I didn't want to hurt me Dad, but I didn't want that to happen with me brother, so I started to follow him. It was easy to see that he was just like our mother. That made me nervous. What if he died early, too?"

Lorna looked at him. "I read about his polo matches and the championship. There was a lovely photograph of you, he, and Brody. I really should have recognized you earlier, but you've changed since your university days."

Aye, he was a scrawny twig back then.

"I read about your wedding, Holly, and the opening of your Christmas Shop. That's when I knew how I could meet me brother and not disrespect me father."

"How?" Holly was on the edge of the couch, in danger of slipping right off.

"I shopped at your shop!" Lorna's smugness over her own brilliance was charming.

"You were in my shop? Did you meet Cameron? Did I say anything to you? Oh, I hope I was helpful."

Lorna laughed. "Oi, were you. I was able to do all me Christmas shopping that year in your shop. It was near the end of the day as I had to work half a day and then the drive down. I was paying when Cameron came in to help. I was stunned at how much we looked alike and was afraid you'd notice. But you went to help a customer, and he finished bagging me purchases." Lorna winked again. "He did give me a double take when he finally looked at me to wish me a Merry Christmas. He asked if he knew me."

Her delight was so expressive, she clapped her hands. "I, of course, told him he didn't, but I did visit that lovely town a few more times, just to run into me brother."

Holly's mouth opened then shut. Then she looked at him, her excitement matching Lorna's.

It was all he could do not to grab her to him and kiss her.

"I can't believe it."

He laughed, the joy in the room making it impossible not to.

A beep sounding in the other room had Lorna jumping out of her chair. "Oh, I almost forgot about the pies." As she bustled off, Holly rose.

"I can't believe I waited on her. Can you?" She didn't wait for an answer as she walked to the tree then turned to face him. "She'd met Cam. Just think how excited he'll be to know that. I bet he could go back in time and watch. At least I think he could."

She walked to the other side of the tree, now looking at the ornaments, probably trying to find one that she sold from her shop. "I'm never sure about all these rules he has. I so want him to enjoy meeting Lorna. I wish he could have stayed to hear all this. Maybe we all could go to her father's, in phased form of course."

He rose and walked over to her, turning her around to face him. "Shh, remember Cameron is gone. I don't want anyone thinking you've lost half your mind."

Holly sucked in her breath. Ethan's words were like a bucket of ice water thrown in her face, except the empathy shining in his gaze took the frigidity from the experience.

Cameron is gone. The phrase reverberated in her head. *Cameron is gone. Cameron is gone.* She didn't want to hear it, but no matter how she shut it out of her mind, her heart heard. He was gone. Cameron's own words flew through her head. *Hen, death did part us.*

She shook her head, but the reality remained. She'd avoided it for four years, and now they were truly going to be parted.

"Lass, what is it?"

She gazed into Ethan's face. It was so different from Cam's. It was less angular, soothing, his light eyebrows lowered in concern, his blond hair falling over his forehead. Without thought, she brushed the hair away from his face. It was a kind, intelligent, caring face. What would she do without him?

A chill raced up her spine. What if he left her, too?

"Holly?"

She blinked. "It's nothing. Just lost in my own thoughts."

He studied her, clearly knowing her well enough to know she wasn't being entirely truthful.

"You're right. We'll have to share this later." She looked meaningfully over his shoulder as Lorna strode back in.

"I hope you don't mind, but I took the opportunity to get dressed for the gathering. You two looked so Christmassy that I felt a bit of a dowd."

Lorna had let down her hair and it fell just past her shoulders. She wore a paisley blouse underneath a tailored jacket over a full maroon skirt that flowed as she walked.

Holly looked at her own outfit. "Now I'm feeling like a wallflower."

Lorna waved off the comment. "You look like Christmas come to life. Now would you like some more tea?"

Ethan looked at her. "No, not for me."

"You will stay until Harris comes back, won't you. I'd love for you to meet him."

"Harris?" Holly moved closer to the couch. "Is that your husband?"

Lorna nodded. "Aye, me second one."

She looked at Ethan. "Do we have more time?"

He glanced at his watch. "Aye, we do."

"Oh good. Please sit." Lorna gestured to the spots they had left. "I must tell you about Harris because once he arrives, I can't talk behind his back any more." She sighed as if it was a real bother then broke into a chuckle.

Holly took her seat on the couch again. Unable to resist, she snatched up a Christmas cookie and bit into it.

Lorna chuckled. "They *are* good. Please have as many as you can, or I'll be eating them into the wee hours of the morning."

She finished the cookie off before speaking. "I wish Cam could have known you were his sister. He would have loved that. He was raised by his aunt and uncle and had cousins, but they were older than him. He always felt like an only child."

"The way you say that, you'd think it was the worst happenstance." Ethan smirked at her.

She chuckled. "I guess I did make it out as terrible when both you and I were only children." She turned toward Lorna. "And Brody, too. We kind of had a club going."

"I understand." Lorna shrugged. "I grew up with siblings, so I wouldn't have fit in the club anyway. Having a big family has been a blessing and a curse. Sometimes you can feel very alone even among the most well-meaning people. I discovered that the hard way after William."

She opened her mouth to ask, but Ethan beat her to it. "Who was William?"

"He was me first husband."

Holly's stomach rolled over itself. "You were divorced?" She was hoping for a positive answer.

Lorna's gray gaze seemed to go black. "Nay, he died. He had my whole heart. Even me Dad approved. William was the opposite of me half-brother. He was calm, distinguished, and very intelligent." She grinned. "I think me Dad approved of him because William talked circles around him."

If she didn't already feel like Lorna was a friend, Holly felt it even more now. They had something in common. Something tragic.

"We were still living in a flat in town. William was expecting a promotion. He was an accountant in a big firm. We were going to buy a house once his salary increased, but we never had the chance."

Holly wanted to ask what happened, but a part of her didn't want to know.

Ethan came to the rescue. "I'm guessing he wasn't a rock climber."

"Oh, nay. William's idea of excitement was watching the Rangers versus the Celtic on telly. Nay, it was nothing exiting, but I do like to think that he gave his life for another. It sounds a bit more heroic that way."

She smiled sadly. "William was walking on the sidewalk. A toddler on the other side of the road got away from her mum and ran out into the road right in front of a car. The driver swerved onto the sidewalk to avoid hitting her, but hit William instead. He died instantly and for that I'm grateful."

Holly felt bile rise up into her throat, every muscle in her body frozen at the suddenness of the tragedy. Moisture gathered in her eyes, making it hard to see Cam's sister.

Ethan put his arm around her, but didn't say a word. He didn't have to. His comfort was more than welcome.

"I was devastated. I didn't even want to get out of bed in the morning."

Holly nodded. She understood that feeling completely.

"Me family started to smother me. They all meant well, but there are so many of them." Lorna smirked. "You can have too much of a good—"The sound of a motorcycle pulling into the front yard interrupted her. "Lovely, Harris is home." A wide smile lit her face as she jumped up to go to the door. "I can't wait for you to meet him."

Holly looked at Ethan. "A motorcyclist?"

Lorna had the doorknob in her hand as she looked back. "Oi, the man refused to put it away with the warmer than usual weather we're having here in the city. He's promised that as soon as a flake hits the ground, he'll give it up for the season." She threw open the inner door as the outer door opened and a large man filled the opening.

Chapter Nine

Holly's first impression was black leather from head to toe, along with black hair and a black beard just beginning to show some white in it.

The man wrapped one large arm around Lorna and pulled her close. "Did you miss me so much, doll, that ye greet me at the door?" He leaned in to give her a kiss, but Lorna put both her hands on his chest.

"Harris, we have company." She turned her head and his lips met her cheek. A soft rosy hue ran from her neck all the way up her face to her hairline.

"What's this?" He lifted his head and looked at them. "On Christmas Eve? That's supposed to wait 'till Hogmanay." He laughed before stepping around his wife. "I guess our luck will start early this year." He strode toward them and Ethan rose.

"I'm Ethan Stewart." Ethan laid his hand on her shoulder. "And this is Holly Douglas."

The big man halted and looked back at Lorna who had just closed the door. She nodded. "Aye, *that* Holly Douglas."

Holly stood as well because looking at the big man from a sitting position was hard on her neck. "It's nice to meet you."

Harris looked at her as if trying to make what knowledge he had of her fit her appearance. "Yer bonnier than I expected."

She let out a relieved breath. "Thank you."

Lorna pushed Harris with her hip. "Stop gawking at her and go drop your leathers. We have to leave soon."

The big man grinned at her before exiting the room to change.

Lorna shook her head. "He can be a bit intimidating, but he has a heart of gold."

Holly was sure she'd missed something. "Your dad approves of Harris?" Certainly, a man who rode a motorcycle would have to be considered in the living-life-on-the-edge category. Cam had a bike for a couple of years, but when he totalled it, she'd convinced him they couldn't afford another. She'd been so shaken up, she'd have said anything to keep him from owning another one.

Lorna waved off her comment. "After what happened to William, me Dad really couldn't say much, and he saw how well Harris took care of me. Still, I don't like to remind him that Harris likes to ride or that I go with him."

She moved forward and picked up the forgotten tea tray. "Honestly, I think me father would have approved of anyone who pulled me out of the dark hole I went down after William passed." She shook her head. "I'll be right back."

With that, Cam's sister left them alone.

Holly was familiar with that dark hole. At Christmas, she often forgot she was still trying to climb out of that hole because Cam visited, but what would she do next Christmas?

Ethan crossed the room to the window. "That's a big bike." He looked back at her and gave her a smile. "For a big man."

She gladly left the path her thoughts had gone down. "Don't tell me you like to ride, too?"

He shrugged. "I rode when I was young before I even met Cameron or Brody." A strange look passed over his face before he smirked. "Haven't thought about it since, but it doesn't mean I don't admire a good-looking bike when I see one."

She threw her hands up in mock impatience. "Men."

Heavy footsteps heralded Harris's entrance back into the parlor, now wearing a pair of dark pants and a brown colored-shirt. He caught sight of Ethan at the window and grinned. "You want to take a look? She rides the roads like a kelpie rides the waves."

Ethan's interest was too obvious to ignore. She was learning a lot more about him in one night than she'd known before. She waved him on. "Go ahead. We have to leave soon, I'm sure, so you might as well get a good look."

At her reminder about the time, he glanced at his watch then smiled at Harris. "Aye, I'd like to take a look."

As the two men exited the house, she was surprised at the niggle of excitement that flowed through her veins at the thought of Ethan on a motorcycle. He was always the safe one in their group, so to learn he'd once ridden rocked her long-time impression of him. Unfortunately, it also made her nervous.

She moved to the window to surreptitiously watch the men. While Harris was like a big black bear, Ethan was like a majestic elk, lighter in coloring and sleek yet strong.

"He's a braw man." Lorna joined her at the window.

"Yes, braw and brawny. The man is a mountain."

Lorna chuckled. "Not Harris, Ethan."

She moved her gaze back to Ethan. "All of them are handsome. They definitely caught people's attention no matter where they went."

"I'm sure, but Ethan, and I mean no disrespect, has a quiet confidence that Brody and me brother lacked. It's much more than looks. Though to be honest, I would *have* to say me brother was the best looking, of course."

Holly turned to look at Cam's half-sister as the woman swept her hair back over her shoulder. She resembled him so much, but Holly had to be fair. Even Cam acknowledged that Ethan was the best looking. Not willing to admit that out loud, she grinned. "I'm thinking you're the bonniest of all of them."

"Psht, now you're telling tales." Still, the woman's face turned rosy once again. Cam never had that happen. Then again, Cam had always been comfortable being embarrassed.

Holly looked back outside. The light was fading and the gloaming was upon them. She couldn't imagine she and Ethan had much more time. She wanted to know all she could for Cam's sake. "How did you meet Harris?"

"At a grief support group."

She snapped her head around to find Lorna turning on a lamp next to the couch. "You went to a support group?"

Lorna sat on the couch and patted the space next to her. "Aye, I did, but only to get me family off me back." She rolled her eyes. "Like I said, a big family can be a boon or a curse."

Holly moved to the couch and sat. "And Harris was there?"

Lorna nodded. "It was his second week attending. He just sat there not saying a word the whole time. I could tell his grief was as strong as mine, and as Harris will tell you, I can't stand to see someone in need."

Holly gave her a soft smile. "And he was in need." Just like Ethan, but unlike Lorna, she hadn't been able to get past her own grief to see that. Or rather not until the Christmas Spirits showed her. She lowered her brows at the reminder of her own self-involvement. She hadn't been like that when Cam was alive, but he was her rock.

Too bad that rock had to fall off the cliff. She stiffened at her thought.

"After the session, I screwed up me courage and approached him." Lorna continued with her story. "I have to tell you, I was really nervous, but me sympathy kept overriding me fear. Still, I made sure we were still in the building. He seemed so angry. You know, the way men get when they're hurt?"

Holly nodded, but she'd never encountered that before.

Lorna sighed. "Poor Harris. He'd lost his younger brother, who was serving in the Royal Air Force in Iraq. They were very close as it was only the two of them. When I approached him, he literally grunted at me."

"Grunted?" Holly couldn't keep her lips from curving up, though she tried.

"Oi, and that was about all I got, too. But I'm pretty persistent. The next week I sat right next to him and after the session was over, I asked him to go out for coffee."

"What did he say?"

Lorna rolled her eyes again. "The thick-headed rock said no. Can you believe it? And it took so much of me courage to ask in the first place."

Now Holly was totally hooked on the story. "What did you do?"

"I did what any self-respecting woman would do. I went home and cried." Lorna grinned. "Next meeting, I sat on the other side of the room. Obviously, I was butting me nose in where it didn't belong."

She didn't say a word, too fascinated to interrupt.

"Of course, that just made me feel worse, like I couldn't even help other people. I was so depressed that I didn't go the next week."

Holly couldn't contain her curiosity any longer. "Then how did you two end up together?"

Lorna folded her hands in her lap, her smile turning smug. "Me Dad begged me to try one more time. He said he'd drive me over there, which of course, I didn't want. So I went. Got there nice and early so I could sit closest to the door. The seats filled up and a young man sat next to me, but he was in no more a speaking mood than I was. I was quite grateful for that. The session was about to start and in walks Harris. He walks right up to the young man and stands in front of him with one eyebrow raised."

Holly giggled. "He didn't."

"Oi, he did. That young man shrugged and left the seat. I was stupefied. The entire session he didn't say a word to me and when it ended, I got up to go, completely lost as to what had been said because of that bear of a man sitting next to me." Lorna pointed toward the window.

"And?" A need had started to grow inside her to know how Lorna had overcome the very grief she suffered from.

"And he says to me in that deep voice of his, which by the way was the first time I heard it. 'I owe you a cup of coffee.' And that was the start of something unbelievable."

"You mean that you fell in love again?"

Lorna's gaze grew serious. "Nay, that I started to live again. First, he gave me a purpose to look beyond myself. Then he gave me company in my misery as well as understanding. I knew he could feel what I couldn't express. It was then that I realized me life wasn't over any more than his was. Once I truly felt that, my heart healed enough to open to the obvious."

"Which was what?" She so wanted to know what the magic was. Deep down, her soul was trying to tell her something, but the shroud around her heart wouldn't listen. Lorna had figured it out.

"I had been blessed with two soulmates. In me bones, I knew our meeting wasn't chance. Somehow William had sent me another soulmate. You may think I'm crazy, but I believe that deep in me heart and no one will ever convince me otherwise."

Holly stared at the woman in shock. William had pushed her toward her second soulmate? Was that what Cam was doing? Could it be true that Ethan was another soulmate for her?

"You don't believe me." Lorna unclasped her hands and shrugged. "It's no matter. You don't have to. But what you do need to do is live." She paused. "Two years ago, I discovered that

Cameron had died. I felt guilty that I had let that part of me life fall away as I enjoyed loving Harris. That Christmas Eve I came to visit you."

"Yes! I know. A…a friend told me, but you never knocked." Her heart thudded with the memory she'd only witnessed because she was in a phased state with the Spirits of Christmas Present. "Why didn't you?"

Lorna sighed. "I had more reasons than I could count. You'd resent me for waiting so long to make contact. You wouldn't want to listen to a stranger about climbing out of the grief hole. Me Dad would find out that I'd contacted you and be very hurt. My heart wanted me to knock, but my brain told me I was too late."

Lorna's eyes misted as she took her hand. "Honestly, I'd given up on ever having a place in me brother's life that night. He had passed. Me mother had passed. I still had me Dad and big family, so I turned away. Will you forgive me for that?"

Holly couldn't get a word past her closed throat, her own eyes watering. Instead, she leaned forward and hugged Lorna like she was her sister, estranged for decades. It didn't matter that their connection was through a half sibling and marriage. The bond went deeper, through grief and beyond the living.

The front door opened and Lorna quickly pulled back, wiping her eyes while smiling at her. "I'm so glad you came."

Harris stopped in front of them and pulled Lorna to her feet, a scowl on his face. "What's this? You're crying. How many times must I tell you there's no crying in this house?"

Lorna laughed and he hugged her to him. "You big bruiser, these are happy tears. Can't you tell the difference?"

He put her at arm's length and studied her before turning his piercing gaze on Holly. "Is this true?"

She sniffed and gave him a weak smile. "Yes."

He dropped his hands from his wife's arms and actually

growled. "Ugh, I hate tears." Then he strode out of the room as if they were catching.

Lorna laughed. "He's such a big baby."

Ethan touched Holly on the shoulder. "Are you alright?"

She nodded, giving him a smile as well. "I really am. We were just having a heart-to-heart girl talk. I haven't had one of those since I last visited my mom."

He gazed into her eyes a moment before giving a short nod. "Harris said he and Lorna need to be leaving for her father's Christmas Eve gathering, so I thought we could take a walk before heading back."

Back to being phased is what he meant, but she was well aware it sounded like they'd driven up from Deervale. "Of course. I'd forgotten." She turned to Lorna. "It was so wonderful meeting you."

Lorna gave her a quick hug. "Thank you for finding me. I feel like my life is truly complete." She turned her head. "Harris, our guests are leaving and there's no more tears, so please come and say farewell."

Her husband returned and after many Christmas wishes, Holly and Ethan left the house of Cam's half-sister.

He took her hand in his and they walked down the street of row houses. She didn't truly see them, her head spinning with all that Lorna had revealed. When Ethan suddenly stopped, she looked around.

"Oh, it's the castle. I've never been so close."

Ethan looked at her quizzically. "And what about the river Ness?"

She turned around and sucked in her breath. The lights in the city had come on, but it wasn't yet true dark and they reflected in the calm waters below them. She moved to the stone wall that edged the sidewalk and gazed at the river as it meandered its way through the city to Loch Ness, home of the famous Nessie. "It's beautiful."

Ethan leaned against the wall facing her. "You haven't said a word since we left Lorna's."

She glanced at him. The golden glow of the lamplight surrounded him, putting his face in shadow. She returned her gaze to the water. "She told me how she was able to live again after the death of her husband. It was…I guess it touched me. Not just my brain, but my heart. I look at myself and realize that I'm so much weaker than she was."

Ethan's hand touched her chin and coaxed her to look at him. "You are not weak. You're stronger than some men I know. You're stronger than I am."

"What? No, I'm not. I've isolated myself. I didn't want to be around anyone, and if it wasn't for the Spirits of Christmas, I would have remained that way."

Now Ethan looked at the water. "Nay, you're still stronger than I am. I've done no better than you, hiding out at my home, only socializing when obligation required it."

"But we've both been out and about this year."

He finally looked at her. "Only because of you. I wouldn't have if you hadn't agreed to go to the music festival, the barn dance, the Branson's Anniversary cèilidh. I only went because you were willing. Otherwise, I would have been home alone those nights, like every night since Cameron left us…with my Scotch bottle."

The image of a drunken Ethan as the Spirits of Christmas Future had shown her flashed through her mind. It had already started?

He closed his eyes and took a deep breath before opening them. "I miss him. It was as if we were two parts of the same soul. I lived vicariously through him even while I worried constantly about him. It was one of the reasons I was always warning him to be careful. I was afraid to lose him."

Ethan looked away and rubbed the back of his neck. "And then I did."

She felt as if her heart were breaking all over again, not for her but for Ethan. He was so good to her. He even loved her. And she… "Ethan, I understand."

His gaze returned to hers. Though she couldn't see his face clearly, the limited light reflected off the sheen in his eyes.

She placed her hand on his cheek and rising on her toes brushed her lips across his in a feather-light kiss. She only meant to give comfort, but a spark of something else hit her heart.

She remained there, her lips close to his but not touching, wanting more but afraid to ask.

Ethan was absolutely still, his breath mixing with her own.

He loved her but would never push her. It wasn't his nature. She could walk away right now, but to what?

Nothing.

She stared at his mouth in the dim light. She wanted to live again. She wanted to feel again. Tilting her head, she pressed her lips more firmly against his, moving her hand down his stubbled jaw and behind his neck to pull him closer.

Ethan's lips opened, and she slipped her tongue between them.

As his arms came around her, it was like waking from a dream. A slow burn flowed through her veins as he took control of the kiss and explored her mouth with his tongue. It was an unhurried exploration and heat built in her belly. When he pulled back to lick the underside of her top lip, she took her first deep breath and as she exhaled, tingles spread throughout her body.

He kissed the corners of her mouth before leaning his forehead against her own. "Ye catch me blood on fire, *mo chridhe*."

She could definitely relate. Her muscles felt like seaweed, and her heart raced faster than a car on the M8 from Glasgow to Edinburg. She stared at the crease down the center of his lower lip as her breathing slowed. How did she never notice how perfectly even his lips were?

He pulled his head back and lifted her chin with one finger. "As I said, ye are the stronger of the two of us."

She opened her mouth to protest, but he gently laid his finger on it. "Nay, ye are. Ye are brave, courageous, and full of life."

Not being able to see the emotions in his eyes made it easier to confess. "Not so full of life. I feel like I've been asleep for four years."

A silent chuckle ran through his body and connected with hers. "That's not so bad compared to sleeping in a bottle."

At the reminder of his coping mechanism, her heart lurched. "I haven't been a very good friend, but maybe we can get through this together."

"I'd like that."

"Good." She stepped back and he let her go. Immediately, she wished she hadn't moved. Did she simply crave human touch? Or Ethan? She crossed her arms at the thought. And what would Cam think?

Suddenly, she flushed with guilt. She was married to Cam, and she'd just kissed his best friend! How could she?

I had been blessed with two soulmates. Lorna's words flew through her mind. Could that be true for her? She knew from Coco that Luca had two soulmates though she'd been surprised they both lived in the area.

Could it be possible that Ethan was her own second soulmate? It was a bit hard to believe, considering how close to them he was. And what would Cam think if it were true? How would she know?

"It would probably be best if we return to Lorna's house now." As darkness had descended, building lights came on, and she could now see Ethan's face in the glow of the castle. He didn't seem happy to be leaving.

She dropped her arms. "Yes, we should get back. Cam doesn't want to waste any of his fifteen minutes having to look for us. He's so excited to be doing this."

Ethan nodded, but didn't say anything as they started back the way they'd come.

She didn't reach for his hand. Her heart was as confused as her head, and she didn't want to make it worse. Maybe Cam's next visits would make things clearer for her. If not, then it would be time for their own heart-to-heart because she was determined to figure out why this was their last night together.

~~*~~

Cameron put his feet up on his desk and crossed them at the ankles. He may have screwed up a bit on the visit to the past and part of the present, but he was one hundred percent sure that he'd nailed it with the visit to Lorna.

Holly would want to learn everything so she could tell him. Lorna's late husband William had been a Spirit Guide for a while, but now he was one of Cameron's many success stories.

"Doctor, heal thyself." He chuckled at his own wit. It was less himself and more his wife that needed the healing.

He'd hoped that Ethan would be a good companion for her, but to discover that he was her soulmate had completely put his own fears to rest. If Holly could just open up and let Ethan in, they could all be together again and this time forever.

For the first time, he let himself imagine what it would be like with his best friend and wife. They could have an immeasurable amount of fun. After all, time didn't exist in the spirit world, and Holly thoroughly enjoyed sex. Just thinking about him and Ethan pleasuring her, had him growing hard.

He waved his hand and an image appeared in his office. It was a king size bed in a lavish room. It was his fantasy, so he included a mirror above the bed and on the wall at the head. Lacing his fingers behind his head, he sat back and watched.

Images of himself, Ethan, and Holly floated in. Holly was in her ass-kicking black boots and a red teddy similar to one he'd bought for her their first Christmas together. Ethan was in a pair of gray sweat pants, and he had himself in a kilt. Holly loved investigating beneath a kilt.

She was so beautiful. Full of smiles and warmth and life, like she'd been when they were married. His image came up behind her and cupped her ass. She exaggerated her surprise and looked back at him as if he'd done something he shouldn't.

Then Ethan turned around and ran his hands down her neck to her shoulders before pushing the thin straps of the teddy down her arms to bare her full breasts. Ethan cupped the large globes in his hands and began to alternately lick each nipple to hardness.

Cameron pressed his hard erection against Holly's rounded ass, knowing how she enjoyed the roughness of the wool against her. Snaking his hand over her thigh to unsnap the skimpy lingerie between her legs, he bared her folds to his touch. Then he ran a finger between them to discover her readiness. He had no reason to resist, so he didn't. He slipped his finger inside her.

Holly arched back, her head against his shoulder as he played between her legs. He stroked the hard nub of her pleasure intermittently then speared her with his fingers. Ethan was sucking on one of her nipples, his free hand playing with the other.

His own erection was hard as a cliff side, and he nestled it between Holly's ass cheeks. Holly's pants grew louder as he and Ethan worked in sync, like they always had in life, though never with his wife. Both of them now were attuned to Holly's whimpers as her tension grew.

She reached back with her hand and grabbed him around the neck. "Please."

Ethan heard her and sucked hard just as Cameron thrust two fingers deep inside her.

Her yell heralded her orgasm as her sheath squeezed his fingers. He pumped them into her harder and kept her literally on her toes as she let go.

No sooner had she finished than Ethan knelt at her feet.

Removing his finger from her opening, Cameron moved both arms around her and cupped her breasts, even as Ethan began to lap at her clit. They were determined to give her all the pleasure she wanted. It was as if they were two parts of the same brain.

He rolled her large nipples between his fingers, causing her to arch again. Then Ethan slid two fingers inside her before going back to lick the hard nub that made her completely lose herself.

He couldn't feel her sheath, but her hips bucked toward Ethan. Taking her nipples between his fingers, he gently squeezed one then the other in no particular order or rhythm, making her anticipate his next squeeze.

Holly began to moan, but as her body readied itself for another orgasm, her sounds rose in pitch and cadence. He increased his squeezes as Ethan increased his rhythm. He held her nipples tightly, and she pressed her hips toward Ethan's mouth, until he brought her thighs over his shoulders.

Cameron held her up beneath her arms while her cries of pleasure fed his own need. Ethan pulled his head away, but kept his fingers inside her as she spasmed in her ecstasy. When her breathing slowed a bit, they nodded at each other and carried her to the bed.

She stretched out, her hands over her head and smiled. "That was nice."

Cameron grinned as he climbed onto the foot of the bed at the same time Ethan dropped his sweats and moved to the head.

Holly looked up at Ethan's large cock and licked her lips. "I think that made me hungry."

Cameron laughed. "Good. Time to eat." He rolled her over and gave her a tap on her ass. "Go ahead, you wanted it."

She got up onto her hands and knees then looked behind her. "How did I get so lucky?"

"You married me."

She laughed before turning to Ethan and licking the tip of his cock.

Cameron's own jumped at the sight. His wife was way too hot, especially from this angle. He could see her thickened folds, moist with her own juices. He knelt up and put his hands on her round ass. It was smooth and soft, and he couldn't help squeezing her cheeks.

She stopped licking Ethan's length to look back at him and wink.

Well, fuck, if she wasn't a vixen. He lifted his kilt up and laid it on her back. Grasping one cheek, he took his cock in hand. Purposefully, he slid himself along her opening, past it and over her clit then back.

Ethan took his cue and pulled his cock from her lips.

"Hey. Now you're just teasing." She whined, knowing full well she'd get everything she wanted.

He ran his length along her opening to her clit again, then nodded at Ethan. The man brought his tip to her lips and as she opened, he slid inside her mouth.

"Hmmmm."

As Ethan slid out, Cameron grasped her hips and positioned himself, then holding her ass, he thrust himself inside her wet sheath."

"Oh, yes." Holly's words didn't last as he pushed her off him and onto Ethan. He pulled her back by the hips again before Ethan held her thick hair as he glided back inside her mouth.

They kept an even rhythm going, pulling her back and forth over their cocks, filling her at both ends until he felt Holly's sheath tightening around him. He wouldn't last now, not with her orgasming.

He pushed into her faster, Ethan following suit, and within a few thrusts, she squeezed him hard. He held her tight against him as Ethan pushed into her mouth at the same time, and she moaned her release around his cock.

Suddenly, the images broke apart as Mrs. Ferrisletter floated through the scene. The vision dissipated as he quickly dropped his feet and kept his excited state below the desk.

The English woman from 1662 had a heart of gold, but if anyone epitomized frumpy, it was her. Her entrance was an ice bath on his cock and within moments he was able to stand without embarrassing himself.

She lowered her spectacles and approached. "Sorry to bother you, my dear, but you requested that I give you my impression of our latest Spirit Guide recruits."

"Aye, I did. Please." Refocusing his thoughts on work, albeit regretfully, he opened his hand to one of the two chairs in the room. He walked around his desk, leaning his ass against it, and folded his arms. "How are our latest recruits doing?"

He listened attentively as the old woman gave him her exact impression of every new student under her wing. She was very perceptive and often delved deeper, suggesting motivations for certain behaviors or recognizing a slowness in accepting the transition. She was invaluable to someone in his position.

When she was finished, he thanked her and walked her to the door. "Could I ask you to think on another important issue? I do value your advice."

The woman puffed up like a tom turkey. "Of course you may. How can I be of assistance?"

"I need to decide on a new Spirit Guide trainer to replace Duncan Montgomerie. I was hoping you could think about who you'd like to work with and who could handle the responsibility, and let me know your top three choices."

"Oh, my." She put her pudgy hand to her large chest. "I'd be honored."

He smiled. "I'd appreciate it."

Her face became very serious. "You can depend on me to give this careful thought and due consideration."

He gave her a short nod. "Thank you."

Mrs. Ferrisletter turned in a rustle of brown silk and white lace. In an instant she phased and floated through the closed office door, her mind obviously already on task.

Cameron brushed the hair from his forehead and floated through the ceiling. Mrs. Ferrisletter's interruption of his future vision was a strong reminder that there was still work to be done before he could truly enjoy any celebratory fantasies. Flying into the ether, he headed for the future—Holly's future, in particular.

As he reached her timeline, he found fewer openings, but now a third one held lights. Not about to ask permission, he quickly floated through it to find himself at a burial ceremony. Confused, he drifted across the crowd, afraid that Holly had once again found herself a young widow.

Since Ethan was her soulmate, he was hoping she was at least in her eighties before she'd be left alone again.

As he approached the casket held above the open hole, he scanned the people there. There weren't many, but they were all her family. He frowned as he found her mother, being escorted by John, stepping toward the grave, a rose in her hand.

She gently laid the flower on the casket before breaking down in John's arms. Her wail pierced his soul.

He scanned the surroundings. This was not Scotland. With unease settling in his veins, he phased through the lid of the casket.

"No!" He pulled back out shaking his head and floating away from it. "This can't be a possibility. How can this be? I refuse to let this happen." Anger burned through him as he floated farther away from the gravesite toward the road where people were walking back to their cars.

Holly could not be dead so soon. He couldn't have messed up that badly. He refused to believe it was even a possibility.

He floated over a older woman dressed in black." I can't believe she sacrificed herself for her father's friend. They say she told her dad that she had nothing to live for but that he did. She wasn't even forty yet. It just breaks my heart."

At the mourner's words, he stilled. The woman spoke of the bank robbery that Malcom had shown Holly in her parents' town in America where her adoptive father's best friend was shot and killed and her father wounded.

If he gave Holly nothing to live for, then she'd put herself in harm's way knowing full well what the outcome would be. He couldn't let that happen.

He sped away from the scene, escaping through the doorway in Holly's future timeline. He had to show her there was so much still to live for. He needed to prove to her that she had a long life of love and laughter still to come, if she'd just embrace it.

If she didn't, he'd never be with her again. His gut twisted at the thought of spending eternity without her. Panic sent him racing through space and time toward an hour after he left her.

Remiel may have tied his hands by not allowing him to show Holly the possible futures in her timeline, but he could create one that was close enough. At this point, he had no choice.

And the final opening that held Holly's future?

He fisted his hands. If he could convince her of the happiness still in store for her, that opening would disappear, and he would never have to know what was in it.

With his determination in place, he broke through the ether to the sight of Ethan and Holly walking toward his half-sister's house. Not wanting to spare a minute, he dropped down in front of them.

Chapter Ten

Ethan felt Cameron's presence seconds before he appeared before them. Something was wrong. There was no ready smile and the energized exuberance that so characterized Cameron was missing. What happened?

Holly jumped then laughed. "Cam, you startled me."

Cameron grinned, but it didn't quite reach his eyes. "Sorry, love, but I wanted to get started on our next visit right away."

"I'm looking forward to it." Holly glanced at him. "Are you ready to be phased again?"

If it was the only way to find out what Cameron was worried about then he was ready. "Aye. Let's see what the future holds, right, Cameron?" A flash of worry crossed his friend's face before he hid it as Holly turned her attention back to him. That didn't bode well.

"I'm more than ready to fly again. Will we have to go through the gray stuff?"

Cameron phased her as he answered. "Aye, but not for long." He turned to Ethan. "Ready?"

He nodded, his concern over Holly's sudden withdrawal compounding with whatever Cameron had encountered. Already, his head was filled with the pros and cons of multiple scenarios. Once phased, he planned on pulling Cameron aside at the first opportunity.

Holly grasped his hand after grabbing onto Cameron's, the touch causing his brain to calm. "I can't wait to see another piece of my future."

Cameron looked at him over Holly's head and grimaced. That in itself was enough to know he must be sharp and on guard. "Now, hen, you know the future is uncertain, so all I can do is show you a possibility." He lifted them upward and into the gray mist.

"I know." She looked at Ethan. "My spirit of Christmas Future, Malcolm, was actually from the future, that's why he was able to tell me the percentages of the chances of a scene becoming reality. Cam doesn't have that ability. Isn't it interesting how each one has different talents? Coco, like I said before, could see soulmates."

Holly blushed and quickly turned to Cameron. "I have so much to tell you about Lorna. Did you know that her husband died young, and he was an accountant! Just shows you that when it's your time, it's your time. So you really didn't have to feel guilty about passing. And…"

As Holly filled Cameron in on all they had learned about Lorna, Ethan watched his friend. Though he made all the right responses, he didn't actually seem surprised. When they had planned the visit to Lorna's, Cameron hadn't let on that he was well aware of all that Holly would learn, but he'd known.

A new respect for Cameron filled him. The man was absolutely dedicated to helping Holly move on with her life. He was doing everything he possibly could. Not every idea worked, but he'd been right about having Holly visit Lorna. The fact they hadn't simply been eavesdropping made it that much more impactful.

But now something had happened that concerned Cameron.

Holly's hand moved his back and forth with enthusiasm as she related every detail. Her liveliness was part of what had attracted him to her. It had dimmed so much after Cameron passed. But here in his presence, she was fully engaged. Could he possibly love her enough for that flame of life to burn so bright?

At the end of the night, Cameron would have to step out of Holly's life forever, or rather for her entire lifetime. For once, he could empathize with his friend. Would it be easier because he'd only seen her once a year? Or because there was no time where he was, did that mean it felt like only four days after he'd died?

What if *he* needed to step out of her life for her to move on? Could *he* do it? His chest tightened at the thought. How could Cameron do it?

Reflexively, he squeezed Holly's hand.

She turned to him. "Did I forget something?"

Not having listened carefully, he grasped for anything. "What about the soulmates?"

"Well, crap. I forgot." She turned back to Cameron. "Lorna said she had two soulmates. Coco said that was a possibility. She also said that she thought William had sent Harris to her. You wouldn't know anything about that, would you?"

Cameron gave his first real grin. "Maybe."

Ethan sensed the tension in Holly as she opened her mouth to ask her next question, but the gray mist parted, and they were flying above his home. Instead of the overcast sky at their last visit, it was sunny, and there was a serious volleyball game taking place on the back lawn.

"We're back at Ethan's." Holly's switch of topic may have been accidental, but he wished she had asked the question she'd planned to. His gut told him it was important. He needed to remember to bring up the concept of soulmates because Holly believed in that concept with absolute certainty and he remembered Cameron mentioning it at some point.

Cameron smiled. "I thought you'd like to go to a picnic." He guided them to the top of a white tent set up on the lawn where people sat beneath them, but there was plenty of activity on the lawn to view.

Holly let go of Cameron's hand and faced him. "This is your house, so what do you think this could be? Remember, it's in the future." She was so excited, she practically burst with it. The dimple in her right cheek deepened with her laugh. "This could be anything because Cameron doesn't know the odds of it occurring."

He smiled in response. The fact that she still held his hand and not Cameron's wasn't lost on him. "Let me see." He scanned the crowd, but he didn't recognize anyone. Could he have lost his family home by mismanaging the money?

He shook his head. "I have no idea. I don't recognize anyone. Do you?"

As Holly moved her attention to the many people and activities, he glanced at Cameron. The man winked, which was a good sign. He brought his attention back to those playing volleyball, but they were moving quickly, so he scanned those playing horseshoes. He was pretty sure his family would never create horseshoe pits on the side of the back lawn.

A boy of about nine turned around and headed for the tent. Ethan stared. The resemblance to himself when he was that age was so striking, he had to remind himself this was the future. The future?

He glanced at Cameron again and raised his brow. His friend nodded, their silent communication just like when they were at university. Warmth filled his chest as he perused the people closer.

These were his descendants.

"Ethan, look." Holly pointed to a teenage boy with wavy brown hair. "That boy just called for Francis."

His heart pounded. Only Holly knew what that name meant to him, and he'd never marry anyone but her. Bloody hell! Without another thought, he yanked her into the sky and headed as fast as he could away from the scene.

Cameron appeared in front of them. "What are you doing?"

He ignored him, his need to put as much distance between the happy scene at his home and Holly, urging him on beyond reason. Swerving around his friend, he spied Loudon Hill and headed for it.

"Where the fuck are you going, Ethan?" Cameron's appearance before them didn't deter him anymore the second time.

Swerving around him with speed born of desperation, it wasn't until he had them descending toward the hilltop that Cameron grabbed his arm. He let go of Holly. "Wait here."

She looked up at him, her brows drawn down. "What's going on?"

As Cameron pulled him away, he yelled. "We have a difference of opinion!" That was putting it mildly based on how hard Cameron gripped his arm. He didn't care as long as they were away from Holly. He had little doubt she'd stay there given her aversion to the ghosts at the bottom of the hill.

As soon as the gray mist enveloped them, Ethan pulled his arm from Cameron's tight grasp. "Stop. You've left Holly alone. You can't do that."

Cameron scowled at him. "I can and I have. Time has no meaning here. I'll return within a second from the moment I left. Now explain yourself and give me one good reason not to leave you here!"

While Cameron lived, Ethan had only seen him truly enraged once. The man got angry as many times as he laughed, but it was always quick, burning itself out, but this was a whole new level and for the first time he felt himself threatened.

He reached for the calm calculation that always stood him in good stead. Quietly, he stated what was obvious. "She's not ready."

"Not ready for what?" Cameron's phased image was growing larger with his anger.

He hadn't expected so much emotion in the spirit world. "Holly isn't ready to see our children and grandchildren."

"And you know this how?"

"I know this because after I kissed her, she was fine until how we both coped with your death came out. The second she thought of you, she stepped away. She's not ready to see an alternative life beyond loving you."

Myriad expressions crossed Cameron's face in a heartbeat from irritation to longing to confusion to hopelessness. It was the last that brought his essence back to normal size, but when he brushed his hair back from his forehead, frustration had settled in.

Cameron didn't say a word. He just hovered there, staring at the grayness. Finally, he looked at him, the desperation in his dark eyes, freezing Ethan to the core. "I have to save her."

His breath left him and refused to return. Save her? Every protective instinct rushed to the fore, and with them, air flooded his lungs. "What do you mean, save her?"

Cameron didn't look away. "I mean save her. If she doesn't see a reason to look forward to her future, she's going to give up and put herself in harm's way on purpose."

"No!" Ethan's phased state reverberated with his demand. He reached for the calm center of his being he'd learned to tap into after years of studying ancient combat. It remained elusive. "She can't. I won't let her. You have to tell me how this happens. I can stop it."

"Not if she wants it." Cameron sighed. "What I learned is that she stepped in front of a bullet meant for someone else…in America. Even if you were able to be with her every moment, that wouldn't stop her from finding another way. I know. I've seen them. The ones who don't want to live anymore." Cameron pierced him with a hard stare. "You know what that's like."

Did he? "You mean the Scotch?"

Cameron raised a brow. "You tell me."

He'd tried to forget those first three years when he'd lost Cameron and Holly shut him out. She'd shut everyone out, so he didn't know how she was doing without going into her shop, which he'd only done occasionally to avoid the pain for both of them. It had been obvious at Cameron's funeral that being around him and Brody just made her cry harder.

He hadn't been persistent, but he did reach out to her only to be turned down until the only invitation he'd issued was to his parents' dinner on Christmas day. His heartache had been complete.

Every night he'd turned to the Scotch and passed out. Without Holly, he'd given up. What would have happened if she hadn't accepted last year's Christmas dinner invitation? "Aye, you're right. Eventually, I probably would have fallen down the stairs and broken my neck, or some such idiocy." Even as he said the words, a chill raced through him as if to confirm his prediction.

He glanced around. Only Cameron was visible. Ethan agreed with Holly. The gray mist was unnerving.

"Are you still drinking?" Cameron's question surprised him.

"Don't you know?"

"No. I don't have time to watch you every second. I've got responsibilities."

He wanted to remind Cameron that he said time didn't matter in the spirit world, but he didn't actually want to know. It relieved him that Cameron didn't hover over him on a daily basis. "No, I am not. At least not while alone…at least not until the night you visited me."

Cameron's lip quirked up on one side. "I *have* been known to cause people to reach for the bottle."

Ethan rubbed the back of his neck. "We have to figure out what will help Holly. I can't lose her now that she's finally back in my life."

"And I can't lose her for eternity. Only if she can let go of me will we be together later."

"And what about me? Does that mean I only have her during

life? Will I lose her later?" Could he accept that? He'd never thought of the afterlife, but with Cameron living proof…or rather after-living proof, it suddenly became very important.

Cameron smiled for the first time since they left Holly on the hilltop. "No, my friend. We both can have her, either separate or together. It's the wonder of this world."

Relief filled him, which brought on a new determination. "Then we need to help her see life is worth living."

Cameron frowned. "Which is why I brought her to your house. I created a scene with all your potential progeny. What more could a woman wish for? She has bemoaned the fact that we didn't have a child, so that should make her happy."

He gave Cameron a quick smile. He had a newfound patience with his friend now that he'd been given all the facts, or maybe he should think of it as information. "Aye, but if she realized those were her children and great grandchildren as I suspect, she would have felt like it was the ultimate betrayal of you. Your presence in her life all these years after you passed has made it seem like you're still alive, and she's still married to you."

"I prefer the word transitioned."

Holly hadn't used that word last time she mentioned Cameron's death, which had to be a good sign. She'd used "passed." It was so like Cameron to avoid the worst, which was that he'd messed up. Though to give him credit, he had admitted it at the start of the evening. It was Holly who didn't understand what he meant. "Very well, so how do we encourage her to let go."

"I could generate an image of me and another woman. Then maybe she'd be so disappointed that she'd let me go."

Ethan squelched his retort. "No, that would just make her angry at the slut and more adamant that you needed her."

"So what? I pretend I'm happy here, that I don't need her? I don't think I'm that good of an actor."

He shook his head. Cameron couldn't even keep a surprise party a surprise, then again, he'd kept a lot from them over the years, so someone had him keeping secrets.

"Let me think."

Cameron sighed. "Please." The hopefulness in his voice weighed Ethan down. Somehow Holly's, Cameron's and his own fate had fallen on his shoulders.

He turned away. The gray mist made an excellent imaginary board on which he could run the pros and cons of multiple scenarios. The problem was, every one ended with an equal chance of success and failure. There had to be a way to tip the scales in favor of success with minimum risk.

If the usual approaches wouldn't work, then maybe he needed to apply strategies outside the typical box. He'd had great success with managing the family finances, so he tried that approach, but the outcomes were the same. It appeared he needed to go further afield. What if he tried the Medieval battle strategies?

Rearranging the imaginary board, he ran a number of battle plans, but they seemed to make it worse. This wasn't about war. This was about love. Would a losing strategy work? What was the opposite of battle plans? Matchmaking plans. He wasn't familiar with those. The only one he knew well was Shakespeare's famous play of Romeo and Juliet, and that didn't end well at all. He racked his brain for other literary plots.

He was an idiot. For all his Uni schooling, he'd missed the obvious. He laughed.

"What? Did you figure something out?"

Cameron's question had him holding up his hand to stave off conversation a few more seconds so he could run the scenarios.

If they confronted Holly with an image similar to what Scrooge had, what were the chances? The odds were greatly improved in his estimation, but still not enough for him to feel comfortable. What if they offered to show her a single happy scene afterward? He went back and forth.

Rubbing the back of his neck, he let out a frustrated sigh. He was definitely missing something. Either it was information he had and was forgetting, or something he didn't know yet.

"What? That sigh doesn't sound good."

Ethan turned to Cameron. "I think I've figured something out that would help without scaring Holly, but it's not perfect. We may have to wing some of this. Are you willing to follow my lead?"

Cameron grinned. "Happily. As you can see, I haven't done so well on my own. I think I just love her too much."

He did as well. Maybe with both their brains thinking in opposite directions, they could figure this out, and for that he was grateful. *You two are like two pieces of a whole.* Holly's words earlier came back to him. Could it be that simple? "We make a good team."

"Aye, we do. Always did and always will…if we get this right. So what do we start with? You need to understand, I don't actually *know* Holly's future. That's been denied to me. But I can create images based on a scene. The people in the scene, however, act according to their character. I can't make them do or say certain things."

That piece of information flooded him with relief. If Cameron orchestrated everything, he could make a mistake that they couldn't fix, not that he'd share that with his friend. The fact was, Cameron's heart was in the right place. "That's fine. That's all we need. Can you show us her family after the scene you saw where she puts herself in harm's way?" He swallowed hard, the words were even difficult to say.

"You mean like days after the funeral?"

He ignored the hitch in his heart. "Aye. That will work. And after that maybe we can see her with one grandchild?" He had to admit, he wanted to see that, too. "But only if I think it's right."

Cameron nodded. "I can do that." He grinned. "As long as her son can be named Cameron."

He chuckled. "Fine, just remember, only if I think it's the right scene."

Cameron slapped him on the back. "You've got it. Thank you." He looked at him with gratefulness.

He understood Cameron's dark gaze. He wasn't just thankful for the idea, but that they were working together to save Holly. He nodded once. "Ready?"

"Not so fast." Cameron's hand clamped down on his upper arm. "What's this about you kissing my wife?"

The question caught him off guard. Wasn't that what the man wanted? "I didn't kiss your wife. I kissed your widow."

Cameron sucked in his breath. "You know how to hit a man where it hurts."

He studied his friend. "I thought you wanted her to fall for me so she would let go of you. Are you saying *you* don't want to let go of her?"

"No, I just…" Cameron moved the hair off his forehead yet again. "No, you're right. Let's go." Without another word, they were flying through the ether and back to Holly.

Ethan's concerns grew. He hadn't imagined, with all that Cameron had done over the years, that his friend might be the one having a hard time letting go. Were his visits for him or Holly? Or what if neither of them could break away?

And if they were successful and she let go but Cameron held on, what could be done? Could he tear her away from Cameron by himself? The answers had his senses on overdrive.

Holly crossed her arms as she floated to a stop on the hilltop. She'd really didn't like this stupid hill anymore. If the boys wanted to talk, why not leave her at Ethan's? She glanced upward to see them returning. Relief that they returned already had her smiling again. She'd forgot about the ether being timeless. It was a concept she didn't even try to wrap her head around.

They landed in front of her, Cam with a huge smile on his face and Ethan looking worriedly at her. He, for one, knew exactly how much she feared the ghost army below.

She dropped her arms. "I'm glad that didn't take long. This isn't my favorite resting space."

A look passed between the two men. How many times had she seen that when they were all together? Her heart warmed. "Can we go back to Ethan's house now."

Ethan stepped forward and took her hand. "No, I told Cameron we needed to focus on you first, not me. Are you ready for a glimpse at a possible future?"

She wouldn't meet his gaze. If it was some happily ever after with him, it would be way too awkward. "I guess."

It wasn't that she was against a future where Ethan was in her life. It was more that she simply couldn't fathom it when Cam remained with her. She wasn't entirely opposed to living as widow all her life until they were together again, yet even the thought of that depressed her. What was wrong with her?

"Ah, come on, hen. Where's your sense of adventure?" Cam took her other hand, his smile one of those he usually used on her when he knew she wasn't going to like what he was about to say.

She'd never told him she could tell that, so she didn't start now. Instead, she steeled herself for the next scene and forced a smile. "I'm up for anything that will get me off this hill."

"That's my love." Cam pulled her up, and they flew into the ether.

When they broke free of it a minute later, they were flying over New Hampshire in the United States where her mom and John lived. Her first thought was Cam would show her the death of the Tinders, her adopted grandparents. She'd spent a lot of time with them last visit, the words of Malcolm still echoing in her ears.

But you're in Scotland and they're here. How much can you really care? You're over there because a man who is already dead means more to you than people who are still alive that you say you love.

For all that Malcolm was harsh, he'd definitely made his point. She'd spent a month in America following that spirit's visit and had plans to do so again. Her family filled her heart, and they were growing by leaps and bounds. Her adoptive father, John, had given her a big extended family. She was looking forward to seeing them all…as long as it wasn't at a funeral or someone's sickbed.

She needed to let Cam know that she'd been visiting, in case Malcolm hadn't filled him in. "When I was here this past summer, Alicia was planning her wedding and Darlene was expecting around Thanksgiving. I'll see them this summer, but it would be fun to have a sneak peek."

She spoke to Cam, but then turned to Ethan. "As I told you, I was an only child who was lucky to get a dad in my teenage years, but I think I forgot to mention that my dad is from a big family. I basically had the best of both worlds."

She rolled her eyes. "And the worst. I totally understood where Lorna was coming from with the big family problems. You wouldn't believe how many calls, electronic messages and even hand-written letters I got from my family asking me to return to America after Cam passed on. It was really hard to resist."

"Why did you? Not that I'm disappointed you did."

She smiled at that. She was glad she stayed, too. She wouldn't have been in Deervale to help Ethan had she left. And just as important was that she wouldn't have seen Cam. Or would she? If he could come to America now, he could have come before. For the first time since Cam passed, she questioned her decision.

But as Ethan squeezed her hand, she had her answer. She had to be there for him, and as it turned out, for Brody, too. "Being in my home made me feel closer to Cam. Plus, I had the One of a Kind

Christmas Shop. We had worked so hard to get it open, I didn't want to give up on it so soon." She quickly looked at Cam. "Not that I would ever give up on it."

He shrugged. "I told you. That was not the legacy I meant to leave you with. It's more work than it's worth. If you wanted to sell it, I'd be fine with that. You can remember me in your heart."

He had said that before, which made her question if she'd been more excited about the shop than he was. "Well, right now I need it to survive. It's my income."

"What about my life insurance policy?"

She couldn't meet his eyes. "That money hasn't come through yet. There seems to be a lot of red tape."

"What?"

"What?"

Both men reacted at the same time. How had she gone four years avoiding that question? She looked down at her mom and John's house. "Oh look, we're here."

Cam brought them to halt right then. "We aren't going any farther until you tell us what's going on with my life insurance. I paid a lot of money for that."

She shrugged. "It's just a lot of hurdles. You know, the death certificate, the marriage license, the proving I have a right to be living in Scotland though I kept my American citizenship. That kind of stuff."

"Holly." Cam's tone was stern, a rarity with him.

"Don't worry. I think I'm near the end of the hoops they make you jump through."

She looked at Cam to see him nodding to Ethan.

Ethan ignored her as he responded to her late husband. "I'll get right on it after the holidays."

She let go of both men's hands and faced Ethan. "You will, will you?"

He gave her a curt nod, not a glimmer of a smile. "I will."

Okay then. So much for standing on her own two feet. Then again, she'd done that for the last four years. If she was honest with herself, it was a relief to have someone's help, especially someone she trusted. "Thank you."

"Are you ready, hen?" Cam held his arm out toward her mom's home.

"Absolutely." She led them both through the roof and into the living room, which was part of the dining area and kitchen in the open-concept home. "John had this built for mom when I went away to school. It's got three bedrooms, one they save for me. Isn't that sweet?"

Her mom and John sat in the kitchen, a big box on the table. She floated behind them, thankful for the tall ceilings. "Oh wow, it's from Brody and Sarah." She didn't realize her friends felt close enough to her parents to send them anything.

Her mom didn't look much older than the last time she'd seen her, but she held a tissue in her hand.

"I don't know if I can open it."

John looked at her mom. "Do you want me to?"

"Yes. No. I don't know." Her mom sniffed. "I just miss her so much. Maybe we could put it in her room?"

John scooted his chair around the corner of the table to be next to her mom and took her hand. "If it's in there, will you be able to forget about it or will you think about it every day?"

Her mom sniffed again and wiped her nose. "I'll think about it every day, but at least I won't know what's in it."

"You always were the one to slowly peel the bandage off the cut instead of making quick work of it."

Her mom laid her head on her husband's shoulder and nodded.

Holly's belly somersaulted as her heart raced. "Are they talking about me?"

"Aye, love."

At Cam's answer, a chill raced up her spine. "What happened?"

Chapter Eleven

Cameron glanced at Ethan who hovered next to her before returning his gaze to her. "You were killed in the bank robbery."

She frowned. "But I was going to keep that from happening. I fully intend to visit next year and call the police with an anonymous tip and go with John and Uncle Jerry and make them stop somewhere before arriving at the bank. I have it all planned." She looked at Ethan. "Uncle Jerry really isn't my uncle, but John's best friend."

"That didn't happen in this future." Cam's words brought her back to the scene.

"Why not?"

Cam lifted his hand to touch her cheek, then dropped it, the need to comfort her clear in his hazel eyes. "Because after tonight's visit, you decided you had nothing left to live for. So you went to the bank with your father and Jerry and took the bullet meant for Uncle Jerry."

She floated backwards, shaking her head. "No, I wouldn't. I couldn't. How do you know that's why I did it? Maybe I was being brave, and I wanted to save Uncle Jerry."

Ethan's hands on her shoulders as she bumped into him let her know he had her back…literally.

Cam shook his head, his eyes turning gray with his sorrow. "You told your father before you died in his arms that your uncle had more to live for than you."

She opened her mouth to deny it. How could that be her? It didn't feel like her. She looked up at Ethan. She had him. She had to help him get over Cam's death. They could do it together.

A niggling doubt made its way into her conscious. What if by sacrificing herself, she could be with Cam sooner? Had that been her thought? She had to know. "So in this future, do I get to be with you forever then?"

Ethan's hands on her shoulders tightened, once again reminding her of how selfish she was.

"No, hen. Because you never let go in life, we would be parted forever."

She shook her head and pulled away from Ethan to face him. She pointed to her mother. "I'm never going to do this. I promise. You must make sure I keep my promise."

Ethan's green eyes lightened. "Aye, I will, but I can't be with you all the time. You have to determine that *you* won't do this."

She crossed her arms, sure she wouldn't sacrifice herself, but the doubt wouldn't go away.

"Open it." Her mom's words brought her attention back to the scene.

"Are you sure?" John still held her mother.

"Yes. Let's get it over with. Then I won't dream about what might be in that box. For all we know it's a box of ornaments they bought from the old shop Holly owned. Then we could put them on the tree." Despite her mother's brave words, tears started down her cheeks.

John didn't say another word. He rose from the table and pulled a pair of scissors from the drawer. He moved back to the box. "Are you sure?"

Her mother nodded, then quickly shook her head as if afraid of what might be in there.

John sliced open the box and pulled out a piece of paper. He held it out for her mom to take.

"I can't. You read it."

He held the paper with one hand that shook slightly, proving once again what an amazing father he was. "Dear Mr. and Mrs. Tinder. Ethan Stewart requested that we send these items to you. He's held onto them for memory's sake, but since Holly is no longer with us and his new fiancée will be moving into Rawdon Manor with him, he asked that we send them to you. He apologizes if these hurt you in anyway, but he didn't have the heart to throw them out. Yours, in our shared grief, Sarah and Brody Hamilton."

Her mother sobbed as Holly spun around to stare at Ethan. "Fiancée?"

His eyes were wide and his face, even in its phased state, had turned pale as he shook his head in denial.

"He couldn't cope with your death." Cam answered her instead. "He had to find a reason to live or die in the Scotch bottle."

She spun around, swallowing to get words past her closed throat. "Is he happy?"

Cam shook his head. "Not really." He looked at Ethan. "Your reason for living was to give your mum the grandchildren she wanted. You did that."

She felt as if she'd been kicked in the gut and stomped on. She couldn't stand the pain. Her mother's sobs filled the room, bringing tears to her own eyes. "So if I avoid this whole self-sacrifice death thing and live a long life, this won't come to pass, right?"

"It's more than that, love." Cameron spread his arms open. "You must feel that living without me is worth it. Do you feel that?"

"Right now, all I feel is afraid and depressed. Isn't there anything happy I can look forward to?"

Cameron looked at Ethan. "Should I show her?"

Ethan, still in obvious shock, nodded.

She didn't wait another moment. It was as if being in that future any longer would make it happen. They needed to leave. Now.

She grabbed Ethan's hand and then Cam's and pulled them out of the house.

None of them said a word as Cameron flew them through the ether. When they emerged, they were back in Deervale and heading to her home.

Relief to be away from her scary possible future helped lift her spirits. There was something about being back in Deervale that made it seem like everything would be alright.

Just above her home, Cam stopped and released her hand. "I'm going to let Ethan show you inside. My time is almost up, but I'll be back in an hour. I need you to do something for me, Holly."

That he used her name told her exactly how important his request was. He rarely called her by her name. "You know I will."

"I know you will try." He smiled. "I need you to not only keep an open mind, but an open heart with this possible future. Can you do that for me?"

At his words, she had an inkling she knew what it might be. It may be what Malcolm and Joy had shown her when they visited Sarah and Brody in the future. She swallowed hard. "If I do, will it mean that we can be together when I transition?"

He nodded, but didn't say a word.

She looked at her home. It was *her* home. Actually, it had been *their* home, but it was hers now. As long as she still owned it, not like the other future Malcom and Joy had shown her, her instinct said everything could work out. "I will."

"That's m—"

Cam disappeared. She held Ethan's hand harder. "I hate when that happens. It's like he has no choice or no control."

Ethan floated in front of her. "I don't think he does. His fate rests in your hands."

She gazed at the man who loved her, though he hadn't admitted it, and who would marry another just for his mom. Every thought, word, and movement of his was centered on her. Could she ever give that to him? Could she get there? Could she leave Cam behind to do that?

"Ethan, I want to be able to love again. I want to feel that amazing feeling, but I'm so afraid that part of my heart will always be with Cam."

His eyes darkened to a forest green and his jaw tensed. "I can tell you I would never expect you to stop loving Cam. No man should. He will forever live in my heart, too."

The knot in her stomach, which formed since first entering her mother's house, eased. Ethan would never ask her for more than she could give. She'd known that. If she could just get out of her own way, they might be able to have something.

Something more than friendship.

Even at the thought, she flushed. The memory of their kiss by the River Ness reminded her that she was still very much alive, even in her phased state.

"Are you ready to see what's below?"

Was she? Cam asked her to keep herself open. "Not yet. I'm nervous. Could you…hold me?"

Ethan's tight jaw eased. "Aye." He opened his arms, and she floated into them.

She sighed. It felt so good to be held. Because it was Ethan or just to be held? She searched her heart. No, she felt loved and safe in Ethan's arms. He'd never let any harm come to her.

And one thing she was sure of, she didn't want him to marry someone else. She cared about him as a friend, but there was more. There definitely was something there. Yet, she held back. Why? Because of Cam? Because she feared losing someone she loved once again?

That thought had her tensing. Ethan never risked his life. So why would she be afraid of that? She leaned back to look at him.

"Have you always been cautious? John told me he preferred being my dad because boys took more risks than girls while growing up."

He continued to look over her. "No."

"No? You mean you were like Cam?" She couldn't keep the surprise out of her voice, her fear taking root.

His lip quirked up. "No, not as adventurous as Cameron, but not cautious either."

She didn't like the sound of that. "Then what changed? Cam said you'd always been cautious."

He finally looked at her. "Aye, by the time I went to university I was, but before that I had to learn my lesson at the expense of another." Guilt filled his eyes.

"Tell me." She had to know.

He let her go, drifting away, almost as if he felt unworthy to be with her. That couldn't be it, could it?

"Remember I told you I had a motorbike?"

She nodded, but kept silent.

"I was in secondary school and was dating a young lady. I was a typical teenage boy and had already had my fair share of mishaps and broken bones, which I thought nothing of. But one night after taking her to a cèilidh for my father's birthday, my blood was up and I decided to race my motorbike along the road like a banshee was after us."

He rubbed the back of his neck, clearly haunted by the memory. "We were laughing, enjoying the breeze as it was a warm summer night. As I sped around the curve just before Loudon bridge, I hit dirt on the road. I have no idea where it came from, but the second my wheels connected with it, I lost all control."

"Oh, no." She floated closer, but he kept his distance.

"That was the least of what I thought as we skidded sideways. I did everything I'd learned to control that bike, but just as I thought I might have escaped the worst, we hit the bridge. The stones of that wall are unforgiving, and we both flew through the air."

She crossed her arms, her heartbeat racing.

"I was the lucky one. I landed on the bridge, the bike on top of me. She flew over the wall and onto the rocky bank of the burn." He stopped speaking as he gazed in the direction of said bridge, though they were too far away to see it.

She couldn't wait any longer. "Please tell me she didn't die."

He looked at her finally. "She didn't die. But while I made it through with a broken wrist, leg and serious concussion, she was in a coma for three days. I thought she would die, and it would all be my fault. I never rode again."

She drifted closer and this time he stayed where he was. "That's why you're overly cautious?"

He shook his head. "I'm not overly cautious. It's one thing to risk your own life without understanding how it would affect everyone who knows you. It's another to almost kill another person because you didn't think through the risks." He cupped her cheek with his hand. "I would never risk your life or mine."

All doubt about losing him disintegrated at his intense gaze. "I believe you."

His gaze turned dark just before he pulled her closer and kissed her. It wasn't the slow kiss of Inverness at all. No, it was passionate and hungry. His tongue breached her lips as he covered her mouth with his own. He commanded that she give way before inviting her to take over.

She wrapped her arms around his neck, pressing herself against his chest, his wool sweater not hiding the hard strength beneath it. Need started in her belly and sent spindles of desire throughout her body. The feeling of being alive grew, filling her veins as pleasure took over.

Ethan pulled away. "Ach, ye make me forget meself."

She gasped for breath, wishing he hadn't stopped. "I'm so glad you…," she paused to take a deeper breath, "have an Achilles heel. I was beginning…to think you were perfect."

Ethan's deep chuckle had her looking up. "I'm far from perfect."

"Really? Doesn't look that way to me."

"Sure, it does. You already said I'm over-cautious. You know I'm a geek and that I wish I had a family of thousands. Not to mention the fact that I don't know how to cook. Never mind that I don't know how to ride a horse, or play polo, or worse, I don't play golf well at all."

She laughed, her heart warming. "Well, I'm not perfect either, so we make a great pair."

"Ach, that's far from true. You're definitely perfect from your small dimple to your infectious laugh."

She rolled her eyes. "You have blinders on, but I refuse to be the one to take them off."

He smiled, the crease in his bottom lip disappearing.

She had a sudden urge to lick that lip, too. What would it be like to have all of Ethan's bulk at her disposal in bed? She heated at the thought, but their phased state probably made that impossible. Besides, she had no idea how birth control would work. She wasn't sure how she felt about children anymore. Reluctantly, she slipped from his arms. She could pursue that thought another day, if she wanted.

"Has your mom been asking for grandchildren?"

Her question caught him of guard based on the widening of his eyes. "Nay. Or maybe…aye. Now that I think on it. She has mentioned it more than a few times this past year. I hadn't thought anything of it, but I may have to pay more attention."

She wanted to ask if he'd marry another just for his mother, but she'd already seen that was the case. He might not think he would, but obviously things changed. That had shocked her. He may love her, but he could and would walk away some day if she couldn't let go of Cameron.

She hoped the visit they were about to start would help her sort out her feelings. "Promise me this visit will be a happy one. No one dying or getting hurt or anything."

He sobered. "It's not supposed to be a sorrowful one, but even Cameron can't fully control these future scenes. Just remember, whatever you see does not have to be. You're still in control of your future."

He always knew exactly what to say to make her feel better. That was a very specific talent that very few people had. In fact, only grandpa Tinder had it before Ethan.

"Are you ready?" Ethan held out his hand.

She took a deep breath. "I am." Grasping his hand in hers, they floated through the roof together.

Below them was the living room fully decorated with a spruce Christmas tree that almost touched the pinnacle of the ceiling. "Wow, you weren't kidding when you said a taller tree could fit in my house."

"I have a good eye for trees."

She had to agree, and obviously her future self had no problem decorating the monstrosity because it was done beautifully. "I love the bows tied on the end of the branches. I never thought of that."

Ethan pointed. "I think you did."

The woman who entered the room was herself, but much older. She had gray in her hair which was pulled back in a ponytail. The wrinkles around her mouth and eyes were deep like she'd laughed a lot in her life. She liked that.

"You're still beautiful."

She would have waved his comment aside, if he hadn't said it in a whisper. Instead, she glanced at him. What would he look like when he grew older?

The older Holly held a pickle ornament and appeared to be looking for just the right spot. Finally, she decided on a lower area and reached her arm far into the branches.

"Oh, she's hiding the pickle." Holly had just learned of that

European tradition last year and had ordered some for the shop. "Don't let me forget to get one from the store. I've been so busy I forgot to bring one home."

"I wonder who will look for this one." Ethan looked at her. "Or yours, for that matter."

She smiled. "Why, you, of course."

Ethan opened his mouth to respond, but was interrupted by a man in his late twenties or early thirties as he walked in with a baby in his arms.

Holly held her breath. The infant couldn't be more than a month old.

"Mum, would you watch the baby for me. I'm being sent home in this frosty cold to retrieve the clootie pudding we forgot."

Older Holly grinned. "Of course, Cameron. Let me have her."

As the man handed the baby over, Holly looked at Ethan. "Well, I know that's not going to come true."

His brows lowered. "Why?"

"I would never tempt the fates by naming a son Cameron." She tried to remain serious, but her lips lifted up anyway. "I think Lorna's dad was right about genes determining personalities, so why not names."

Ethan nodded as if what she'd said made complete sense, which it didn't.

Turning back, she floated closer to get a good look at "Cameron." He was tall, with sandy brown hair. He looked familiar, which made sense since he was supposed to be her son. He was also very handsome, which gave her an odd sense of pride.

Her son waited until her older self was seated with the baby in her arms then he kissed both his daughter and mother on the cheek. "I'll be back in no time."

"Don't rush. Your father will have my head if you get in an accident over clootie dumpling."

"I won't, mum." He grabbed his wool coat and was out the door.

Holly floated around to the back of the chair to get a look at what was her granddaughter. It didn't seem like such an unbelievable occurrence now like it had when Malcolm had revealed that she could have a son. Maybe that was because she could imagine herself as a grandma easier than a mom, which made no sense at all.

The baby had light blonde curls, a squished nose, and dark eyelashes that rested on her chubby cheeks. She was fast asleep.

Grandma Holly was clearly taken with her granddaughter.

Suddenly, a little boy ran into the room, his pudgy hand stretched out ahead of him, a sugar cookie shaped like a Christmas tree in his grip. "Grandma, cookie for you!"

Holly's heart melted at the sight. With Ethan floating above the little boy, it was clear who he took after. This could be their family if she wanted it.

"Shh, your sister is sleeping."

The little boy pressed his hand to his mouth, the cookie still in his grip, and blew. "Shh."

Grandma Holly smiled. "You're a good boy, Alexander."

The little boy walked closer and handed over the cookie before peering at his baby sister.

"There you are." As an older version of Ethan walked into the room, Holly caught her breath. He still looked young for their age, but he had a peacefulness about his face that she'd never seen.

The little boy put his finger to his mouth. "Shh."

Grandpa Ethan covered his mouth and crouched down, his knees cracking a bit with the movement. "We have to be quiet."

Alexander nodded seriously.

"Why don't we go back in the kitchen and finish helping mummy set the table."

At Alexander's nod, grandpa Ethan picked the boy up and bent over to drop a kiss on grandma's cheek. Alexander wanted to as well and once he did, they both exited the room.

Holly looked at Ethan whose gaze was still on the open doorway where the two disappeared. Even from where she was, she could see the sheen of moisture in Ethan's eyes.

She finally understood what her future could hold. It was this and more. It was the love of another good man who would never forget Cameron. "Ethan?"

He turned toward her, and the love in his eyes took her breath away.

Without thought, she drifted to him. "This could be us."

He swallowed, his Adam's apple moving above the collar of his sweater. "Aye, if you want it."

Did she want it? The answer came slowly, not in a burst of light, but from a small glow inside her heart that grew larger, showing her the way. "I do."

Ethan's smile was tender. "I know you may not be ready now, but I can wait."

She nodded, once again amazed at his understanding. If it had been Cameron—

The scene suddenly dissipated and they were back in her house, Mac sitting on the arm of Cam's chair, staring at them.

Holly floated to the floor. "Mac?" The cat jumped down and stretched before walking out of the room. "So much for a welcome home."

"Will this do?"

She spun around to find Cameron by the fireplace, a piece of mistletoe in the hand above his head. She laughed. "That will do just fine."

Ethan studied Cameron's face. He was relaxed, which had to mean they were successful. Holly was free to live her life, and they all would be together in the future. It was exactly what Cameron had hoped for and more than what *he'd* hoped for.

Cameron dropped the mistletoe, which disappeared and waved his hand at Holly who became solid again.

Ethan quickly lowered himself to the floor before Cameron did the same for him. He rolled his shoulders. He was grateful he'd never have to be phased again.

"What did you think of your visit?" Cameron drifted toward them.

"I liked it very much." Holly blushed.

Cameron turned his attention to him. "Did you as well?"

"Aye. It was a pleasant possibility."

His friend laughed. "Very true." Cameron's gaze returned to Holly. "It was just a possibility, but if you're willing for it to happen, love, it could come true. I couldn't ask for a better man to take care of you."

Holly looked at him, her brown gaze warm. "I agree." She turned toward Cameron. "But I'm not tempting fate by naming a son Cameron."

"You're not?" It was obvious Cameron was more than a little hurt by that.

"No, because I want my son to live a long time. You understand, right?"

Cameron didn't look at her. "I guess."

Ethan couldn't believe his friend was so caught up in having a child named after him that he couldn't see Holly's fear. It was similar to what she'd expressed to him on the roof top. She feared losing anyone she loved again.

Holly grasped his hand, drawing his focus. "It's almost like everything was meant to be. I have to know, Cam. Is Ethan a second soulmate?"

Cameron wiggled his brows, but didn't say anything. Instead, he moved toward the tree. "Hey, this is a new ornament." He pointed to a Scottish fold cat sitting with a sprig of holly between its paws.

Ethan had given Holly the ornament last Christmas. It was specifically painted to look like Mac. "Aye, I've been giving her one for every year since you've been gone."

Holly chimed in. "It's a new tradition."

"A tradition." Cameron didn't move as if he'd frozen and Ethan's senses went on alert. His friend clearly was not happy with their new tradition. Because he wasn't part of it?

"I like it." Though the words were positive, Cameron jerked away from the tree as if the ornament had lashed out at him in some way. He covered his movement up by scanning the room. "Where's Mac?"

At Holly's crestfallen look, Ethan frowned. Now Cameron was ignoring Holly's question. Ethan couldn't let that pass. "Mac's in the other room. Is Holly right? Are we soulmates?"

"Fine, fine, I just wanted to say goodbye to my cat before leaving for good."

Holly crossed her arms. "Cameron Douglas, you're stalling. Is Ethan my second soulmate or not?"

Cameron wouldn't look at them. "The thing is I'm not allowed to say either way."

"Why not?" Holly wasn't letting him off the hook, which only proved how much the issue meant to her.

"It was all part of the deal I struck so I could visit you one last time."

The hairs on the back of Ethan's neck stood on end. Cameron was acting strangely. His movements and tone didn't match his words.

Holly dropped her arms and her shoulders sagged. Tears made her warm brown eyes shimmer in the light from the tree. "So you're going to leave without telling me. I'll never know because I'll never see you again."

Cameron floated toward them, stopping mere feet away. "Ah, hen. Please don't cry. You've got this braw man with you now. And it won't be forever."

Ethan squeezed Holly's hand, willing her not to give in. It was critical for all of them that she stay strong.

"I know, but what about you? It will be so long for you and you're all alone."

"Not so long." Cameron lifted his arms in the air. "There's no time where I am. In the next second I can be meeting you after you've had a long and happy life." Now the man was almost flippant.

"Really?"

He nodded. "Absolutely." His voice was strained, overly happy.

"And if I have a happy life with Ethan, what happens then? Will I still see you? What about Ethan?"

Cameron turned his back on them, floating back to the fireplace.

Something wasn't right. Ethan answered for him. "When we pass into the afterlife, we will all be together again."

Holly's eyes widened. "Really?" She turned. "Cameron, is that true?"

"Aye." He spoke to the fireplace.

Ethan let go of Holly's hand and walked to where Cameron hovered. He put his hand on the man's shoulder and it went right through to his chest before he pulled away. The essence he felt was conflicted.

Bloody hell! *Cameron* was the one who couldn't let go.

He should have seen it. He should have listened to his conscience when he first doubted. He had to save this. "Cameron, it's time to say goodbye. As you said, in the next second you can see us again."

"I know." He swept his hair from his forehead then spun around and gave Holly an odd grin. "But how much more fun would it be if I could visit every Christmas Eve?"

"No, that won't work." He stepped between Cameron and Holly. "It's time to move on. You said so yourself."

Cameron phased right through him and the desperation left Ethan stunned for a second. "Love, would you like that? Would you like it if I could come back? I think I might be able to make a deal."

Ethan ransacked his brain for a way to save them all. "What about forever? Would you sacrifice that for a few more seconds? Time is of no matter. You said you can see us in a matter of seconds."

Cameron was staring at Holly. "What do you think? Do you want that?"

A loud crash came from the kitchen.

"What the hell?" Cameron frowned.

Holly spun. "Mac!" Her fear had her running from the room, proof just how much the cat meant to her.

Ethan sucked in his breath and strode through Cameron.

"Ach." Cameron floated away. "Why are you angry? I could make this work."

Ethan shook his head. "No, you can't because I won't be a part of it."

"What are you saying?"

He felt the tick near his temple throbbing. He needed to calm, but this was Holly's life at stake. He had no time to weigh the risk. "I'm saying, if you do this, I won't be in Holly's life. Either she lives for your dead spirit or she lives with me for herself. It can't be both."

"You don't know that."

"Aye, I do because you told me. You were desperate to help her so you could be with her forever and now you're going to ruin everything for her. Don't you care about anyone but yourself?"

Cameron scowled. "Of course I do. I care about Holly."

He glared at the spirit. "Not enough. If you care about her, you'll say goodbye. The man I knew may have been a risktaker, but he loved his wife more than anything. Whatever you are, it's not Cameron Douglas."

He stared hard at the spirit before him, noticing the tiredness Holly had mentioned. What Cameron was trying to do was against the laws of the spirit world. That was why he was frayed.

The spirit's hazel eyes turned almost green in its anger. "I know what I'm doing."

Ethan tried for calm. "You don't. You asked me for my help. I'm telling you, you'll fail. Let her go. If you don't, I walk out of here now and out of her life. She won't move on if you're still visiting her and after she passes, you'll never be together."

A flicker of doubt showed in Cameron's eyes before he shook his head. "I won't leave her…ever."

Ethan strode across the room and grabbed his coat from the rack. He yanked open the door, flooding the room with cold air then paused. He looked back at the spirit that floated before the fireplace. Shaking his head, he walked out into the falling temperatures, the frigid air no match for the ice that settled around his breaking heart.

Chapter Twelve

Cameron's anger cooled as he stared at the closed door. Ethan would be back. He loved Holly. He wouldn't leave her alone for the rest of her life. Would he?

"Poor Mac." Holly strode into the room. "I don't know how he did it, but he got into the top cabinet where I keep all the cookie sheets and roasting pans and such. He must have jumped and knocked them all out right on top of him."

He turned at Holly's entrance and looked at the heavy gray-striped cat. Its bronze eyes seemed to blame him for the incident. "Is he alright?"

"I don't know." Holly sat on her chair and lifted a paw to examine Mac. The cat didn't like it and went spastic before jumping to the ground.

"Ow! Well, crap." She stood, holding her wrist. "I have to wash this. Promise you won't leave until I'm back?"

He nodded, his focus on the cat who sat staring at him with an accusatory gleam. "What? I didn't make you fall."

Holly left the room, the sound of water in the bathroom, infiltrated his mind for a moment as he stared at the cat.

A gray mist seemed to surround Mac. As it grew larger, Cameron backed up. The gray cloud spread from the chairs to across the Christmas tree, blocking the lights. A perpendicular, long narrow darkness at the center of it began to glow and soon two large white wings appeared.

Fuck. This wasn't good.

The dark center solidified and the glowing eyes of Remiel pierced his soul. *What have you done?*

He wanted to deny what he'd said, but he knew better. "I couldn't stand to see her so sad."

No. Try again.

Try again? "I don't understand."

The arch angel pointed at him. *You refused to let her go.*

"Me?"

A white wing brushed through him and the truth burned inside his head.

He hadn't come to Holly to help her get over him. He'd come because he couldn't let go. He couldn't do it.

His vision started to blur as he looked into the eyes of Remiel. "I love her." Tears rolled down his cheeks, the pain bending him over, too harsh to endure.

I know. The voice inside his head was softer. *I will send her to you, but you must first let her go. She is ready to live, but she's wavering. If she doesn't move forward, you will never have her again. It will be beyond even my control.*

Fear sliced through him at the threat. He nodded, unable to form words as agony at what he had to do filled him.

Again, the white wing brushed over him, releasing him from his pain and clearing his head. The angel's form darkened into a black cocoon again and the wings wrapped around it melding with it to form a gray mist that vanished as Holly's footsteps approached the doorway.

"I can't believe Mac spazed out on me like that. He must be hurt." Her brow was furrowed with concern as she approached him.

Cameron forced a smile. "No, I don't think he is." He moved toward the cat who had bounded up onto his old chair. It didn't even look at him. Cameron reached his hand out, but it flowed right through the animal, who hissed at the contact.

Remiel must have been in the cat every time he visited. That's why he could touch it before.

"What's happened? You can't touch Mac anymore." Holly moved to calm the animal. "It's just Cameron, Mac."

He shook his head. "No, I can't. Not anymore. It's time for me to leave. I'm afraid I won't be back like I thought."

"They won't let you?"

He steeled himself against her forlorn look, his heart hanging on Remiel's promise. "No. I've done what I came to do."

"You mean show me that I can have a life with Ethan until I see you again? Hey, wait a minute. Where's Ethan?"

He cringed. "I messed up."

Holly folded her arms. "What did you do now?"

"Ah hen, don't be mad at me. One of you angry with me is more than I can bear."

"You made Ethan angry?" She gave him a shrewd look. "That's not easy to do."

He sighed. "I know. I was being selfish. I may have suggested that you didn't need him to have a happy life."

"You what?" Holly's eyes narrowed. "What were you thinking? He said he'd wait for me to be ready. Now he thinks I never will be?"

"Ach, sorry. Maybe you should let him cool off before you talk to him again. He was pretty pissed."

She headed for the coatrack. "I have to find him."

Cameron smirked behind her back. *See Remiel, I can do this when well-motivated.* He had no idea if the angel heard him, but he still felt pretty smug. He'd finally learned the easiest way to get his wife…no, widow…to do what he wanted was to tell her to do the opposite. That was information he could take into eternity with him.

She had her coat on and was crossing the room to get her purse when she halted and stared at him. "What am I thinking? You're only here a few more minutes and here I am racing off after Ethan."

"That's how it should be, love. Remember, time is nothing to me."

She smiled. "I'll miss you."

"I won't miss you since I'll see you in a second."

She snorted. "Smarty pants."

He laughed, finally feeling right about letting her go. "Be good to him. He deserves it."

"I will. Can you phase through me one last time?"

"Aye, I can. I love you."

"I love you, too, Cam."

He drifted toward her until he'd engulfed her, letting her feel all his love and good wishes, then he floated through the ceiling and into the ether.

Ethan strode into his study and dropped his snow-covered coat on the love seat in front of his desk. He'd lost his best friend all over again and with him, the woman he loved. If ever he needed a scotch, it was now.

Picking up the decanter, he opened it and splashed some in a glass. Halfway to his mouth, he stilled. "Bloody hell!" He threw the glass at the wall.

"That's going to stain."

Spinning around, he brought his hands up and bent his knees, ready to defend himself. "Who are you and what are you doing in my house?"

The man with long dark hair and features that could only be described as beautiful, shrugged. His dress was exactly that of the warriors Ethan had seen at the bottom of Loudon hill. "You can consider me a friend or your worst nightmare, whichever you choose."

His gut was telling him something wasn't right. This was no ordinary trespasser. It couldn't be Cameron in disguise because he remained phased. This man was definitely solid and he sounded like a movie script.

"Come on, lad. Aren't you gonna fight for yer lassie?"

Now the Scottish accent was extra thick. An actor? "Who sent you?"

The man looked at the ceiling before shrugging again. "A friend."

"My friends don't send strange men to my house in the middle of the night."

The stranger pointed to the clock. "The night has just begun. Brody will be expecting you."

He glanced at the time. It wasn't even nine yet. How could that be? "Is this some kind of trick? Did Brody send you?"

"Silly man, tricks are for kids."

For fuck's sake, this was getting him nowhere. "You need to leave now or I'll throw you out."

The man strolled toward an original Renoir statue on one of the bookcase shelves. "If you must know, I'm a friend of Cameron's."

Ethan stepped around to the front of his desk. "No, *I'm* a friend of Cameron's. You're an intruder."

The man turned and leaned against the bookcase. "You *were* a friend of Cameron's. But he passed into the wild blue yonder."

"That's it." Ethan jumped over the love seat and lunged.

The man was fast, but not fast enough.

In less than six seconds Ethan had him in a head lock. "Now tell me—blast!"

The man disappeared as in simply vanished.

Ethan scanned the room. At least now he knew what he was dealing with. It was someone who was being made solid and then phased, which meant the man was alive, and Cameron could well be behind it. What was he playing at now?

"Aren't you going to fight for your woman?" The man stepped from behind one of the window curtains, now dressed in the leathers of a biker.

What the hell? Had some spirit gone rogue, but then how could he be solid? What did it matter? He was done with all of it. Turning on his heel, he headed for the door.

The man laughed. "So you're a coward."

Ethan froze. Slowly he turned, the tick near his temple starting to throb. "I suggest you leave."

"But you haven't answered my question. Are you going to fight for your woman? You, who knows every Medieval battle fought on Scottish land?"

A chill raced up his spine. No one knew about his recent accomplishment. "I can't battle for her. It's not an even battlefield, Mr...."

The man strolled forward, the chain at his waist that held his wallet, slapped against the leather. He stopped as he reached the couch. "Call me, Rem. Surely there's a battle plan for evening the odds."

He shook his head. "The Scots won battles when they chose the ground. They knew their land. That was their advantage."

"But you're thinking only of those battles fought for power and land. What about the more subtle battles fought for love and FREEDOM!" Rem chuckled. "Always wanted to do that. Are you going to simply walk away from your woman? Sound the retreat?"

Not a little baffled by the man's strange behavior, he shook his head. "She's not my woman." Even as he said the words, a stab of loss struck his heart and took his breath.

"So you're going to play it safe again. That's what you always do. You accuse Cameron of risking so much, but you never take a risk. How can you tell Holly to live when you don't even know how?"

Huh? "I'm living, which is more than I can say for you."

Rem laughed, the sound filled with joy that tickled Ethan's senses. "I'm far beyond life and death, my friend." He sobered. "But you. You haven't really lived. That's one reason why you're so attracted to Holly. That woman knows how to suck out all the marrow from life." He shook his head. "Too bad she's loved by idiots. First, Cameron and now, you."

Fury filled him at the insult, but underneath was a fear that Rem was right. "She's down to one idiot now. Just Cameron and only him." He turned away and reached for the doorknob, not having the stomach to talk about the raw opening inside his chest with Rem or anyone else.

"Soulmates."

He stilled, the knob cold beneath his hand. He refused to turn around. "What did you say?"

"I said 'soulmates'." The man's voice had softened.

He should walk out. He turned the knob, but couldn't get his feet to move.

"Humans have soulmates. Some find one, others don't. And still others find more than one. Holly has two."

Holly believed in soulmates. He finally turned. "What are you saying?"

The man sat on the edge of the desk. "I'm saying, you're Holly's other soulmate. That's not something you walk away from."

Frustration burned inside him. He was being played by forces far beyond anything he could understand, and he detested it. "You do if another has already claimed her."

"He left."

He studied Rem. The man swung one leg back and forth as he picked his teeth with a switch blade. He focused on the spirit's face, determined to separate the lies from the truth. "He'll be back."

"Nope." The word, said nonchalantly, didn't change the man's expression at all.

Ethan looked away. There were no visible cues. "So what are you trying to tell me?"

A heavy sigh filled the room, its force so strong, it ruffled his hair. "Cameron has done his part. Now you must do yours. She needs you."

The room grew brighter, and Ethan looked back at Rem. The man was no longer sitting on the desk. He floated as a solid being, light surrounding him.

Ethan Alexander James Stewart, your soulmate needs you. She's on her way here, but ice and Loudon Bridge stand between you.

Fear filled him and sent adrenaline rushing through his veins. He pointed at Rem and scowled. "I'll get to her, but you bloody well better protect her until I do."

Without another thought, he threw open the study doors and ran down the hall to the front door. Within seconds he was racing along the road in his car, his heart beating faster than a tenor drum in a tattoo. If he could cross Loudon Bridge before she did, she'd be okay.

As he hit a straightway, he pressed the gas pedal, ignoring the flakes that tried to build up on his windshield. A curve had him breaking, the vehicle fishtailing. Fuck, everything was icing up.

As soon as the road straightened again, he gunned it. If Rem thought he'd lived a safe life, he was in for a surprise tonight. Just one more curve and a straightaway and he'd be at the bridge. He slowed again then accelerated, watching for lights in the distance, letting him know a car was approaching, but it remained dark.

As the curve to Loudon Bridge appeared, he slowed before turning onto its slippery surface. No car approached from the other side. He'd done it! Relief washed through him. As he approached the other end of the bridge, fresh skid marks caught his lights despite the snow's attempt to cover them.

"No!" Pulling the car to the side of the road just beyond

the bridge, he jumped out and shivered, not at the cold, but at the headlights shining underneath the broken ice of the burn water.

"Holly!" Running down the embankment, he could see her hood was submerged, but the rest of the vehicle remained on land… for now. "Holly!" He slid the last few feet, careful not to jostle the car.

Pulling his phone from his pocket, he shined the flashlight on the window. The airbag filled most of the front seat driver's side, but Holly's shoulder was visible. It must have happened just before he got there.

We had a deal Rem. Honor it!

"Holly? Can you hear me?" There was no movement in the vehicle. Fuck, if he lost her now, he wouldn't care if he lived or died. Carefully, he pulled on the door handle, hoping she didn't lock her door. At first it didn't budge, then the locking mechanism clicked and the door opened.

Not wanting to take time to contemplate that odd occurrence, he nudged the door slowly until it was wide open. The car slid another couple inches, but stopped. His heart skipped a beat before he was able to move back to Holly. "*Mo chridhe,* can you hear me?"

Holly moaned, but didn't move. What if he pulled her out and she was critically injured? He started to weigh the risks in his head. "For fuck's sake." Shining the light on the seatbelt, he pushed the button to release her. As it slid back, it caught the air bag, crinkling it up before springing free..

"Ethan?"

Holly's groggy voice was all he needed to hear. Relief rushed through him as he bent and extracted her from the seat. He slid down the slope himself as the car moved another foot then halted again, but he had Holly.

Snow caught in her hair as he set her on an exposed boulder. "Holly, does anything hurt?" He needed to take her to hospital.

"Ethan." Her eyes opened and she smiled. "Ethan! Don't believe anything Cameron said. I *do* need you in my life. Please say you'll stay with me."

He looked up toward the sky. "Thank you, Rem."

You're welcome. Now live.

He grinned at Holly. "I will."

She wrapped her arms around him and kissed him, heating his blood despite the cold. When she broke away, she brought one hand to his face. "I love you."

Joy filled his chest as he wrapped her in his arms. "My heart."

Holly left her wet clothes in a heap on the floor and padded across the room to the closet in her bra and panties. She opened the door. "Oh, holy crap." The closet was as big as her bedroom in town. She definitely needed to explore it further at another time. She'd known Rawdon was big and old, so she hadn't expected this particular update.

Walking in, she found what she was looking for. Pulling one of the white collared shirts from its hanger, she brought it into the room with her. Quickly, she added her underwear and bra to her pile of wet clothes and slipped on the shirt.

She was well aware if Ethan came back with the food and she was in bed, he'd insist she rest. She felt anything but tired. In fact, the accident had her feeling more alive than ever. She didn't want to spend the night in bed without him.

Walking over to the two upholstered chairs, she sat in one and crossed her legs demurely. No, that wasn't it. She jumped up and sat on the arm of the chair, but she lost her balance. "Real graceful, Holly." She re-evaluated. The fireplace might work.

She moved in front of it. There was no rug, so laying down

seductively wouldn't work. Maybe she should be at the window, but even at the thought, she shivered. The temperatures outside had turned frigid, at least that's how it had felt in her wet clothes.

She and Ethan had climbed up the rest of the hill to the bridge, but not without incident. They'd slipped so many times, they were both soaked by the time they reached his car. He immediately drove her to Rawdon, which was exactly where she wanted to be.

She'd probably totalled her car, but she'd do it again to have Ethan. When her car started to slide on the ice, her heart had pounded with fear. She thought she would die as the vehicle headed over the side. In that instant, she wanted to live more than anything. She wanted to live so she could be with Ethan. Her last thought before she blacked out was of him.

The door to his bedroom opened, and he stepped in carrying a tray of food and drinks, and wearing nothing but a pair of black sweatpants. He started for the bed. "I brought you some—Holly?"

So much for her seductive pose. "I'm right here. I had too much energy to crawl into bed right now."

Ethan turned at her voice and stared.

When he didn't say anything, she grew nervous. "I hope you don't mind. I wasn't ready to go to bed, so I grabbed this out of your closet." She fisted the shirt in her hands on either side of her.

Ethan's Adam's apple bobbed as he swallowed. "Maybe you should step away from the fireplace."

She looked behind her. "I'm okay. There's a fire guard."

He set the tray on the end table and strode toward her. "I don't think you understand. The firelight is revealing every beautiful curve you have, and I'm only human."

His gaze was so dark as he stepped in front of her that her breath hitched. He wanted her. Inside she was jumping up and down, but somehow, she held it together. "I've been among spirits too long. I need human. I need you."

Ethan growled low in his throat, sending a shock of desire through her. "Ye tempt me, lass, but yer rattled from the accident. Rest is what ye need."

He was right. She should be rattled and want to rest. She might even be sore tomorrow, but the only thing she felt was excitement. Ethan's switch from his usual stiff speech to the heavy Scottish accent even had her fingers tingling.

She let her gaze roam past his tense jaw to the large pectorals that made up his chest. Beneath those were abdominals that rippled before disappearing into the waistband of his sweats. The waist was barely tied as if he'd been in a rush to return to her and it dipped low, teasing her. She wanted to see him, all of him.

Walking slowly onto the area rug between the two easy chairs, she laid her hands on his chest. Heat sped from where she touched him to her belly, starting a chain reaction in her whole body.

"We shouldn't." He grasped her hands and stepped back, holding her away, but his nostrils flared and his chest expanded as he breathed deeply. "You could be hurt."

"I'm not hurt. I'm fine. And I want you to help me feel alive again." She pulled his hands to her, resting them beneath her chin. "Ethan, I want you."

His gaze didn't leave her for a second and he turned his hands to cup her face as he stepped closer. "Ye know I have no power to resist ye."

She gazed into his eyes, his own desire clear. "Then don't."

A low groan came from deep in his chest. Then his mouth was on hers, tasting her with a fervor of need.

She wrapped her arms around his neck and pressed herself against him, letting him lead her where he would. Every nerve ending came alive at once as his hips moved against her, and she felt his erection press against her abdomen.

An ache started between her legs, and she grasped his hair, pulling herself tighter to him as if she could crawl inside him.

Ethan pulled his mouth away suddenly, leaving her breathless. "I want to see ye."

She was too busy pulling air into her lungs to register his words.

When he stepped closer again and undid the first button of the shirt she wore, she found her breath growing shorter again. His fingers lightly touched her skin as he moved them down through her cleavage and to the next button. When that one was loose, his fingers again traced a line over her skin and at the top of her belly, he unbuttoned another.

His shirt was long on her, and so his fingers moved lower to touch her abdomen making the butterflies inside fly into a tizzy. Another button was let free and his fingers traveled farther, over her mons to the next button where his movements brushed lightly against her folds.

She forced herself to breathe after the zing of excitement flew to her core. Then his fingers were against her inner thighs as he undid the next two buttons, leaving her weak-kneed and almost panting.

"So soft." His whispered words brought her attention to his face. She swallowed at his intense gaze, which was riveted to the strip of skin showing the length of the unbuttoned shirt.

When he raised his hands to the center of her chest, she held her breath. He slowly moved the shirt aside, his hands separating it, running over her breasts, across her nipples, to stop at her arms. He held the shirt open like that and stared at her.

Her cheeks warmed at his perusal, but the heat in her belly fanned out, causing her skin to tingle.

"Ye are all woman. Bonnier than I could have imagined. I want nothing more than to be inside ye."

Her breath left her in a whoosh. Relief, combined with anticipation, had her standing a little straighter.

Ethan pushed the shirt off her shoulders then down her arms until it dropped at her feet.

"I want to see you, too."

He shook his head the second before he swept her off her feet and brought her to his bed. She had little time to worry about her weight before he gently laid her on the cool sheet. Since he'd turned down the bed before he left for food, his aim had been to entice her to rest. She was pretty sure that was the farthest thing from his mind, now, thankfully.

He climbed up on the bed and covered her with his body, leaning on his elbows to hold her head in his hands. "Ach, I've dreamed of this so long, I almost canna believe this is real."

She touched his bare back, the solid muscle moving beneath her hand. "Oh, it's very real." She let her hand travel down toward his butt only to be stopped by his sweat pants. "I know I haven't done this in a very long time, but I think you need to take these off, right?" She tugged on the waistband of his sweatpants.

His lips quirked up. "Aye, but I want to savor every moment."

He captured her lips even as he pressed her down into the bed.

Yes! Her body revved with anticipation, and she made her excitement known by thrusting her tongue into his mouth.

His groan warned he was ending the kiss, but only on her mouth. Within seconds, his lips were kissing her neck, her collar bone, the side of her breast.

She buried her hands in his hair even as his mouth moved to her nipple.

Ethan's tongue wound around her hard peak, teasing her beyond sanity. She lifted her chest, wanting more. He took the hint and nibbled at her nipple, his tiny nips winding her up until he finally sucked it into his mouth.

She moaned, unable to keep her pleasure silent. His mouth worked her hard nub, sending thrills straight to her core and causing her sheath to contract. Just when she thought she'd orgasm right there, he let go and moved to her other breast.

"Ye taste too good, lass."

Before she could think to form words, his mouth performed his magic on her other nipple until she was squirming with need. She pulled his head from her breast. "Ethan."

He looked at her. "Aye. Did I hurt ye?"

She wanted to laugh, but she was too wound up. "You're torturing me. I need you. Now."

Understanding dawned, and his gaze took on a determined gleam. "Aye, I will bring ye to bliss."

Her body relaxed a bit at his promise until he knelt back and blew on the curls above her folds.

Holy crap.

He coaxed her legs farther apart before burrowing his hands under her butt. Bending low, he lifted her to his mouth.

She was going to die right there, with his breath heating her folds.

As his first lick crossed her center to the tip of her clit, she jerked, the intense feeling, after so many years, a shock. She grabbed his hair. "I'm not sure."

He didn't meet her gaze. Instead, he pressed her folds apart with his tongue and made a wide swipe past her opening but lifted before he hit her hard nub.

She loosened her grip on his hair. That was better. Maybe she just needed to go slow.

Ethan did move slow as he savored her like a fine wine. His tongue explored every fold, her opening and all around her clit, as if he couldn't quite get enough. What she thought was relaxing turned exciting, and she could feel her sheath tensing as it readied for him.

His tongue swiped across her clit again, and a spike of pleasure hit her core. He may want to savor her, but she was too close. "Ethan, please. I want to be with you. I don't want to be alone."

He stilled and his face came up. "I'll never let ye be alone again."

Rolling off the bed, he pulled the string on his sweats and they fell to the floor.

She stared, hoping she wouldn't orgasm just from staring at him. The muscles in his thighs were even harder than his abs, and with his erection so stiff, she could imagine him pumping into her.

He picked up a glass from the tray and drank.

She watched his Adam's apple move with his swallow and imagined the liquid flowing over his body. Quickly, she looked away to focus on breathing. She wanted to come with him, not before him.

At the sound of the glass being set down, she turned back to find him crawling into bed between her thighs. She lifted her arms. "Please. It's been so long. I want to feel you around me. I need to hold you."

His gaze softened. "I need to hold ye, too." He laid out over her again, his hard chest pressing against her sensitized breasts. He leaned on his elbows once more and looked into her eyes as he lifted his hips.

She rested her hand at the base of his back, her anticipation making her tense.

He lowered himself until his cock touched her opening. "My heart." His words came out on a breath as he started to enter her, sending a shiver of desire through her.

"Relax. There's no rush."

Oh, but there was. She wanted him now. She caught herself. What about what Ethan wanted? Thinking of him helped her relax, which aided him as he slowly spread her. Every inch that entered her filled her, and in an odd way, took the edge off her frantic need.

As Ethan's pelvis touched her own, she took a deep breath. Finally, she was surrounded by him.

He gazed into her eyes. "Are ye okay?"

"More than okay. I feel whole."

"Ach, ye fill my heart when ye say things like that."

She liked that. She wanted to fill his heart every day. "Love me."

He lowered his head and kissed her, his tongue mating with her own, tasting faintly of Scotch and filling her with the scent of Christmas. Then his hips began to rise, and she grabbed onto his back as fire raced through her veins with the friction.

As soon as he retreated, he pushed back in, a little faster causing the wonderful friction that fed her need. He thrust again, and she had to break off the kiss, her body pounding with excitement.

His thrusts continued, filling her, faster and faster, her body melding with his until she couldn't tell who was moving. All she knew was it felt better and better until her sheath tightened and he shouted.

Her world blasted apart. She held onto Ethan as a wall of pleasure hit her hard, sending her heartbeat into overdrive, her pulse pounding out every thrill and exquisite feeling. It was his endurance, pushing her along until she neared the end, and she drifted away in contentment with the man she loved.

Ethan held Holly against his side, too content to believe it was true. He'd waited so long, given up hope—twice, but she was finally his. He wanted to yell it from the top of his roof at the same time he never wanted to leave the room. He wanted to keep their love safe.

Rem's words echoed through his mind. *So you're going to play it safe again. That's what you always do. You accuse Cameron of risking so much, but you never take a risk. How can you tell Holly to live when you don't even know how?*

Whoever or whatever Rem was, he had a point. If their love

was true, nothing could come between them. Instinctively, he gave Holly a squeeze. He understood now. "Soulmates."

"What did you say?" She looked up at him.

"I said 'soulmates.' I was told by some kind of spirit tonight that we are soulmates."

"You were?" Her brown gaze was intense as she twisted around to lean on his chest. "Do you believe him? Was it a him? Or was it a her? Was the spirit phased? Alone? Was it—"

He placed a finger on her soft lips and smiled. "Aye, I do believe him. He protected you tonight until I could get to you." He moved his hand to stroke her cheek. That she was truly his and not hurt was still sinking in."

Her gaze softened. "I think I knew it deep down. Only a soulmate could make me this happy."

He cupped her chin. "You deserve to be happy."

She grinned. "Well, so do you."

She was silent for a moment as she gazed at him before barely shaking her head. "Wow, soulmates. My mom will be torn because now I have an even better reason to stay in Scotland, but she'll be thrilled I'm in love again. And I know Brody and—Oh, no!" She sat up, and his gut tensed.

"What?"

She stared at him, her eyes wide. "Sarah and Brody's Christmas Eve party." She turned her head, obviously scanning the room for a clock.

He touched her bare shoulder, purposefully ignoring her beautiful bare breasts which were too great an enticement. He didn't want to hurt her by being too active on their first night together. It had been a long time.

She looked at him, her brow furrowed in concern.

He gently brushed her hair away from her eyes. "No need to worry. When I pillaged the kitchen, I called them to let them know what happened. I reassured them you weren't injured but would be resting at Rawdon."

She winked. "I'm not sure I could call this resting. Oh." She blushed. "You mean, they know I'm with you?"

He nodded. "I told them we finally came to our senses and asked them not to tell anyone as I wanted you to decide how you wanted to do that."

She crossed her arms, making it very hard to ignore her rosy nipples. "Do you always think of everything?"

His chuckle came out tight as his cock was already reacting to her naked state. "Not at all. Only with mundane things like calling the police to report the accident and calling my parents to let them know I wouldn't be over tonight."

She suddenly crossed her hands over her chest, hiding it from his view. "Wait a minute. Do your parents know I'm here with you? Oh, crap."

He frowned. "Nay, I wouldn't reveal that. I'm a gentleman. I simply told them you were here resting after your accident." He raised his left eyebrow. "At the time that was what I expected you to be doing."

A sly smile lifted her lips. "Are you complaining?"

"Nay." He pulled her down against him. "Showing ye how much I love ye has made me the happiest man in Scotland. Nay, make that among all men living."

She smiled and maneuvered one of her hands out from between them, only to bury it in his hair. "I'm sorry it took me so long to realize my own feelings."

He cupped her cheek, still a little in awe that she was here, with him. "*Mo chridhe,* all that matters to me is that ye love me."

She returned his smile just before she tugged on his hair. "Okay, you have to try and translate that phrase. You keep using it, so it must have some meaning that rings true at least to you."

He chuckled, loving her playfulness. "Aye, it does have a true meaning now."

"Wait a minute. How come it has a meaning now and not when I asked you this past summer?"

He stifled a grin, recognizing her growing frustration. "Because it's Scottish Gaelic for *my heart*. Only now that I know you love me in return can I truly say you are my heart."

"Oh, Ethan. You're going to make me cry."

"Please, no more tears."

She smiled, though he could see her eyes watered.

Best to distract her. "I have something for you."

That did it. "You do? What?" She looked over her shoulder as if he had something in his hand that held her back.

"It's in the nightstand drawer."

Her gaze flew to the furniture, and she immediately scrambled over him to open it.

He gritted his teeth as her leg brushed his cock and her breast, his arm. If his need for her continued like this, they'd never leave his home again.

She plopped back onto the bed, sitting up crossed legged in all her naked glory.

He stifled a groan and focused on her face as she stared at the small package.

She put her finger on the wrapping then stopped and looked at him. "Can I open it now?"

"Please do."

The excitement that filled her face deepened her dimple, filling him with joy.

She ripped the wrapping off and threw it aside, then opened the box. Lifting the cotton filling, she pulled out the ornament. "Oh, wow. It's me."

"Aye. The painting is from a photo I took of you last year at

Sarah and Brody's party. You looked so festive in your green sweater and skirt that I couldn't resist."

She held the ornament to her chest. "Thank you."

"Ach, lass, not tears again." He had to stop causing her cry.

She shook her head, carefully laying the ornament back in its box and setting it on the night stand. "They're happy tears. There's nothing wrong with them."

"I think I like making you happy without the tears better."

She grinned. "I know how you can do that."

"Then tell me." He'd do anything to make her happy.

Before he could guess her intention, she'd thrown back the covers and straddled him. "Why, ye can make love to me, lad." She laughed at her own language, vibrating him in places that were already interested.

He grasped her hips. "Are ye sure?"

She nodded. "I am. This has been such an amazing night so far. I want to make it a one of a kind Christmas in all ways."

He needed no other encouragement. Rolling her over onto her back, he proceeded to make them both happy into the wee hours of Christmas morning just as she requested.

Epilogue

Rawdon Manor, Christmas Eve

Holly added her Christmas Eve present to the tree next to the ornament of Inverness Castle. The new ornament of a spruce tree that Ethan gave her after dinner was a warm reminder of the night that started them on the course they were on today. So much had happened in two years.

A noise behind her had her turning quickly. "Mac, what did you do?" Striding over to Ethan's desk where the cat sat on one end, she walked around it. Spotting a pen on the floor by a bookcase, she retrieved it and brought it back to the desk. Mac now lay sprawled across the paperwork Ethan had last been reading.

"Mac, you know Ethan doesn't like you up on his desk. Don't think that because it's Christmas Eve he's going to cut you some slack."

The cat stretched, pushing a piece of paper onto the floor.

"Really?" She walked to the other side and picked it up. Glancing at it, she smiled. It was the offer on her house in town next to the One of a Kind Christmas Tree Shop. She and Ethan had finally convinced Brooke to lower her offer. They were so thrilled that the house would stay in the Douglas family. Brooke had done an awesome job running the shop over the past year, so they convinced her the difference in price was her bonus.

Holly pulled the rest of the contract out from under Mac and put it in the top right-hand drawer. "Now behave or you won't be getting any Christmas treats this year."

Mac reached his paw toward her, his amber eyes looking sleepy.

Without a thought, she stroked him before scratching the side of his face. For a ten-year-old, he was in great shape, now that he had the run of the house. The staff said they found cat hair in every single one of the twenty-two rooms. He probably knew the house better than she did.

Not that the staff minded. He was spoiled rotten by all three of them. It had been an adjustment, getting used to having people in her home during the day, but since it gave her more time to spend with Ethan, be it riding his new Harley or meeting up with Lorna and Harris in Glasgow, she was thankful. They were alone in the evenings, and she'd absolutely drawn the line at a nanny.

Mac moved his head and pushed her hand away with his paw. "Demanding, aren't you?" She stopped petting him, and he curled himself into a ball and closed his eyes. She had obviously been dismissed.

Since she was no longer needed by her cat, she moved to the couch, which now faced the tree instead of the desk. She was looking forward to telling Ethan about her discovery.

As if she'd conjured him up, he strode into the study. "They're both asleep."

She twisted to look over the back of the couch, her gaze flitting to his fantastic calves beneath the red Stewart kilt before making eye contact. "Who fell asleep first?"

"Cami." He walked toward her. "You were right. It's as if Francis is already looking out for his little sister."

She grinned. "I think that would be wonderful. I'd always wished I had an older brother to protect me."

He chuckled. "I'm not sure four minutes counts as an older brother."

"Oh, yes, it does. I'll bet he pulls the older brother card on her every time he wants to get his way."

Ethan sat next to her and pulled her close. "If he looks anything like his father, he's going to have a hard time convincing anyone of that."

She laughed. "Yes, you look so incredibly young that soon people will start thinking I'm a cougar."

"Not a chance. You're too full of life to ever look old." He gave her a sly grin. "Now being a cougar in bed is a completely different matter."

She felt heat rise in her cheeks. "You do know how to get on my good side." She laid her hand on his thigh, itching to pull the wool up. "Did you notice your desk?"

"Nay, why?" He looked over his shoulder and sighed before turning back. "It's Christmas Eve. I'll let it go this time."

"Oh, no. Not a good idea. Once you give in to him, he'll expect it."

"Not this time." He laid his hand on hers. "You said you discovered something important today. What was it?"

"Well, crap. I almost forgot." He was such a distraction sometimes. "I found another link in my family history." She smirked. "But it's highly controversial."

Ethan pulled back to look at her. "Why? Was someone on the wrong side of the law?"

She wiggled her brows. "No, worse. The wrong side of the bed." She laughed. "It turns out my female ancestor had an affair with John Campbell and bore him a son. She insisted on him supporting the child and giving the boy his name. It happened while he was Governor General of Virginia."

His eyes had grown wide. "You're a direct descendent of the founder of Deervale!"

"Not exactly. I mean I am, but nothing official. It's only in my ancestor's record that it happened. I couldn't find anything on the Campbell side. It simply shows him as never married."

Ethan grinned. "Your ancestor's word is enough for me." He pulled her back against his side. "Speaking of those who've passed, I was thinking about Cameron today."

Her heart skipped a bit, but the awful ache she'd lived with for years was gone, leaving behind only fond memories. "And why were you thinking about him?"

"I was reviewing our finances, and I received the annual statement on the investment we'd put Cameron's life insurance money into and it's now available to withdraw if we want. Have you thought about what you'd like to do with that money? There's a nice amount there."

Nice? Only Ethan would think half a million pounds was nice. She'd thought she'd invest it for her children's education until she'd fully grasped exactly how much money Ethan had. He'd never acted like he had money. "I don't know. Do you have any ideas?"

"I might."

She looked over at him. "Well, tell me."

He chuckled. "Ever my impatient American."

"Aye, ye should be used to it by now, lad."

He laughed at her attempted accent. "I am and I wouldn't want that to change, ever." His smile was so loving, she had to grin.

Making him laugh had become her second favorite past time. Making the twins laugh had become her new first.

"I thought it would be appropriate to honor Cameron in some way. There are a lot of young people in Glasgow that never have a chance to leave the city and experience the nature of Scotland. There's a camp up north that gives teenagers like these a chance to go hill-walking, rock-climbing, hang-gliding, and bungee-jumping, but they also learn teamwork, self-defense, and how to meditate."

He shrugged. "I admit, it would be a tribute to Cameron, but a slight nod to our friendship."

Her eyes suddenly turned moist. "Oh, I love it! How many could we fund?"

"I'd have to run the numbers, but probably six or seven. That would leave the principle to grow and possibly send more in the future. It's a month-long experience so it's well worth it."

At his defense of such a low number, she shook her head. "I was thinking three would be a lot. You are simply a financial genius."

He looked away. "Nay. The camp is a charity that keeps costs down. I'd already been thinking about making a capital donation for new cabins. I'd still do that." He turned back to her, a gleam in his eye. "I was thinking I could insist that one of the scholarships go to Thea's boyfriend next summer. That would keep him from infecting Sophia's little sister, correct?"

"Oh, wow, it would! Then she'd have the bone marrow transplant. At least that would give her a fighting chance. That's perfect!" He never ceased to amaze her.

How could she have ignored such a kind heart for so long? She'd spend the rest of her life making up for that. She pulled his head down and kissed him.

It was a loving kiss, born of mutual respect and caring. When she broke away, she rested her hands on his chest. "By the way, thank you for the Christmas tree ornament. Will you ever tell me where you find these wonderful gifts?"

He shook his head. "Nay. But I promise to give you one every year for the rest of our lives, even if I have to make it myself."

Did he? Could he? She turned her head to look at the tree, studying each of the five ornaments he'd given her so far.

He lowered his head to speak into her ear. "Do you like it?"

"I love it. It means so much to me. I like the idea of ornaments that reflect our past *together*." She looked back at the tree, resting her head against him. "However, I think this will have to be the last year we have the tree in the study. Next year Cami and Francis will be old enough to really participate in Christmas day, and I just know your parents will want to be here when they open their presents."

"You're right as usual." He gave her a light squeeze. "Do you think we could entice your parents to come as well?"

Excitement raced through her at his idea, and she sat up to face him. "Oh, yes! And maybe we could have Sarah and Brody, too. Their little boy will be almost a year by then. And we certainly have enough room." She threw her arm out to include the whole manor. "So which room? Should we have it in your mom's parlor? Or do you think we need it in a bigger room, like the formal living room, but then we'd have to re-decorate because it's a little stuffy for kids running around with toys. I wonder if we could get Lorna and—"

His lips came down on hers and her excitement found a completely new avenue. As Ethan laid her down on the couch and started to unbutton her red blouse, she looked at the ceiling, envisioning her two children upstairs sound asleep and dreaming of sugar plums. Well, maybe not sugar plums since they weren't old enough to know what those were yet. She sighed contentedly. "Soon."

Ethan looked up at her. "What?" His eyes darkened. "If it's speech, ye need, I can do that for ye, lass. I'm happy to tell ye what I want to do with ye."

She grasped his head and pulled him closer. "Enough talking."

No sooner had she opened her mouth to kiss him, then he took control, showing exactly how much he loved her, heating her from the inside out, now…and forever.

Cameron marked the file completed and waved it away to the file cabinet. "Next case."

Another file appeared on his desk. He opened it and with another wave of his hand, the life story of a young man played out before him. At the end, he groaned. "Another widower." They were the hardest.

He sat back to determine which Spirit Guide would work best when a form phased up through the floor.

Remiel, impeccably dressed in a black suit, floated to one of the chairs in front of his desk and turned solid.

Fuck, what had he screwed up this time? Standing, he kept the desk between him and the arch angel. It wouldn't protect him, but at least he didn't feel so close. He tried to think of what it might be, but nothing came to mind.

"Do you feel lucky, Cam?"

At Remiel's harsh tone, he stepped back. "Lucky?"

The angel crossed his legs at the ankles and looked at the fingernails on one hand. "Yes, are you a betting man?"

He shook his head. "No. I tried that once on the London Exchange and lost my shirt."

"I know." Remiel smirked. "You're not good with numbers."

He had to agree. Maybe if he had been, he wouldn't have taken so many chances in life. A twinge of regret hit him, but he let it go. He'd had a good life. Better than expected.

"But you are good with Spirit Guides."

The unexpected compliment caught him by surprise. "I am?"

Remiel finally looked at him. "You are. You saved more than a few I thought we'd lose. You've come a long way."

That was two compliments in a row. Not that he didn't trust his supervisor, but the angel's knowledge and abilities were so beyond his own that he remained on guard.

Remiel linked his hands behind his head. "Did you ever wonder about that last shrouded opening in Holly's future?"

Tension rifled through him. He knew better than to relax around Remiel anyway. "Aye, but I've let it go. You told me to let her go, so I did. Do you bring it up to torture me some more?"

"I just thought you might be curious what her third future looked like."

He didn't respond. It didn't matter. She chose the future with Ethan. It was what was best for her and that's what he wanted.

"Oh, come on, Cameron, ask me what it was. No, never mind, I'll just tell you. It was a future where she lived out the rest of her life as a widow after selling the shop and moving back to America."

"That wouldn't have been a terrible life. Why couldn't I see that?"

Remiel sat up straight. "Is that what you wish she'd done instead of loving Ethan?"

"No." Two of the people he loved most had a life together now. "She deserved more."

Despite his solid form, Remiel began to drift upward, still in his sitting position. "Exactly. She was special. She *did* deserve more."

Was? "What do you mean was?"

Remiel grinned as he started to glow. "I mean after sixty years she transitioned just two weeks after her husband. Can't you feel it?"

Light started to surround him, moving up from his feet. He did feel it! The light, the love, the peace. "I'm moving on!"

"Aye, lad. It's time. You deserve it." Remiel's voice sounded far away.

Within seconds he could no longer see the arch angel and all his cares left him. Then he sensed others. Was that Ethan? Ethan and…"Ah, hen."

For updates, sneak peeks, and special prizes, sign up to receive the latest news from Lexi at http://bit.ly/LexiUpdate

A CHRISTMAS CAROL SERIES:

Pleasures of Christmas Past
Desires of Christmas Present
Temptations of Christmas Future
One of a Kind Christmas

Read on for an excerpt of Passion of Sleepy Hollow

CHAPTER ONE

Present Day, Sleepy Hollow, NY

"Brom." The tortured whisper escaped Katrina Van Tassel as she stared at the back of the man waiting by the reception counter of her inn.

He must have heard because he started to turn in her direction.

Panicking, she retreated two steps and swung around the corner of the hallway, plastering herself against the floral wallpaper. Her heart beat faster than the wings of the monarch butterflies of summer, and she folded her arms across her stomach as a chill filled her soul and tears blurred her sight.

It couldn't be him. He was dead. Long dead. It was someone else, a Newtimer, that's all. But his build was so exact that she didn't want to see the front. What if he looked just like Brom? She would faint. Yes, she was sure she would. No, she wasn't. She'd never fainted. Of course, there was always a first time.

Brom had been her first, her only, her intended.

Her gut twisted at the remembered pain of sitting on the church steps realizing something terrible had happened. That was long ago. Too long ago. She needed to get a hold of herself.

Ignoring her agitated pulse, she stepped away from the wall, tucked stray hair back into her braid and straightened her shoulders.

This man was probably lost. That's all. No reason to make a mountain out of a molehill. She brushed down the apron on her cotton dress.

The little bell on the counter rang again.

"Well, hold your horses," she murmured under her breath as she strode around the corner to face her visitor. Her feet slowed of their own accord. The striking man with amber eyes and the build of the only man she ever loved tapped his long, blunt fingers on the counter. He looked so much like Brom, and yet not.

Irritation with herself and him brought her heart back on track. Stepping behind the counter, she nodded once, her lips refusing to smile her usual welcome. "How can I help you?"

"I need a room."

She ignored his smooth baritone and the goose bumps it sent along her arms. "I don't have one."

He had the audacity to raise one eyebrow. "Really. I see three rooms right here."

"That would be the parlor, the breakfast room and the kitchen." She glanced down, searching for the stool she used when dusting, wishing she could step on it now to meet the man eye to eye. She settled for craning her neck and catching his gaze. "I'm sorry. I thought you wanted a bedroom."

His brows drew downward, giving him a menacing look, but he didn't say a word.

She didn't even blink. She hadn't been running the Sleepy Hollow Inn by herself since her grandmother's death because she backed down from a little conflict. Besides, staring at him was pure pleasure. Like her former betrothed, his face had all the right masculine angles from his straight nose to his lightly bearded chin. His dark brows, lowered as they were, set off warm, amber eyes, and his wavy black hair gave him a polished air that Brom never had. The fact that this man was just as tall and broad as her only lover proved she still found that physique attractive. More than attractive, if the warmth suffusing her body was any indication.

The man's mouth quirked to one side, causing her heart to stutter. His lopsided grin could melt ice. "I *am* looking for a bedroom." He sighed and ran his hand through his hair. "But I can sleep in the parlor if I have to."

Oh Lord, he needed to stop being nice or she would be ready to give him the whole darn inn. She shook her head. "I'm sorry. I'm full, but you can find a room in town or even try Tarrytown. That's just down the road and they have a lot of inns."

"No. I already checked. They're full too. I didn't know this festival thing was such a big deal." He rubbed one side of his face with his large hand.

He had no calluses. Just another way in which he was different from Brom. She simply had to keep finding differences until he left, and he needed to leave soon. His continued presence was shattering her nerves. She pulled out her reservation book. "It's always this busy. That's why people book rooms so far in advance." She turned the page. "If you like, I can check to see if I have a room available for the next festival."

His hand came down hard next to hers, effectively covering all the names listed there. "I need a room tonight. Just tonight. I have to play at being this stupid Headless Horseman at midnight."

She snapped her head up, her voice barely a whisper. "The Headless Horseman?"

At her undivided attention, he squirmed and glanced away. "Yeah. Stupid, I know. But my brother asked me and since he can't do it, I promised him I would."

Kat's hand on her book gripped the pages into a crumpled mess as she croaked, "You're Stephen's brother?"

"Hey. Are you all right?" He covered her hand with his, its

warmth relaxing the muscles between her fingers, as well as those around her heart. All she could do was shake her head.

He took her hand and kneaded it. "You aren't going to faint on me or anything, are you?"

"Is Stephen hurt? I know he loves being the Headless Horseman. He wouldn't miss it. He'd move mountains to get here. Something must be terribly wrong." She squeezed the man's hand like she wrung out the laundry, but she couldn't help it.

Stephen's brother wouldn't meet her gaze, but his face had definitely closed off that conversation.

"What's your name?"

"My name?" His eyes found hers again and his devastating smirk returned. "I'm Braeden Van Brunt, temporary Headless Horseman, only as you can see, I have my head."

She dropped his hand. "Braeden Van Brunt?" Brom Van Brunt. "But you look nothing like your brother." Not even slightly. Yes, his brother had dark hair and was tall as well, but that was where the resemblance ended. Stephen had a softer face, was small-boned and very thin. Even his eyes were hazel, which had made her think he was a distant cousin of her Brom. But Braeden, even in the loose garment he wore—

"Yeah, we get that a lot. He takes after our uncle and I take after our dad." He stood straighter, his whole body stiffening. "Stephen had open heart surgery and asked me to fill in. I'm guessing no one will mind who rides tonight as long as there is a Headless Horseman."

Kat's mind tried to grasp Braeden's words, but her heart beat too loudly for her to focus. Stephen's heart? Kind, sweet Stephen's heart was bad? His brother, Braeden, so like Brom. She didn't want this. To feel like this again for him. No, not for him. For Brom. For—Argh. His baritone words finally penetrated her thoughts.

"I have to stay here. There isn't enough time to find another place." Braeden ran his hand through his hair again.

"Fine." The word was out of her mouth before she could stop it.

"Fine?" His voice softened. "You'll let me stay?"

She shook her head but refused to meet his gaze. "Wait here." Without checking to be sure he remained, she spun on her heel and headed down the hall to her room. She needed to remove herself from his presence to find her brain again.

Once behind her closed bedroom door, she looked around. *God in de Hemel*, what was she doing? She had no rooms available. Her inn was filled with Oldtimers every festival because Newtimers simply couldn't stay at the Sleepy Hollow Inn. But Braeden was the Headless Horseman. If she turned him out, the festival wouldn't be complete. He had only asked for one night. One night shouldn't hurt. As long as he didn't want to stay Sunday night, it would be fine. After midnight Sunday the whole village disappeared. That secret could never be revealed to a Newtimer, or so it was said.

Kat glanced around her room, the only room not occupied—well, not by a guest. Worrying her bottom lip, she took a shrewd inventory. She could have the room made up in an hour.

Then what? How could she let a Newtimer, who reminded her so much of Brom, stay in her room? How could she let a descendant of Brom sleep in her bed?

How could she not?

Braeden leaned back against the check-in desk, his elbows resting on the wooden surface. The diminutive innkeeper was his biggest surprise of the day. At least a foot shorter than his six-foot-five frame, she had the curves of a larger woman packed into a concentrated package, easily assessed in her historical outfit. Her pale golden hair didn't like to stay in the loose braid she wore and it teased her round blue eyes as they danced with her changing emotions. Too bad he couldn't tell if he irritated her or attracted her, though he had a hunch it was the former. That in itself was strange. He couldn't remember the last woman he irritated, not counting his mother. After high school he'd found his ridiculous muscles attracted women. He hadn't minded that until he'd lost his best friend, or rather half of his best friend.

Why hadn't his brother suggested he stay here? Because it was always full? He could sleep in his car tonight if he had to, but he'd be sore tomorrow. He hadn't ridden a horse in over a year.

Braeden surveyed the tiny interior of the inn. He doubted it had more than eight bedrooms. The parlor had two settees and an armchair. The breakfast room, as she had called it, was only set for six. The entire building was like a dollhouse. He straightened. Maybe the beds were small too. He'd never fit anyway.

"Just great." He glanced at his Rolex and tensed. It was already past nine. He wanted a shower before putting on the costume Stephen had designed. He still couldn't believe he'd let Stephen talk him into this. If his brother hadn't been in the hospital, he would never have caved. But seeing his brother sitting in bed, wearing that crappy hospital gown with his wife and four kids all in the room with them, he couldn't say no. He might not see his brother in person very often, but he'd do anything for him, even be the Headless Horseman for a night.

"I have made the arrangements." The innkeeper's voice had him turning as she strode up the hallway toward him, hips swaying with purpose in the full skirt of her dress. "You can have a room in one hour. If you want, you can go next door to the pub until then."

Not likely. His bulk tended to challenge smaller men, especially while they were drunk, and the last thing he needed was a fight tonight. He glanced at the parlor as a possible place to wait, but when he looked back at his hostess, it was clear she wanted him out. Not wanting to push his luck, he nodded. "Great idea. I'll be back in an hour, Miss…"

Silence greeted his polite inquiry. If she pursed her lips any tighter, they might just disappear altogether.

She glowered. "Do you want a room or not? Now go while I get it ready."

He turned away before she caught him smiling at her. It wouldn't do for her to see he found her interesting. She appeared immune to his physique, a breath of fresh air for him. That was at least one bright spot in his day.

Striding out the door without looking back, he walked by the building next door and glanced in the window. The bar was dimly lit, but even so, it was clear there were plenty of people inside. Ignoring the inviting feel of the place, he continued along the darkened dirt road.

He didn't like having to be out among so many people. Luckily, not many strolled around the village. Most seemed to be at the other end of the road where tall lanterns shed light over stalls and tents. He should check in with the stable. His brother had told him where to retrieve the horse, but never said how much it would cost.

Braeden strode farther down the road until he spotted a wooden sign touting a horseshoe. Since his brother had been playing the Headless Horseman for years, the least the organizers could do was provide a horse free of charge, but since Stephen had a soft heart, Braeden doubted the man ever suggested it.

Stepping into the wide opening of the wooden stables, he stopped and took a deep breath. Despite his best intentions, the scent of hay and old wood had excitement growing in his chest. Anticipation built at the remembered feel of a horse beneath him. It had been too long.

"Do you need somethin', sir?" A bulky man with a balding head and a large nose emerged from the shadows to the right of him. Some kind of suspenders held brown knickers up over a white shirt with the sleeves rolled up to the elbows.

Braeden turned and the man stopped, both hands out in front of him, shaking his head. "No, don't come no closer. I be a good man."

Braeden looked behind him to see what caused the man's fear, but there was nothing. "What are you afraid of? There's no one there."

The man lowered his hands and stepped forward hesitantly, squinting. "Who are you?"

"I'm Braeden Van Brunt. My brother Stephen rides as the Headless Horseman?"

The man broke into a smile. "Ah yah, Stephen is a good man. You are his brother, huh?" He took a lantern off the hook and brought it closer, holding it high. "Hmm, I don't see much 'semblance."

"Yeah, I know. We look different. I understand I don't have much time, so I thought I'd better make arrangements to pay for a horse to ride tonight."

The man reached out his hand. "I'm Ludo Van Ripper and you don't pay for the horse. You just ride it. You know how to ride, yah?"

Braeden shook Ludo's hand, the hard calluses on the palm telling him this was a hardworking soul. "Yes, I do."

"Good. Come. You need to meet Daredevil."

Braeden followed Ludo down a short row of stalls. The man lifted the lantern and pointed. "This here's your mount."

The huge black stallion lifted its head high before bringing it down in short bounces.

The blood sped through Braeden's veins at the sight of the beauty walking toward him. The horse lifted its head over the stall door and sniffed him. Braeden didn't blink. Now, *this* was a horse. Braeden stepped forward and lifted his hand slowly, so as not to spook the animal. When the horse nudged him with its nose, he stroked its neck.

"I'll be a barn swallow's baby, I never seen Daredevil take to no one like that except his master."

Braeden continued to stroke the majestic beast, sensing its need to run. "We'll be out soon, boy. Just a bit longer." He gave the horse a final pat and turned to Ludo. "Didn't my brother ride Daredevil?"

The older man shook his head. "Nah, he couldn't get near him. He always rode Gunpowder."

Braeden followed the man's nod to see another black beauty across the way, but that horse stood at least a hand shorter and was smaller-boned than Daredevil. Daredevil took the opportunity to nudge Braeden's shoulder. He grinned and gave the horse another stroke.

"Yah, *that* is the horse you need to ride tonight." Ludo ambled away. "Yah, it's a right match, it is." His chuckle hung in the air and despite his loose cardigan, Braeden felt a chill.

Zipping up, he returned his attention to the horse. "We'll have a great ride tonight, Daredevil. I promise."

Kat examined her room one last time, her gaze resting on her armoire. Buried in the back of that piece of furniture was the wedding dress she'd worn on what was supposed to be her wedding day. Seeing Braeden reminded her she had yet to sew it into something else. It was such a waste of material to be sitting in there, but somehow, she just hadn't done it. Closing the door to her room and straightening her back, she made her way to the kitchen. It was just one night. It couldn't be wrong to help the village's Headless Horseman so he could do his work, surely. The more she reassured herself, though, the more doubtful she grew.

Setting a pot of water on top of the two-opening stew stove, Kat jumped when the kitchen's outside door flew open.

"Kat, Kat, you've got to see what they've invented now!"

Kat put one hand to her chest and another to her hip. "Maxwell Vandend, you just about scared the life from me. What do you think to come into my kitchen like a witch on a broom?"

Max's shoulders fell. "But Kat, I always come in this door, and you have to look at this." He held out his ever-present sketchpad. "Kat? Is everything all right?"

She quickly dropped her hands and pulled a bowl off a shelf. Max must think her a bit touched to be so surprised by his entrance. It was her nerves and her conscience telling her nothing good would come of her good deed this night. "I'm fine. I just can't be expected to know who is coming through my door."

He lowered the pad and her stomach clenched. Now who was being a witch? "I'm sorry, Max. I had a bit of a surprise already tonight. Let me see what crazy new invention the Newtimers brought with them this time." She smiled encouragingly.

Max suffered the most of all the villagers. Though a strapping young man of twenty, his curious mind longed for the excitement of invention instead of the local young ladies. A situation much bemoaned by not a few mothers.

His mercurial mood rose as he stepped closer to show her his sketch. He always shared his discoveries with her. Not only did it help her keep abreast of the Newtimers' culture, but it gave him someone to share his excitement with. His grandmother wanted no part of Newtime.

"What is it? What does it do?"

"This is the dashboard in one of their cars." Max pointed to his drawing. "Irwin said he tells the car to do something and the car answers and then does it."

"No. How can that be?"

She grinned as Max proceeded to tell her how it worked, a regular routine for them. When he was done, his cheeks were flushed with his enthusiasm. His youthfulness made her feel older than her twenty-eight years. "That is astounding. Have you—"

A shadow fell over them. A very large shadow. Kat looked up to find Braeden in the doorway, his body overwhelming the opening and his face serious. "Excuse me. I rang the bell but no one came. Is my room ready?"

Her tension returned full force at Max's quiet gasp.

"I'll be right there."

Braeden nodded and retreated.

Kat spun. "Max. You mustn't tell anyone." She grabbed his arm. "I had to let him stay because he is the Headless Horseman tonight."

Max's face grew paler as he moved his gaze away from the door to meet hers. "That was Brom." His voice was barely above a whisper.

"No, it wasn't. It's just one of his descendants. He's Stephen's brother."

Max's color started to return. "That is Stephen's brother?"

"Yes. I know it's hard to believe, but he is." She glanced toward the closed door. "He's only staying tonight so he can be the Headless Horseman for us. Stephen is not feeling well and asked him to do it. You know Stephen would never let us down, so I couldn't send his brother away."

Max suddenly looked his age. "But Kat. That's against the rules."

"I know." She latched on to his arm. "But what could I do? If I didn't let him stay, we would have no rider tonight. Please. Don't tell anyone."

Reluctantly, he nodded. "Very well. I suppose it will be all right for one night."

She moved her hand from his arm to his cheek. He was truly becoming a man. "Thank you. Now I better show him to his room. He doesn't have much time."

"Right. I'll be by tomorrow."

As Max strode to the back door, she untied her apron and headed for the front counter. But Braeden wasn't there. "Now where did you go?"

"I'm in here."

His soft-spoken voice came from the parlor, but she didn't see him. Walking into it, she found him looking at a painting on the wall shared by the entryway and the room. No wonder she hadn't seen him. He stood with his arms behind his back, contemplating the scene with the Catskill Mountains rising above a stream where two men fished. His build, so much like Brom's, had her heart aching again. But Brom would never have stood still long enough to study a painting. Hanging on to that fact, she steadied herself. "I can show you to your room now."

He turned his head to look at her—no, study her. From the top of her head to the bottom of her dress. She swallowed, wishing she could fan herself. She raised her hand to put her hair back in place but stopped herself, placing it on the top of the settee instead. She hated that he could rattle her so easily. "Are you going to want breakfast in the morning?"

He cocked his head, as if he wanted to determine if there was more meaning to her question. Finally, he stepped away from the painting, walking toward her like a bear bent on his prey. "No, thank you. I just drink coffee in the morning. So where is the room you were able to conjure up despite being full?"

She glared at him before spinning on her heel to lead him down the hall. "If you must know, it's my room."

His hand on her arm stopped her cold, or rather hot, as heat streaked from the place where he touched her all the way to her toes. "Your room? I can't do that. I'll sleep back there."

She pulled away and he let her go. Putting her hands on her hips, she focused on her irritation instead of the heat building in her belly. "Oh no. You are not staying in my parlor. First of all, in case you haven't noticed, you're big. My biggest settee could sleep an eighteen-year-old at best. Second, I just spent the last hour making the room ready for you, so you will use it. Understand?"

His mouth started quirking at the corner again, and she quickly turned. She needed to stay mad at him for at least another twelve hours. She strode down the hall quite confident he was right behind her. His weight alone on the old wooden floorboards made that clear enough, but even without the creaks and moans, her body was well aware of his presence. When they reached her door, she thrust it open before she could change her mind. "Here you are."

She stepped back while he walked through, directly to her bed. The thought of him in there, naked, asleep, had her body warming all over again.

He turned slowly and looked at her. "That's a large bed for such a small lady."

She shrugged, trying for nonchalance. "It was my grandparents'. I saw no reason to change it." She brushed by him to the washstand. "There is a pitcher here if you want to wash before your ride. This village is set in the 1790s and we keep everything authentic. That's why you won't see any electric lights here. Just turn down the lanterns before you go to bed. Now, is there anything else you need?"

He was still staring at the lantern by the bed when she asked the question, but his gaze found hers and it was filled with curiosity. "No, I'm good."

"Good." She started back through the room, anxious to shut the door behind her, but he stopped it from closing.

"I need to retrieve the costume from my car. Is there a key to the room?"

"A key?" She lowered her brows. Why would he need a key? Oh, right. Theft was common in Newtime. She looked up to find him gazing at her hair. He was only a foot from her and she stepped back.

It was easier to meet his eyes while standing farther away. "No, I'm afraid I have no key for this room. But don't worry, your baggage will be safe." She turned to leave but his hand on her shoulder stopped her. His palm covered her entire shoulder easily, just like Brom's.

"Wait, I need to thank you."

She didn't want to turn and look at him. He would have a friendly smile for her and she'd melt completely.

"I don't even know your name." His low voice caressed her nerves, making them settle.

Ducking out from under his hand, she forced herself to walk away even as she spoke over her shoulder. "I'm Katrina Van Tassel, proprietor of the Sleepy Hollow Inn."

Read on for an excerpt from Pleasures of Christmas Past (A Christmas Carol #1)

Chapter One

Jessica Thomas floated near the ceiling of the small Christmas ornament shop, anxiously waiting to find out who would be her mentor on this, her first case as a Spirit Guide. She had no idea what it would entail, which irritated her a little. When she was alive, she'd been an excellent social worker because she read the case file *before* meeting the client. The Spirit Guide position was very difficult to obtain, but her past expertise had helped her land the job and she was anxious to prove she deserved it.

Having the file would certainly help that.

She scanned the shop, liking the feel of the place. It was cozy, with ornaments everywhere in every conceivable shape and size. With just three days until Christmas the store was full of people, all with lovely Scottish accents. She'd never been to Scotland while alive, though she'd planned a trip once, but had to cancel. She'd just been too busy to take a vacation for any length of time. Yes, it was one of her many regrets she had about her short life. At least *she* felt thirty-three years was short.

As far as time went, her mentor was late, or at least it seemed like it. There was no time in the afterlife, a fact that had thrown her completely off balance, but she was learning to cope…somewhat. Maybe her mentor was still in class answering questions. One of the many instructors from the intensive training she'd gone through would be her mentor on this first assignment. She really liked old Archibald. He was an American from the 1880s. Mrs. Ferrisletter, from 1662 London, was very sweet and would be a lovely mentor. Jessica crossed her fingers. As long as she didn't get Dr. Marley, she'd be happy. That man could put a saint into a depression.

"Are you ready for your first case?" The lilt of a heavy Scottish accent behind her caused her to turn.

Duncan Montgomerie floated there, not close enough to touch, but near enough she caught the whiff of pine that was so much a part of him.

Oh no, not *him*. The man was the hottest instructor she'd had and even now she couldn't remember a word he'd said. She'd been too busy having her libido stroked by his voice while her eyes feasted on his rugged looks and ripped body. He'd never told them what time period he was from, but his accent gave him away as Scottish and some of his vocabulary made her think it might be centuries back, even though he dressed in modern-day clothes.

Nervousness tamped down her excitement. There was no way she'd be able to concentrate on this assignment with him around. She was bound to screw something up.

"Jessica?" His blue eyes sparkled with an unearthly light as one brow rose. "Are you with me, lass?"

"Yes, of course." She tried not to focus on his wavy brown hair that fell past his strong jawline or on his scruffy chin that led the eye to his quirking lips.

His arm stretched out past her as he pointed below them, revealing his forearm muscle flexing as he moved his finger. "That's our case. Mrs. Cameron Douglas."

Despite the butterflies tickling her stomach as Duncan's breath passed by her left ear, Jessica snapped her focus to the people below. There were many women in the shop. Mrs. Douglas could be any of them. She leaned away and looked her mentor in the eyes. "What's her first name?"

"Huh?"

Jessica pushed her glasses back up the bridge of her nose. "What's Mrs. Douglas' first name? To get a client to trust you, you must show an interest in them and knowing the person's first name is the very tip of the iceberg."

Duncan frowned. "I dinna teach you that."

She took a deep breath. "No, you didn't. It's part of the experience I bring to the job. Do you know her first name?"

He shook his head, clearly perplexed by her request.

"How long have you been a Spirit Guide?" It was really none of her business, but she wanted to be sure her mentor was, in fact, more experienced than she was.

He shrugged broad shoulders, drawing her focus back to his build.

"Since we have no time in the afterlife, I cannot tell you how long I've done this, but I can assure you it is no' my first case." He pulled the neck of his t-shirt away from his skin, as if it were too tight.

As far as she was concerned, the entire shirt was too tight with the way it molded to his chest muscles, showing a significant valley down the middle. Heck, if he just wanted to take the whole thing off, she certainly wouldn't complain.

"Holly." Duncan grinned and her insides turned to melting ice cream.

So why did he point out holly? It was Christmas. There was holly everywhere… And mistletoe. Oh, maybe she could find some mistletoe and Mr. Distraction here could catch the hint and kiss her.

"Holly is her first name." Duncan nodded to confirm his statement. "It's also what that older woman down there just called her."

Her? Oh right, the case. Jessica forced her gaze from Duncan and looked below. "Which one is she?"

"She's the owner of the shop. The one with the shoulder-length brown hair and red Christmas hat on."

Jessica forced herself to focus on the woman. Her straight hair was a very deep brown, like dark chocolate, and she had a round face with an adorable smile, but it didn't quite reach her eyes. There was a quiet sorrow about the friendly shop owner. She looked perhaps thirty years old, max. What could have caused such a poignant hurt in one so young? "She definitely has the Christmas spirit. Why does she need us?"

Duncan chuckled, a warm sound that sent pleasure from her heart to her fingertips and everywhere in between. "No' every case is about some old Scrooge character. Each person we're assigned needs something different, but it has to be very important for them. Cameron—he'll be our supervisor on this assignment—received special permission for us to tackle this. You can equate him to Marley in your Scrooge story. There is always a Sprit Guide supervisor who preps the person receiving our help."

"Cameron?" She couldn't resist looking at him again and was surprised to see him frown, an unusual occurrence for him.

"Cameron Douglas is—excuse me—*was* her husband. There is a strict rule about handling personal cases, but I guess Cameron made a good argument with the boss."

Even frowning, Duncan was gorgeous. His cheekbones were strong, but his nose did have a slight bump that kept him from being entirely perfect. Genetics? Or was that from an injury? She could see him modeling for a highland wool sweater catalog, looking scrumptious in a white turtleneck and tartan kilt. Oh. Just the idea of seeing this man in a kilt had her body flushing. What did they say about what a man wore under—

"Jessica? Are you listening?"

"What?" Oh no. She was afraid of this. "Sorry, my mind drifted. What were you saying?"

He studied her for a moment before explaining. "I said, we, or rather you officially, are one of three ghosts who will visit Mrs. Douglas. Our goal is to remind her of the happy times before she lost her husband. Cameron's wife is no' truly living, just going through the motions."

Jessica's heart melted for the woman. She'd had cases like this, but never tackled them with the ability she had now. The possibilities excited her, causing her adrenaline to kick in. "So we literally take her to wonderful moments in her past. This is going to be fun. I can already imagine her smiling and laughing." She couldn't help her own grin at the thought of bringing a client such joy.

Duncan raised his hand. "Hold on, it's no' that simple. Remember what I said in training?"

"Uh, you said a lot. What part?" Not that she remembered any of it.

"You cannot get too attached. You need to keep some distance. We only have one night to work our magic, so to speak." He grinned.

"Do you really believe that?" How could he be a trainer of Spirit Guides if he thought they could do any good staying detached?

His grin faded. "I wouldn't teach it if I dinna believe it. Trust me, lass, you cannot get too involved in someone else's troubles. If you do, your soul will become entangled with your case."

She stared, open-mouthed. Had she really missed how shallow he was in the training? Or maybe he was talking from experience. She studied him closer. Was there something substantial behind those good looks?

His grin returned. "But dinna worry. I'll be there to help." His comment was said with such arrogance that for the first time she found herself not liking him at all.

She wasn't exactly a novice at this. It may be her first case as a

Spirit Guide, but she did have years of experience as a social worker. Maybe she needed to focus on the client and not on Mr. Distraction. "Where's the file?"

"Dinna worry about that. I can give you all the basics." Again he smiled, but this time, she noticed it was the kind a person gives to a child when humoring them.

He had little faith she could accomplish this assignment. Well, he was in for a surprise. She had a mission of her own and that was to prove Duncan Montgomerie was no more than a redundancy on this mission. Pasting on a fake smile, she took charge of *her* case. "I appreciate that, but I'd like to read through the file anyway. Sometimes, as a woman, I can catch a clue or two when trying to better understand a female client."

He shrugged once again and she forced herself to focus on his face.

"I left it on your desk. When you're done looking for *clues*, let me know and we can get started." He was clearly laughing at her.

She gritted her teeth. This wouldn't work. She would have to request another mentor because it was obvious the two of them had radically different ideas about helping people. She forced her jaw to loosen. "Fine." Without another word, she floated through the ceiling and back to her office to plan her attack and have a talk with her new supervisor.

Duncan watched Jessica drift away and chuckled. The lass was "wound too tight," as he'd heard Cameron say. Even her look was too professional. Blonde hair pulled back into a loose ponytail, wire-rimmed glasses hiding very bonny green eyes and a buttoned-to-the-neck Oxford shirt that made her look more like a scholar than a counselor. Her navy-blue pantsuit was boxy, hiding her entire body, and reminded him of a Christmas candle, rectangle bottom with a bright round flame at the top.

There was no way she would get through her first case without messing up. Good thing he was her mentor. He couldn't see any of the other instructors dealing well with her. He dinna doubt her heart was in the right place, but helping the living while dead was very different from helping them while alive.

He had a hard time remembering what it was like no' having the ability to move through space and time at will. It had been so long since he died. He frowned. It was difficult remembering the exact year, but he was confident it was long ago. He'd trained too many recruits. No' that it mattered. Time meant nothing now.

He grinned. Training new Spirit Guides was a fun adventure and he was perfectly happy where he was. It would be entertaining to watch the lass handle her first assignment. And when she stumbled, because she definitely would, he'd be there to catch her. The idea of what she might feel like under all those clothes had his smile widening. First, she needed to lose the glasses and the ponytail. Then he'd be happy to help her change into something more comfortable. Something he would do as soon as this assignment was over. The clothing in his time period was much less confining, but dressing according to the year of the client helped keep the person from running away in pure horror when he showed up.

Activity below caught his attention and his smile faded. He watched their client as Holly helped a teenager choose a unique ornament for his girlfriend.

Cameron and his wife had had one of those rare love stories that deserved a happily forever after, no' just a happily for thirteen months. Duncan had no idea what that was like, but he respected it. To see two people so in love suddenly separated by death touched even his hardened bachelor's soul.

Though he'd only known Cameron for a short while, probably almost a year, it was clear the man was a brilliant supervisor, but like his wife, sadness emanated from his spirit. Holly deserved a wee bit of happiness herself and Cameron could benefit from a little peace. If Duncan could do this small service for him, he would.

And there was no blasted way he would let Miss Jessica Thomas bumble their assignment, bonny eyes or no'.

~~*~~

Jessica closed the file. It wasn't very detailed. She'd expected—hoped—for much more information that would help her understand the Christmas shop owner. She'd bet a gallon of ice cream her supervisor had kept important information out of the file. After all, Holly Douglas was his wife.

The problem was, with so little information, she would be more dependent on Mr. Distraction, a situation she seriously needed to avoid. Between his attitude toward her and their client and his hot physique, it was a recipe for disaster. Not only did she not want that to happen to Holly, but as her client was her new supervisor's wife, she was doubly motivated to do a great job.

Picking up the file, she walked down the hall toward Cameron Douglas' office. She was still more comfortable in a solid state, so she had to knock on his door when she arrived.

"Come in." The Scottish accent reminded her of Duncan.

She opened the door and halted. "Oh, I'm sorry. I didn't know you had someone with you."

Cameron motioned her forward. "No worries." He looked at the woman sitting in the chair before his desk. "You were just leaving, correct?"

The woman rose gracefully. "Yes, I was. Thank you for the advice." Then without turning, she phased and disappeared through the floor.

Jessica hesitated at the woman's disappearance then walked forward.

"Still getting used to phasing?" Cameron smiled encouragingly.

She shook her head. "Not me, but seeing others do it."

"That's normal."

She studied her new boss. He was about her age with sandy-brown hair that fell across his forehead but was cut short above the ears. He had hazel eyes, a narrow nose, and shoulders to rival Duncan Montgomerie's. Despite the sleeveless t-shirt he wore, which made him look like a bouncer, his smile was friendly and not condescending, like another spirit she knew.

"Mr. Douglas, I'm Jessica Thomas. I was assigned your wife's case."

He walked out from behind his desk. "Yes, I know who you are." He reached out his hand. "Call me Cameron. Welcome."

She shook his hand, and when he gestured to the chair recently vacated by the other spirit, she sat. "Thank you. I wanted to talk to you about this case."

He raised his brows at her as if she'd taken him by surprise. "I'm confused. Didn't you discuss it with Duncan?"

His assumption that Duncan had filled her in bothered her. "About Duncan."

Cameron turned and returned to his seat behind his desk. "What about Duncan?" Her boss's smile disappeared.

Not a good sign. "I was wondering if I could be given a different mentor."

"No."

"No? Why not?"

Cameron sat back in his chair. "Duncan is the oldest and best Spirit Guide trainer I have. I chose him because I wanted the best for my wife; however, trainers are not allowed to serve as Spirit Guides, so I chose you out of our new recruits. Duncan is who I want on this case. Would you prefer to be given another one?"

He would take her off his wife's case? That would mean she'd failed before she'd even begun. "No, no. I would like to help your wife. Perhaps you can fill me in a bit more?" She held up the file. "This appears to be a bit sparse."

Cameron leaned forward. "I'm sorry, Jessica, but that's Duncan's job. I have a lot to do here and I assigned you to him to insure this assignment would be handled successfully. So if you don't want another assignment then I suggest you find Duncan and talk to him about my wife's file. That's *his* job."

"Oh, I see." She didn't. Not really.

"Good. I look forward to hearing how well everything goes." Cameron turned his attention back to his desk and started writing on a piece of paper.

Obviously dismissed, Jessica rose and nodded at him, but he didn't look up. Great, not only was she stuck with Mr. Distraction and a file of no information, but she'd pissed off her boss. Good start. She turned and walked toward the door.

"Oh and Jessica."

She spun. "Yes?"

"When you see Duncan, give him a message for me."

"Of course." Maybe this was a chance to redeem herself a bit.

"Tell him my team won and he owes me three beers."

Really? He wanted her to deliver a message about a bet?

He grinned at her, making him look a whole lot younger than she'd first thought. Men.

Too angry to speak, she nodded and turned back to the door, closing it decisively. If he thought she slammed it, that was his interpretation. The chances of her delivering his message were about one in a hundred million. A nagging piece of conscience reminded her he *was* her supervisor. But really, how important could a bet be? Cameron may be her boss, but she wasn't his errand girl.

She skipped going back to her office and headed for home. There had to be another way to learn more about Holly before they started the case. With time at her disposal, she might just have to bop on down to see Holly…without Duncan Montgomerie. Or was that allowed?

~~*~~

Duncan sauntered into Cameron's office and sat, crossing his legs at his ankles. "I have to thank you."

His friend smiled and rose before walking to a side bar. "Scotch?"

Duncan nodded.

Cameron poured a splash of water into two glasses and then filled the glasses three-quarters full. Picking them up, he handed one to Duncan before sitting on the corner of his desk.

Duncan raised his glass. "To women."

"To the right woman."

Duncan grinned at their regular toast and took a sip. There was nothing like good Scotch.

"So what are you thanking me for this time? Did you fall in love with a new recruit?"

Duncan laughed. "No' likely, but I will admit to falling in bed with a couple."

Cameron shook his head. "Two at a time isn't going to find you the one."

Duncan shrugged and looked away. That would never happen. He'd accepted that fact while he was still alive. The truth was, he couldn't love beyond those he'd been born to, like his parents and brother. He just didn't have it in him. "But my new mentee has definite possibilities. She's a bonny one for sure."

"So if it's not love, what do you have to thank me for?"

He grinned again at the memory of his conversation with Jessica Thomas. "Jessica. That woman will be quite the challenge.

It's obvious she thinks she knows what to do and I think she may have slept through my trainings."

Cameron took a sip of his drink. "Funny you should say that. She was just in here asking for a new mentor."

Duncan spit his sip. A bloody waste of liquor. "What? I wasn't even trying to get her into bed yet." His ego as a trainer took the blow hard. "Did she say why she wants a new mentor?"

"No. I wouldn't let her. You're the only one I trust with this visit, so she's stuck with you. You may want to handle her differently than you did. I don't want this assignment screwed up. Maybe you should turn on that legendary charm of yours."

Duncan raised an eyebrow. "I won't let her mess this assignment up. I'll fix her mistakes and everything will go well." He looked his friend in the eye. "Cameron, I won't let anything get in the way of your wife's happiness. You have my word."

His friend and boss looked down at his glass before swirling around the liquid and taking a sizeable gulp. The man's sadness was like a cloud about him. When he brought the glass back down, he continued to stare at it. "I appreciate that. She deserves it."

Duncan took another swallow of his own drink to push down the lump in his throat. He was more determined than ever to help Cameron's wife.

Cameron looked at him. "So what did you do to piss her off?"

He snapped his head up. "I dinna ken."

"Don't know, not ken."

"Blast." He finished off his Scotch. "The language of your time is too harsh." He pulled at the neckline of his t-shirt. "And the clothes are stifling."

Cameron finished his drink and stood. "Holly is used to kilts, so you can change into yours after the first visit or two. I'm hoping your accent and Jessica's experience will put her at ease."

"We will help dispel some of her grief. Dinna worry about that."

Though who would help Cameron was another matter entirely. He smirked to lighten the mood. "I'm sure once I have Jessica bending to my will, all will go according to our plan."

"I don't think she's the type to be told what to do."

Duncan winked. "Then I will just have to woo her to my way of thinking. I have been known to charm a lady or two…or score."

Cameron looked at him quizzically. "Exactly how many women have you had sex with?"

Duncan shrugged before giving his friend a sly look. "Too many to count."

"Get out of here." His boss shook his head and returned to his chair, the paperwork on his desk making Duncan cringe.

"As you wish." He gave his friend a nod before he phased and floated through the roof, Cameron's last question bothering him. Why did he ask?

Duncan would be the first to admit he enjoyed life. At a young age he'd discovered he would never have what Cameron had, though he'd tried, his heart always hoping, but by time he was a score and eight, he'd realized he simply didn't have the ability to love a woman like that.

But there had been more to life than love and he had a brilliant life. That he was able to continue in the afterlife as he had with women, drink and his favorite pastimes was more than he'd hoped for.

And now he had a new woman in his sights. A bonny woman with emerald-green eyes, hair like spun gold, and based on his vast experience, he would wager a cask of single malt Scotch she had a body made for pleasure. Just the thought of kissing her rose-colored lips had him smiling with anticipation. Aye, he was anxious to lie with her and enjoy her feminine attributes.

"Jessica." He even liked her name. It was soft with a hard edge and he'd bet a hundred pounds sterling that was exactly what she was like. He just needed to get beneath that edge.

He hesitated. She'd had a fiancé, which could be an issue. He had to respect her feelings on that. A lover he was, but he'd never come between two people who loved each other like Cameron and Holly.

He continued floating toward home. He didn't like that she'd requested someone else. He'd been very patient with her. Maybe that was too subtle for her. Aye, that made sense. His best approach now was to be obvious. He would charm her into enjoying herself a bit with him, then they could work together to help Holly.

A new energy surged through him at the prospect of his challenge and he grinned. He couldn't wait to discover every enjoyable nuance of Jessica's being.

Holly Douglas closed the safe then turned off the lamp on her desk. It had been a long day of customers. As usual, Christmas Eve had seen her store packed from open to close and for the third year in a row, Mr. Branson had shown up just as she was about to lock the door. He took his usual half hour picking out the perfect ornament for his wife. It had to be an ornament with motion involved. He said it was because now that his wife had a scooter and electric wheelchair, she moved around even more than when she was younger.

She had to agree with the man. Mrs. Branson did seem to be out and about a lot more since she'd finally given up the walker two years ago. She would love the singing cardinal with the flapping wings he'd bought her. Holly could almost picture the older woman opening the gift-wrapped box. Of course, she had been so tired she'd cut the ribbon too short and had to start over. But it was a "holiday tired" as Cam always said.

She smiled sadly as she turned off the lights in the little shop and walked around her ceramic ornament display to the tapestry that hid the door to her home next door. It'd been *their* home just last year.

When everyone heard about Cam's accident, they had been so kind, visiting her every day, bringing her food and company. Later, people invited her to watch the Old Firm Derby between the Rangers and the Celtic or to come to a local ceilidh. But as the year wore on, people became too busy with their own lives and their own challenges.

Except for Cam's two best friends. Ethan and Brody had both remembered her. Brody had invited her to his flat where he was holding a Christmas Eve party with all their friends. Ethan had invited her to his parents' house for Christmas day. Their invitations were just like them, completely different. Brody was like Cam, always ready to jump into another adventure while Ethan was cautious, weighing all the pros and cons before making a decision, yet the three of them had been inseparable since their university days.

She turned both offers down. She had a feeling they both sensed her hesitation to be around them. They reminded her too much of Cam and the good times they all had together. To be in their presence would be torture without him there.

She flicked the switch as she entered her little home. Mac jumped off the couch and stretched his feline body by digging his claws into the area rug before sauntering over to say hello.

"Did you miss me, sweetie?"

The cat insistently rubbed against her leg, arching his back as she gave him the mandatory stroke.

"Well, I didn't have time to miss you. We were so busy today." She moved to the side table by the door and dropped her keys. As she looked up into the mirror above it, she froze. Her late husband stood behind her. "Cam?"

She spun around, her heart beating a tattoo, but no one was there. She looked back at the mirror. Just her round face flushed by her scare stared back at her. "Good job, Holly, now you're seeing things."

With her adrenaline pumping overtime, she took a couple calming breaths and walked into the kitchen. It was nothing a cup of tea couldn't soothe. She switched on the electric tea kettle and opened the refrigerator. She scanned the contents, ignoring the little Cornish hen she'd bought to cook for dinner the next day, and instead stared at the clootie dumpling Mrs. Bell had dropped off the day before. "That's not exactly Christmas Eve dinner."

Mac ignored her as he munched on his own dry food, his teeth crunching down on the hard pellets.

She dug deep for her willpower and forced her hand to move past the dessert to the container of leftover pasta from the night before. Scooping some onto a plate, she set it in the microwave for a minute.

Her family back in New Hampshire had pressured her to visit during the holidays. They didn't want her to be alone so far away, but she just couldn't bring herself to leave. Cam loved Christmas so much. To not be here where they had celebrated their only two Christmases as a married couple had just felt wrong. But her family wouldn't have understood, so she told them she couldn't get anyone to cover her shop. It was actually *their* shop. Cam had come up with the idea and the name "One of a Kind Christmas Shop." She'd just implemented it. It was his brain child. The only child they had. Her living link to him…sort of.

The microwave binged, keeping her from going down the dark path her thoughts always traveled when remembering her late husband.

Pulling out her dinner, she set it on the table before pouring the hot water over a tea bag and letting it steep while she ate. When she was finished with her meal, she made her tea and headed into the parlor to turn on the Christmas lights. Setting her cup on the end table next to her comfy recliner, she went about flipping all the switches.

Finally, she turned on the gas fireplace. Walking back to her chair, she stared down at Mac, curled into a large ball in the middle of the cushion. "I don't think so." She bent over him. "You're not fooling anybody. I know you're not sleeping."

The cat didn't move a muscle, so she reached over and lifted her mug from the coaster. The cat's ear twitched toward the sound. "I knew it." Putting her cup back down, she picked him up and deposited him on Cam's chair. "That's your chair. You inherited it from Cam, so enjoy it."

Once comfortable in her own spot, Holly took a sip of tea and critically reviewed her Christmas display. Just because Cam wasn't with her anymore, didn't mean she should change their decorating tradition. Ever since their first Christmas Eve five years earlier, they'd always decorated the main living room to the max. They'd both thought the same thing when they found this house three years ago, which was that with a ceiling so high, like in their shop next door, it meant lots of room for decorations. The room glowed with a pink hue from all the lights, while the firelight kept it moving.

The flames weren't the only things moving. She had the electric train going around the tree, the various motion ornaments she'd kept instead of selling in the shop, and of course the blinking lights. Some moved in a continuous pattern, others stopped and started, and some simply changed from one color to the next. Her Santa's Workshop on the bookcase was busy with elves working and even the electric candles in the windows flickered. There was only one thing missing to complete the decorated room. The star.

She looked up at the top of the tree where the twelve-inch star belonged. Cam always placed the star on top. She'd tried every night for two weeks to put it up there, but started crying every time, so she gave up. She even put it back in its box and returned it to the closet.

The fact was, she could pretend all she wanted, but Cam wasn't here for Christmas. The room was his shrine, but he would never see it.

Holly's chest tightened and she tried to take a deep breath to stop the inevitable tears, but it was no use. It just made her cough as her nose started to run. Why couldn't she get through just one night without crying?

Because half her heart was buried six feet under.

The pain in her chest intensified and she doubled over, the sobbing starting all over again. Even as the tears flowed, her heart filled with hurt until she couldn't breathe. If she'd known this would happen, this was how it would all turn out, she would never have smiled at Cameron Douglas that fateful day at the Highland Games in Lincoln.

Irritation raced through her veins. How could he die on her? He was only thirty-two. She felt robbed, cheated, betrayed. Holly sat upright as her chest eased but her stomach tensed with anger. She grabbed a tissue from the box on the end table, mad at Cam and at herself.

Also by Lexi Post

Paranormal Romance

Masque

Passion's Poison

Passion of Sleepy Hollow

Heart of Frankenstein

Pleasures of Christmas Past (A Christmas Carol Series: Book 1)

Desires of Christmas Present (A Christmas Carol Series: Book 2)

Temptations of Christmas Future (A Christmas Carol Series: Book 3)

One of a Kind Christmas (A Christmas Carol Series: Book 4)

On Highland Time (Time Weavers Inc. Series: Book 1)

Sci-fi Romance

Cruise into Eden (The Eden Series: Book 1)

Unexpected Eden (The Eden Series: Book 2)

Eden Discovered (The Eden Series: Book 3)

Eden Revealed (The Eden Series: Book 4)

Avenging Eden (The Eden Series: Book 5)

Beast of Eden (The Eden Series: Book 6)

Contemporary Cowboy Romance

Cowboys Never Fold (Poker Flat Series: Book 1)
Cowboy's Match (Poker Flat Series: Book 2)
Cowboy's Best Shot (Poker Flat Series: Book 3)
Cowboy's Break (Poker Flat Series: Book 4)
Wedding at Poker Flat (Poker Flat Series: Book 5)

Christmas with Angel (Poker Flat Series Book: 2.5/Last Chance Series: Book 1)
Trace's Trouble (Last Chance Series: Book 2)
Fletcher's Flame (Last Chance Series: Book 3)
Logan's Luck: (Last Chance Series: Book 4)
Dillon's Dare (Last Chance Series: Book 5)
Riley's Rescue (Last Chance Series: Book 6)

Aloha Cowboy (Island Cowboy Series: Book 1)

Military Romance

When Love Chimes (Broken Valor Series: Book 1)
Poisoned Honor (Broken Valor Series: Book 2)

About Lexi Post

Lexi Post is a New York Times and USA Today best-selling author of romance inspired by the classics. She spent years in higher education taking and teaching courses about the classical literature she loved. From Edgar Allan Poe's short story "The Masque of the Red Death" to Tolstoy's *War and Peace*, she's read, studied, and taught wonderful classics.

But Lexi's first love is romance novels. In an effort to marry her two first loves, she started writing romance inspired by the classics and found she loved it. From hot paranormals to sizzling cowboys to hunks from out of this world, Lexi provides a sensuous experience with a "whole lotta story."

Lexi is living her own happily ever after with her husband and her cat in Florida. She makes her own ice cream every weekend, loves bright colors, and you will never see her without a hat.

www.lexipostbooks.com

www.ingramcontent.com/pod-product-compliance
Lightning Source LLC
Chambersburg PA
CBHW070630170726
48291CB00003B/950